*Acclaim for David Plante's*

# ABC

"David Plante writes in a restrained, classical style that's
a relief from the excessively digressive work the kids all
seem to prefer these days. . . . Simply beautiful."
—*New York* magazine

"A novel about the globalization of grief. . . . The wisdom
and beauty of [its] closing pages are striking."
—*The New York Times Book Review*

"Powerful. . . . A clear-eyed look at the isolating nature
of grief."                    —*The Providence Journal*

"A quiet, realistic chronicle of death, grief, and perhaps
redemption."                        —*The New York Sun*

"Resonates with the quiet passion of an artist restoring
order to his own life."        —*San Francisco Bay Times*

# David Plante

# ABC

David Plante is the author of more than a dozen novels, including the Francoeur trilogy—*The Family* (a finalist for the National Book Award), *The Woods*, and *The Country*—and the nonfiction *Difficult Women: A Memoir of Three* and *American Ghosts*. His work has appeared in *The New Yorker* and *The Paris Review*. Plante teaches writing at Columbia University and lives in New York and London.

## Also by David Plante

# ABC

BIBLIOTHÈQUE HISTORIQUE

# JAMES G. FÉVRIER

DIRECTEUR D'ÉTUDES A L'ÉCOLE PRATIQUE DES HAUTES-ÉTUDES

# HISTOIRE
## DE
# L'ÉCRITURE

*Nouvelle édition entièrement refondue*

### Avec 135 figures

## PAYOT, PARIS

# ABC

a novel

## David Plante

Anchor Books
A Division of Random House, Inc.
New York

FIRST ANCHOR BOOKS EDITION, DECEMBER 2008

*Copyright © 2007 by David Plante*

All rights reserved. Published in the United States by Anchor Books,
a division of Random House, Inc., New York, and in Canada by
Random House of Canada Limited, Toronto. Originally published in
hardcover in the United States by Pantheon Books, a division of
Random House, Inc., New York, in 2007.

Anchor Books and colophon are registered trademarks of Random House, Inc.

Owing to the limitations of space, permission to reprint previously
published material may be found on p. 251.

The Library of Congress has cataloged the Pantheon edition as follows:
Plante, David.
ABC / David Plante.
p. cm.
1. Children—Death—Fiction. 2. Alphabets—History—
Fiction. 3. Domestic fiction. I. Title.
PS3566.L257A23 2007
813'.54—dc22 2006103288

**Anchor ISBN: 978-0-307-27801-2**

*Book design by Iris Weinstein*

www.anchorbooks.com

Printed in the United States of America
10  9  8  7  6  5  4  3  2  1

For Al Sabatini
With fifty years of friendship

All the dead have come to hear the concert
in this half-lit oasis of Time.
—Siegfried Sassoon, Diaries

# ABC

# ONE

From the canoe, stilled on the still cove of the lake, the land was reflected in detail in the water: branches and leaves and pinecones, berry bushes, and the stone-and-timber house on the steep bank among trees. The house was abandoned. For all the ten years Gerard had been spending his summers on the other side of the lake in the house his wife, Peggy, had inherited from a rich uncle, the cove with the abandoned house overlooking it had been the end of every canoe ride. The cove, as calm and warm and peaceful as it was, instilled in them the calm and warmth and peace that they went out on the water for: Peggy at the front of the canoe, Gerard at the back, their dripping paddles resting lengthwise across the sides, and sitting on a cushion on the bottom halfway between them was their six-year-old son, Harry, who seemed to be in the same drifting state as the canoe, or so Gerard imagined.

For the first time, Gerard was struck by how Harry's bones, which he had up until now seen as delicate, were beginning to enlarge, his vertebrae pronounced, his shoulder blades almost disproportionately large in the way they stuck out, and yet his shoulders were small and smooth. Harry was motionless, which meant he must have been thinking, drifting, Gerard again imagined, on his thinking. Gerard liked to drift on his thoughts, and his son, he was sure, took enough after him to like to too—that is, until Peggy, as Gerard always counted on her doing, stopped the drifting. She did so now by dipping her paddle into the water, a sign for Gerard to get to it and paddle. He did, and they continued in slow ripples deeper into the cove, towards the abandoned house, some of whose wide, many-paned windows on the second story were broken.

Raising his thin arm with a large elbow, Harry pointed to the house and asked, "Who lives there?"

Not turning, Peggy answered, "No one does."

"Why doesn't anyone live there?"

His high voice sounded in the silence like one of the natural sounds of the lake, a heat bug trilling or a bird flying overhead.

Gerard said, "Harry, here we go with your question why again. I'd like to answer, but I have to tell you I don't know why."

"Did the people who lived there die?"

Turning her head a little, so the thick bunch of her frizzy, tied-back hair swung against her bare shoulders, Peggy said, "No, they didn't die."

"How do you know?"

Amused, Gerard also wanted to ask how she knew.

"I just know."

As a matter of simple fact, Harry said, "You just know a lot of things."

"I do."

"I wish I knew a lot of things."

"You will, darling. You'll know a whole lot of things."

"I want to know everything."

"That's not possible," his mother said. "You can know this and that, you can know a whole lot, but you can't know everything. Everything is too much to know."

"But that's what I want."

"Well, I hope you get what you want, darling. I do."

Peggy again rested the paddle across the canoe, and Gerard did, and again the canoe drifted, now among water-lily pads that made a slurring sound along its thin bottom; and Harry, silent, seemed to Gerard to be once more drifting in his mind.

Below the abandoned house was a rotted dock, the remaining weathered boards tilting into the water.

Harry suddenly asked, "Can't we go see the house?"

"No," Peggy said abruptly.

"Why not?"

"I'm not going to answer one more question of yours that begins with 'why'!"

Harry was bemused, seriously so. "Why won't you?"

Now Peggy did turn enough to look at Gerard and say to him, "You've got to help me answer Harry's why this, why that, why everything."

Smiling, Gerard said, "But that's his way of learning."

"If I had answers, he'd learn something, but I don't. Maybe you do."

A little petulantly now, Harry asked, "Why can't we go see the house?"

"You tell him why not," Peggy said to Gerard.

"I'm not sure why not," he said. "To be straightforward, why not?"

"Because I don't want to."

"Why?"

"For God's sake, don't be like Harry."

The boy was deeply attentive to this bantering between his parents.

"Maybe I'm more like Harry than you think, and have a whole lot to learn—more than a whole lot, a whole everything," Gerard bantered. "I want to know why not."

The canoe was arrested among the thickness of the lily pads, with white lilies, swarming with small black flies, rising among them.

Peggy clearly didn't want to banter. "In all the years we've been coming here, you never once said you'd like to see into that old, broken-down house. Let me ask you, why now?"

"I want to now because Harry wants to."

Harry had his father on his side. He bounced on his butt. "I want to, I want to."

His father said, "The boy's at the age when he's drawn to a little adventure."

"I'm sure there's nothing in that house, or if there is, it'll be nothing but broken-down furniture and rubbish."

"Then he'll see that."

Peggy turned away to look, Gerard saw, up at the house, in the shadows of trees, with small flashes of sunlight. He heard her say, "I really don't want to."

Harry chanted, "I want to, I want to, I want to."

Without saying any more, Peggy stuck her paddle into the lily pads, and Gerard followed suit. At this, Harry knelt on the cushion and turned to his father and gave him a wide, bright smile, one that made Gerard place his paddle across his knees and lean forward and reach out and with both hands take his son's head into his hands and hold it. With a sudden rush of love for his son—love for him because, for some reason he only glancingly wondered about, he realized his son was right now more his son than he had ever been before—he would have kissed Harry if the canoe hadn't swerved because of Peggy's continuing paddling. Gerard sat back and righted the canoe, so it slithered over the lily pads to the shore, where, with a soft bump, it was stopped by weeds and mud. Kneeling before him, Harry was still smiling at his father, with a look in his eyes as of his too seeing something in his father he hadn't seen before, something that pleased him a lot.

In nothing but shorts, Gerard stepped out of the canoe into the muck that oozed in gray-green clouds about his feet and held the side steady for Peggy, in a bathing suit, to step out. Now Gerard could hold his son, his naked, narrow, flat chest against his own naked, rounded, and hairy chest, to heft him out of the canoe and place him on the shore, where the roots of pine trees were exposed among stones. That contact between his and his son's body was, to Gerard, a contact he had never before noticed with his son, and once again he wondered, however glancingly, Why now? While Harry watched, Peggy helped Gerard beach the canoe up the slope beyond the shoreline.

There was a path up the slope, so covered with dry pine needles it was hardly distinguishable. Harry ran up it.

"Harry," Peggy called. "I don't want you out of our sight. You hear?"

The boy laughed and ran on more, but, in sight of his parents, stopped by the trunk of a massive pine tree on which was attached a verdigris-gray bell with a rope dangling from its clapper. Harry studied it.

Peggy said to Gerard, "Why I don't want to go into that house is—well, because I'm sure all kinds of acts have been performed there that I wouldn't want Harry to know about, not at his age."

"How would he know?"

"There'll be graffiti all over the walls, and, Harry being Harry, he'll ask what they mean. I don't want him to know. As long as he's my baby, I don't want him to know."

"Is he still your baby? I think he's beginning to know more than you think he does."

"Not as long as I can stop him from knowing."

Gerard laughed a little.

"Don't laugh," Peggy said.

Gerard pressed his lips together and shook his head, then said, "I'm not laughing."

"Yes, you are."

"Yes, I am."

"Why?"

"I guess, thinking of everything Harry will learn."

Peggy slapped Gerard lightly on his bare shoulder and she too laughed. "And what's that?"

With a lilt to his voice, Gerard said, "Those strange acts performed in the house you're apprehensive of Harry finding out about—he'll find out sooner or later, and God bless him for what he finds out."

"Did I say strange? You did. You are such an innocent, Gerard. Not being so innocent, I can think of some pretty sordid acts performed there."

"I block those out, and so will Harry." As they approached Harry, who was holding the rope and looking up at the bell, Gerard took Peggy's arm and pulled her towards him for a moment and whispered, "The fact is, the house makes me think of an act I'd like to perform with you." She smelled of fresh lake water, and all her clear, taut skin, exposed on her shoulders, the slopes of her breasts, her abdomen and her back and her thighs and legs, looked as if it had the sheen of water.

Laughing more, Peggy shoved him aside, saying, "Remember, this is Harry's adventure, not yours."

"That's right, Harry's adventure."

And that moment, the boy jerked on the rope and rang the bell, and to the resonant clang throughout the woods birds flew out from everywhere. Laughing, Harry continued to ring the bell.

"Stop that," Peggy called, and rushing up the needle-covered path she slipped and fell, and lay sprawled on the depth of pine needles, laughing.

As if in celebration of his mother laughing, Harry rang the bell all the more.

Gerard, laughing too, helped Peggy up.

Harry, laughing with all the freedom with which his mother and father laughed, rang out the celebration of their laughing all together.

"Stop it, Harry," Peggy called and, no longer laughing, strode quickly up to the boy.

But Gerard asked, "Why stop him? Why not let him ring the bell?"

At Harry's side, Peggy grabbed his arm to stop him. The boy continued to laugh, now at the naughtiness of something he shouldn't have done but did anyway.

Approaching then, Gerard again asked Peggy, "Why shouldn't Harry ring the bell?"

"Someone may hear."

"Who?"

"I don't know, someone."

"And if someone does?"

"If someone does and comes—" She didn't finish her thought.

"You know this countryside from your time here when you were growing up. Can you think of anyone for miles and miles around who'd care if we came to see this old house, much less if Harry rang the bell?"

"I'm tired of all this questioning, really tired of it. First Harry, then you, as if you were taking after your son, not your son after you. Well, maybe you are. Maybe this is all an adventure for you too."

Gerard grabbed the frayed rope and rang the bell, rang and rang it, so that the reverberating clanging, all together, vibrated the air, and the more he rang it the more Harry laughed, and Gerard loved his son for laughing, and longed for him to go on and on laughing, for all his life, no matter what he learned. Mocking her disapproval, Peggy pressed her hands to her ears.

Crying birds darted in and out of the trees, but the moment Gerard stopped ringing the bell the birds disappeared and stopped crying, and a silence came over the woods. The silence was so deep that not only Gerard but, he noticed, Peggy, and even Harry were attentive to it. It was as though the woods had become filled with people who themselves were the cause of the silence, and Gerard, Peggy, and Harry, standing motionless, were waiting for one of these people to step from behind a tree and appear before them, and do what?

Harry began to walk back down the path to the canoe.

"Don't you want to see the house?" Gerard asked him.

Turning round, his face set in a frown, he said, "Maybe not now."

"Why not?"

"Ma is always telling me not to ask why not," he answered, with a maturity that startled Gerard.

Not only startled, Gerard was a little offended that his son should so suddenly leave him, as though the adventure had all been Gerard's and his son decided he didn't want to have anything to do with it.

"Well, I'm not giving up," Gerard said and, making a show of throwing out his chest, he continued up among the trees, sometimes stepping on a pinecone with a bare foot and wincing. He was aware of his son, and his wife too, behind him, and he had the fantasy of his back causing a current of power that would draw them into it and to him. It didn't happen. He reached the top of the slope and the level land on which the house was deeply shaded by the trees close about it. The porch along the front had pillars made of field-stones and screens that were torn and bulging; the screened door was hanging off one hinge. Gerard wouldn't look back to see if his son and wife were following him, and as he looked at the house with some of its timbers rotting, and some of the stone fallen off onto crumbling concrete, he thought he would not go any farther, but would go back to Harry and Peggy and the canoe. The silence that had followed the ringing of the bell was more profound than before, the silence and the stillness, which he imagined kept by invisible people, aware of him standing there. And he had the acute sense that those people were in the house, also aware of him, and that, like those outside, they were holding back from making them-selves visible to him, until, suddenly, one of them would. A shock shot through him when he felt a hand grasp his hand, and he jerked his arm away; but the hand held on to his, and when he looked down he saw Harry was beside him.

"So I guess we're both up to the big adventure," Gerard said.

Harry didn't reply, but he walked along with his father to the stone stoop that led up to the porch, and, as if lifting him a little,

Gerard pulled on Harry's arm to help him to go up the steps first. Inside the porch, Harry kept his hand in his father's. On one side of the porch was a rusted glider, only one of its cushions remaining and this torn and its dirty stuffing scattered; beside the glider was a pile of moldy newspapers and magazines, and before it was a wooden steamer trunk on which were crowded many beer bottles, some fallen to the floor and shattered. On the other end of the porch was a heap of automobile tires. Gerard, looking down at his son, saw the boy's eyes enlarge, taking in everything as if everything— the wrecked glider, the torn cushion, the beer bottles, the moldy newspapers and magazines, even the worn automobile tires—was vitally meaningful to him. It was clear that the things—or perhaps the meaning they had for him—frightened him. Gerard was reassured when Harry held his hand more tightly as Gerard brought him to the door of the house, a large wooden door inset with four panels and with a black porcelain knob, shut. Even Harry's fear reassured Gerard—reassured him that he was still very much his son—and if Gerard himself had been a little, just a little, frightened of the silence and stillness, he gave up all fear to show his son that he could simply turn the doorknob with his free hand and open the door wide.

It opened into a room that was wrecked beyond repair. Because the plaster was in large patches off the walls, down to the lathes, the spray-painted graffiti Peggy had predicted were in incomprehensible fragments; some of the floorboards were up; the furniture was so broken it was unidentifiable.

"Who did all this?" Harry asked.

"People," Gerard answered.

"What people?"

"Not the people you ever want to know."

Clutching his father's fingers tightly, Harry said, "Daddy, I don't want to go in."

"Are you scared?"

"No, I'm not scared."

"I think you are."

"I'm not."

"All right, you're not. But I am. So we'll leave."

But when Gerard drew back, Harry, staring into the room, stood firm and, not letting go of his father's fingers, kept them both from leaving.

Peggy appeared behind them and, looking between them into the room, said, "This is worse than I imagined."

"Well, we're leaving," Gerard said.

Harry stood motionless, holding on to his father's fingers.

"Harry," Gerard called him.

Pointing into the room, Harry asked, "What's that?"

"What's what?"

"That."

Peering between them to see for herself, Peggy said, "An old bicycle."

"I'll bet it works," Harry said.

"I'm sure it doesn't."

"I'll bet it does."

"You can see from here that it doesn't work," Gerard said. "Are you just using it as an excuse to go into the house?"

Harry didn't seem to understand this, and he pulled at his father's hand as he stepped up into the room. Inside, he let go of his father's hand.

Peggy followed them in, and Gerard was aware of their near nakedness, the three of them standing together in this destroyed house. The summer light beamed through a window in a heavy, almost solid block, in the midst of the broken furniture. She said, "Be careful, Harry, where you step." He went ahead of them, into the effulgent light, where he seemed to disappear, without a shadow.

"I think your adventure, as all adventures, has ended in disappointment," Peggy said to Gerard. "I told you so."

"Thank God you're always right in telling me so."

She knocked her forehead against his and smiled, then she turned round and asked, "Where's Harry?"

Gerard was just able to see, through the block of light, his son entering another room, and he called out, "Harry, wait for me before you go anywhere else."

"Please go after him," Peggy said.

Gerard too entered the block of light, where he was blinded; when he emerged, it took a moment for his eyes to focus. Ahead was a large fieldstone fireplace, with a high mantel made of a rough plank of wood and, above, a wide fieldstone chimney. The mantel was covered with beer and whiskey bottles, dusty and strung together by cobwebs. The stone hearth was littered with charred bits of floorboard, and within the fireplace was a heap of crumpled papers. Gerard noted that there was writing on the papers, which must have been torn from a notebook, maybe a school notebook, and he leaned to get a closer look. On the top of the heap, not crumpled, was a sheet of writing, and Gerard leaned closer to try to decipher the meaning. He couldn't, and he reached down to pick it up. Frowning, he saw what he assumed must be letters, but he had no idea in what script, because it was not any he was familiar with. The letters were drawn very carefully, maybe by a child.

य द ड ऋल्ल ए डी क र ग
घ उ च छ ज द्म अ ट ह उ
ढ रा त य द ध न य फ ब
ब म प र ल ब य ष म ह
ग र ड ऋल्ल ए डी क र ग
घ उ च छ ज द्म अ ट ह उ
ढ रा त य द ध न य फ ब
ब म प ट ल ब श ष म ह
य द ड ऋल्ल ए डी क ख ग
घ उ न छ ज द्म अ ट ह उ
ढ रा त य द ध न य फ ब
ब म प र ल ब श ष म ह

Gerard held the page closer, and the more he studied it the more its incomprehensibility took hold of him, and the more the incomprehensibility took hold of him the more he believed it *must* have a meaning.

"Harry," Peggy called, for she was, Gerard realized, more attentive to their son than he was at that moment, and, the torn-off page in hand, he looked to the side, into another room that gave off from this main room, a room that was completely empty, and just when he looked he saw his son, with a look on his face of astonishment, fall through the floor. Gerard stood back for a second, not able to register anything beyond the vision—for that second was disconnected from any reaction—of his son disappearing. Gerard's visual impression remained that of his son's face, suspended in its astonishment, in its amazement, in its wonder, at what was happening. Peggy bumped against Gerard as she ran into the room, where many floorboards were torn up, to a gap, where, looking down, she screamed.

Crumpling it, Gerard shoved the page of script into a pocket of his shorts and ran to stand beside Peggy. Looking down he saw, through the ragged gap in the floor, his son lying spread out, his arms open, on the concrete floor of the basement some ten feet down.

Peggy screamed, "Harry, Harry!"

The gap was narrow, between beams, but, bruising his hips and shoulders, Gerard jumped through it to the floor below, and, on impact, fell to the side with a flash of shocking pain in the shin of his right leg and the knee of his left leg. Whatever the pain, in his panic he got up immediately, but the pain almost knocked him down again, and he had to lean against one of the wet, lichen-covered walls of the basement to steady himself enough to look down at his son, lying, totally motionless, on the wet concrete, blood spreading in a vivid circle around his head.

From above, Peggy was screaming, "Don't move him, don't move him."

His impulse, in the midst of his pain, was to reach down and take up his son in his arms and bring him he had no idea where, because he knew of no exit from the dark cellar, but bring him out into the daylight, bring him out into the light, bring him out to someone who must be there to help him, someone who was waiting for him, for them, just to help Gerard's son, to help his son and to help Gerard too; someone, or even some whole world of people, waiting for Gerard to appear with his son just because those silent and still people had known that something would happen to Gerard and his son and that they would need help.

Above, leaning over the gap, Peggy was screaming, "Don't touch him, don't touch him!"

Though the pain was so great it shocked out of him all other feeling, Gerard nevertheless knelt before his son, and as he reached down to pick up his son's body—Peggy screaming, "Don't move him, you'll kill him!"—Gerard, his knuckles scraping against the rough concrete, reached his arms out under his son and picked him up and raised him and held him, blood running from his son's head and down his back and onto Gerard's arms and legs, against him. He rocked back and forth, back and forth, groaning.

# TWO

At night, he lay in the hospital bed and, on a painkiller, felt his body suspended, leaving only his thoughts, which seemed to expand and contract and then expand on their own.

The thought all at once occurred to him that he and Peggy were very different. Different? he asked himself. His assumption had always been that they were, if different in small ways, similar in the big ways—ways big enough to have kept them happily together for ten years, two of them graduate-student years at Boston University when they lived together in an apartment off campus, and eight of them as husband and wife in their house among maple trees on a hillside above Manchester. The more he tried to concentrate on the similarities, the more they gave way to differences.

Why these differences had never before occurred to him as expansively as they did now, he didn't know.

Maybe everything that had made them believe they were essentially similar, so similar that they were as parents the same person, was in their love for Harry. Since his death, nothing made them similar, and they were two people who had nothing to do with each other.

When Peggy came, she reassured him that the college dean wanted him to know he must take all the time he needed to recover and that if, after the summer break, he wasn't yet able to teach, someone from the department would take over his classes until he was well enough to. Gerard nodded.

She sat beside his bed and asked if he was in pain.

"No," he answered.

She closed her eyes, and with them closed, she said quietly, "You should know that Harry has been buried." She kept her eyes closed.

As if to hide himself away, Gerard raised both arms and crossed them over his face.

Peggy remained as she was, her eyes closed. She remained as she was until Gerard stopped sobbing.

She said, "I thought I shouldn't be alone. I've been going to Henrietta's, who has asked me to stay over."

His throat and sinuses filled with tears, he said, "You should do that." Then she sat still and silent until he said, "Don't sit like that, Peg. Go home, or go to Henrietta's."

She kissed him, and after she did he slowly turned his head away.

Most of her daily visits, she sat still and silent on the chair. He knew that she would not talk about Harry unless he did, and he was not going to talk about Harry. When he was able, she walked with him, he on his crutches, along the hospital corridor with its shining floor, and she spoke only in response to questions he finally felt he must ask her to show her some attention. How was Henrietta? She was, Peggy said, supportive. Gerard did not take this as a reproach that he was not supportive, because Peggy did not expect support from him. She respected his withdrawal, even from her, and, as he asked her to, she told people he didn't want anyone to visit him. For all her silence and stillness, he could not feel she was someone whom he could give way to in his grief. He wept alone, at times simply staring into space and not thinking anything, and almost not feeling anything.

But he must show Peggy his appreciation for everything she had done. Peggy had helped him as much as anyone could help anyone else. He appreciated this—he more than appreciated it, he felt he owed her his life, for it was Peggy who had gotten the paramedics to the site of the accident. She never explained to Gerard how, as if she hadn't wanted to concern him with such an exercise. All he remembered was the long, long wait, holding Harry, dead, in his arms for hours, while he, his body a body of pain, lay flat on the con-crete floor with Harry lying on top of him, he kissing, over and over, the face of his son, as though kissing would revive him. Peggy still wanted to help him, and he did try to show his appreciation by saying, "Thank you, darling," for the flowers, for the grapes, for, when he was able to read, the books. But his appreciation didn't go deep, and he knew she was aware of this.

She came to take him home. In the car, he looked at the Merri-mack River as Peggy drove along, at the boulders over which the water flowed and foamed, and at the old, abandoned mills, some turned into offices, one even a museum of the history of the textile industry. Across the river on the West Side, the poor side of the city, was where he had grown up.

He asked, "Do you mind driving round my old neighborhood?"

Without questioning him, she did as he asked, and crossed over at the next bridge. The street of large, square tenement houses, some listing at odd angles, with looping wires crisscrossing from pole to pole across old asphalt here and there exposing old cobbles, led to the church. This had once been his neighborhood, his parish, of French Canuck immigrants who had come from Canada to work in the textile mills owned by the Yankees.

As if he realized this was the reason for his having wanted to come here, Gerard said, "Let's stop in front of the church."

Peggy did, and Gerard looked at the Gothic façade through the windshield.

"Would you get my crutches from the backseat," he asked, "and help me out?"

She did this also, and walked beside him, taking his arm to help him up the stone steps. The vault of the church's nave was narrow and high, as was the apse over the altar which rose in gold and pink Gothic arches, with white marble statues of saints standing in niches around the altar. His crutches thudding on the floor, Gerard went towards the altar, all the while looking around at the interior, which appeared to him both familiar and strange, and, holding out his crutches for Peggy to take, he sat heavily in a pew. This was the church where he had been baptized, where he had received his First Communion, where he had been confirmed, but he had not been married to Peggy here, and it was as if this ceremony, performed elsewhere, made his entire past in the parish disappear. And Harry had not been baptized here, had not received First Communion here, or confirmation. Harry had been brought up, as agreed by Peggy, without any religion. That agreement—that Harry should not be brought up with any religion, not his Catholic religion, not her Presbyterian religion—had, he once thought, made them deeply similar. He couldn't ask, but he supposed that Harry had not had a religious funeral service.

Peggy stood in the aisle by Gerard, who closed his eyes and lowered his head, then, after a moment, he opened his eyes and raised his head and saw a girl, a dark girl wearing a sari, a red sari with a golden border and golden stars, part of it draped over her head, walk, with a slight undulant movement of her body, towards the altar. She was wearing sandals. She knelt below the steps to the altar, pressed her palms together, and bowed in, Gerard assumed, prayer. He watched her for a long while, for all the while she prayed, and he watched her leave the church, passing by him down the main aisle.

He said to Peggy, "Let's go," and as he pulled himself up by holding on to the back of the pew in front of him, she held his crutches ready for him to place them under his arms.

In the car, they were silent, and they were, it seemed to him, because they were both thinking of that girl in the sari praying in the church, and they couldn't think what to say about her that was in any way relevant to them.

Their home—or, rather, her house, a Victorian mansion that had belonged to her great-grandfather, a Scottish Yankee who was a banker—was on the East Side of the Merrimack, in the North End. The North End had once been inhabited entirely by rich Yankees, but now also by rich-enough Jews, Italians, even a few French, many of the Yankees having moved to the bedroom community of Bedford outside Manchester. Gerard felt that to call Peggy's house his was pretentious, and maybe he had been pretentious in marrying her, knowing he would be living in this house.

She got him into the living room, where the lamps, on tables and floor, had large shades of pleated and stretched tawny silk and fringes of tiny beads. He fell back into the middle of a large, overstuffed, dark brown mohair sofa, his legs in casts sticking out.

As if, finally, she could address him directly because she had gotten him into the house, Peggy said, "Look, Gerard, I know you didn't want to see anyone, but that isn't good, not for you and not for me. I've asked Joe to come over for a drink."

"You're right, of course you're right," Gerard said. "Of course I should see people, both for your sake and mine."

She didn't address what they were both most aware of: that he had not only not seen Harry's grave, he had not mentioned Harry's name since their son's death.

"I'd like to see Joe," Gerard said.

Joe was from Manchester, a big, rough guy, who had only once been as far as New York, and who taught Spanish in the modern language department of the college. When he arrived, Peggy left Gerard alone with him in the living room. Joe sat in an armchair, and told Gerard that he'd take over his classes until he was ready to teach.

He said, "You won't believe it, Gerard, you won't believe that this year we've got even more students from more races than you knew existed enrolled in the college, this college of one-story buildings in the boondocks that can't even dream of having a graduate program. My first day, I asked my students what languages their parents or grandparents spoke, and, you know, almost every student came up with a different language. Never mind Canuck French, Dago-Italian, Mexican Spanish, Midwestern German. We've got Cantonese and Mandarin Chinese, we've got Tagalog, we've got Bengali, and we've got Hindi."

"What's Tagalog?"

"I didn't know myself. It's spoken in the Philippines."

Gerard called for Peggy, who came in from the kitchen with snifters of whiskey on a silver tray, along with a bowl of peanuts and little napkins. She placed the tray on the coffee table and turned to leave.

"Won't you join us?" Joe asked her.

"I'll let you two talk," she said.

"Peg," Gerard asked, as if calling her again, "do you know what happened to the shorts I was wearing at the time of the accident?"

Shocked, she frowned. "Your shorts?"

"Those shorts."

"I think I threw them away."

"You did?"

"You need them?"

"There was something in one of the pockets I want."

She was shocked, he saw, that the first time he should mention the accident in which their son died was to ask for the shorts he had been wearing. As she looked about the room as if for something to explain his request, her frown became a wince that contorted her face. Then she looked at him and said, "I may have left them in the basement, and forgot to put them into the washing machine."

"Would you go look, please?"

"Look for your shorts?"

"Yes."

"Look for them now?"

"Yes, please."

"Why now, Gerard? What could be in the pocket of your shorts that you want to have it now?"

He tried to temper the urgency he felt to have the sheet of paper with the strange script he had found in that house. He must more than temper it, he must suppress it, because Peggy was right, to have referred to the accident for the first time by asking for the sheet of paper he had crumpled into the pocket of his shorts was not only irreverent, it was sacrilegious. This word came to Gerard's mind on its own, without, it seemed, his having to think. And yet, he did want that sheet of paper.

But he said, "It's nothing."

Peggy was too shocked to let that go. "Nothing? It's nothing? It must be something if you asked for it now."

Gerard raised a hand. "Nothing."

"Don't tell me that." And she voiced what he had thought. "The first time you refer to the accident in any way, it's for something you put in the pocket of your shorts. Well, it must be important."

Joe pressed the tips of the fingers of both hands together and let his head hang down.

"I'm sorry," Gerard said, his hand to his forehead. "I don't know why it came to me—why I want to see some writing on a sheet of paper I found in that house. Maybe it only shows how unwilling I am to face anything about Harry's death. I can only face something that happened then but doesn't have anything to do with it."

Peggy knelt by the side of the armchair. She said, "I've been waiting for you to mention Harry's death, Gerard. I can't tell you how much I've been waiting for that."

This, to his own shame, struck Gerard as banal. He didn't want to think of it as banal. He had always thought of Peggy's feelings as deeper than his for being oh-so-open to expression, while his were closed to expression. He was cruder, emotionally and intellectually, than Peggy. He let his hand drop from his forehead and his arm fall across the arm of the chair towards her, as if he had become too weak to hold it up. Peggy took his hand in hers. Gerard, biting his lower lip, didn't look at her, didn't look anywhere.

Releasing his hand and standing, Peggy said softly, "I'll go see if I can find those shorts." She went out.

Joe remained as he had been, his fingertips pressed together, his head lowered.

Gerard said to him, "I'm sorry, Joe."

"Nothing to be sorry about," Joe said. "I wish I could help."

"Help yourself to the whiskey."

Reaching out awkwardly because of his big bulk, Joe did take up one of the snifters, studied it for a moment, then sipped. He was trying to be as delicate as he could.

Gerard sat up when Peggy came back into the room.

"I found the shorts," she said, holding out in one hand, as if not to him but to someone who might come into the room and ask for it, the rag of old shorts, cut off at the legs and frayed, sweat-stained and pouched at the genitals. In the other she held the sheet of paper that had been crumpled in his pocket; she had smoothed it flat. "I found them in an old hamper where I put clothes I plan to throw away."

Now Gerard didn't want to see the shorts, torn from old dungarees, that he had been so eager to see, and, more, he didn't want to see the sheet of paper. He wished that Peggy had thrown the shorts and the paper away. And yet, too eagerly, he reached out for the sheet of paper.

She didn't hand it to him. "They have blood on them, the shorts," she said. "I don't know why, but I hadn't been able to wash them because of the blood, so I shoved them into the old hamper and forgot them."

Gerard kept his hand held out.

She looked at the paper, frowning. "What is the writing on this?" she asked.

"I don't know."

"You kept it even though you don't know what it is?"

"I don't know why."

It took him a long while to raise his hand again to take it, and when he saw it, that strange script so carefully written out, tears filled his eyes. Holding the paper close, he mentally traced what he assumed to be letters, though maybe they were not letters, but symbols. His tears dripped from his cheeks onto the paper. Peggy remained at his side. She would not, she could not, understand the expression of his feelings, so much shallower than hers, Gerard thought, because even he could not understand them.

Joe stood and said, "I think I should go."

"No," Gerard said to him, "don't go, please don't. It's good for me, as Peggy knows, to have company."

"I'd like to help."

Gerard thrust the paper towards Joe and asked, "Do you have any idea what this could be?"

Swinging his big body, Joe came round the coffee table to take the paper. Looking at it, he said, "I couldn't say, Gerard. I've never seen anything like it." And he held the paper out for Gerard to take it back.

"Do you know of anyone who might know?"

"I'd have to think about that. I don't know anyone in the college who's a philologist."

"Think about it."

"You want me to take this away and try to find out what it means?"

"That'd be a big help to me."

Joe shook his head. "I'll give it a try."

Joe let himself out, and Peggy was left holding the bloody shorts. She asked Gerard, "What do you want me to do with these?"

"What would you do with them?" Gerard asked.

"I would throw them away."

"Just like that—in the garbage?"

"What should I do with them?"

"Burn them."

"Burn them?"

He tried to laugh. "I guess I was thinking of an old nun in my parish grammar school telling us that the only way to get rid of holy objects—blessed holy cards, dried up palms from Palm Sunday, rosary beads—was to burn them and scatter the ashes."

"That is stupid."

"It is stupid, and, you know, I never realized before now what a stoical person you are for saying it's stupid."

"Stoical?"

"Stoical."

"Do you mean that I'm not showing enough feeling for this"—she held the limp, faded, but blood-stained shorts out to him—"relic of our suffering, the only object you have ever mentioned with any significance to you that has to do with the death of our son?"

"It was the sheet of paper I really wanted," he said. "You can do what you want with the shorts."

"And that has more significance than anything else?"

"I don't know why."

"You mean, it *does*?"

He could only answer, "I don't know why."

"Gerard, Gerard, Gerard."

"You're right to get angry at me. I want you to get angry at me. I want you to tell me that I'm a person of no feeling, if all that I can think about, after the horror, is a sheet of paper with writing on it I can't understand. I should call Joe back, should tell him to throw it away. I should tell you to throw out those shorts, which I was going to throw out anyway, they're so old. Call Joe yourself, please, and tell him to tear up the sheet of paper, and wash the shorts to get the blood off them, just that, and then throw them away. You may think I don't have much feeling, and maybe you're right, but I do at least have this feeling—that I couldn't stand Harry's blood being thrown out into the garbage."

Peggy pressed the shorts to her face. "I can't wash his blood away."

They balanced there for a moment.

"But at least call Joe and tell him to get rid of that sheet of paper."

Lowering the shorts, Peggy said, "I can't do that, either."

"Why?"

"Because, however much I don't understand, it *means* something to you."

A low howl broke from Gerard, the howl of giving in to something Peggy was allowing him to give in to, and he should have loved her, loved her more than he ever had, for allowing him to give in; but, the howl fading as if over a vast, snowbound landscape and heard by no one, he dropped his head back against the chair and stared past her, past all his love for her, into a distance he was drawn out to and would go out to beyond his love for her and her love for him. Maybe out there, where Peggy was allowing him the freedom to go, there was no love at all.

Peggy left him.

Joe telephoned Gerard the next afternoon to say, "Listen, I asked around the college, even asked those students I was telling you about, and, would you believe it, one of them, from India, said she recognized the writing. It's the alphabet in Sanskrit. Her father can read Sanskrit, but though she can't, she recognizes the alphabet.

That's all the writing on the paper is. It's the alphabet in Sanskrit, written over and over."

"That's all," Gerard repeated.

"Do you want the paper back?" Joe asked.

"You can throw it away."

Gerard hung up with a sense of defeat, a sense that his expectation had been more than disappointed; it had been made impossible to realize. Peggy would have told him as much. She was with her friend Henrietta. He got up on his crutches to walk from room to room, asking himself, well, what had he expected? That the incomprehensible writing would have had a meaning for him just because it had been incomprehensible to him? All his life, he had been drawn, as naïvely as a boy was drawn by the adventure of exploring an abandoned house, by what was beyond his comprehension, and he didn't know why. He must stop that. He owed it to Peggy, to her and to their future together, to stop.

When he asked himself, with as calculating a mind as he was capable of, how a page of Sanskrit letters got into an abandoned house, he answered himself, because there were people now in Manchester for whom the Sanskrit alphabet was familiar, and one of those people had, for some reason, gone into that house to practice the script and left the page in the fireplace. That was the explanation.

# THREE

The Valley Cemetery in Manchester was the old Protestant cemetery. Though Peggy's parents were buried there, unless a person was a hundred and ten years old and had had a plot reserved since the beginning of the nineteenth century, no places were free. Peggy took Gerard to the other big Protestant cemetery, the Pine Grove, where Harry was buried in a plot that Gerard assumed she meant also, one day, for herself and for him. Still on crutches, walking just behind Peggy between the rows of grave-stones, Gerard noted names that could not have been Yankee, some of them even French, and he stopped for a second before one that had incised in it his family name, Chauvin, with the surprise that distant relatives of his, very distant, would have found their way into the Yankee world of the dead, reminding him of how he had wanted to find his way into the Yankee world of the living; in that world he had expected to have everything he wanted. He came up abruptly behind Peggy standing before a dark granite stone, nar-row, the head of an angel and wings outspread carved into the stone at the top, and Harry's name, Harold McGregor-Chauvin, her family name and his hyphenated, which, as far as he knew, had never occurred while Harry was alive. She turned to him, and all he could say was, "Why? I don't understand." Not understanding what he meant any more than he did, she walked away, and he, the ends of his crutches sinking into the sod, followed her.

As if he were alone, at meals with Peggy in their dining room, he would suddenly sit back and, weeping, ask, "Why?" On Peggy's insistence, which he always deferred to, they would go out for meals at the homes of friends, and at their dining tables he would, in the midst of a low-level conversation among the others, begin to weep, and, again as if he were suddenly alone with his grief, ask, "Why?" Peggy would excuse them both, everyone around the table understanding, and drive Gerard home and lie next to him in bed and hear him weep more, asking, "But why?" In a soft voice, she would say, "Don't ask yourself that question, Gerard, please don't ask yourself that question." This made him weep more and almost shout out, "But *why?*" even though he gave in to her putting her arms about him and holding him and, as if he were her baby son, rocking him and saying, "Shh, shh."

On crutches, he resumed his teaching, again because Peggy said he had to, and sometimes, while elucidating a point of the language—writing on the blackboard letters that, once drawn, appeared to him strange when he stood back from them and studied them, as if he wasn't sure for a moment what they meant any more than he had known what the Sanskrit alphabet meant when he had first seen it—he would turn away from the class and weep, and, turning back, his face dripping with tears that he did not hide, explain when the past participle agreed with the verb *avoir* and when not, depending on the placement of the object. The students, whether or not they understood, listened attentively. And he would dismiss them early.

Peggy spent more and more time with her close friend Henrietta, and sometimes when he got home from the college he found the house empty, she still at Henrietta's. She always appeared, apologizing that she was late, but he never reproached her, and he told her that she should stay with Henrietta as long as she wanted, he would get his own meal, and read for a while or not, and go to bed.

"But you must count on me, as always," she said.

He would kiss her on the forehead and thank her.

An autumn evening, when Gerard got home from work, without knowing whether Peggy was at home or not, he went upstairs and stood before the closed door to Harry's bedroom, which had not been opened since his son's death. He stood for a long time. His hand seemed of itself to reach out for the knob and slowly open the door. The bed was unmade, and on the floor, scattered over the carpet, was a miniature city destroyed: tiny cars and train engines and wagons, overturned houses and gasoline stations, and stiff-limbed men and women lying among the ruins.

His knees up, Gerard sat on the low chair at the table on which were books, many with torn pages, and broken pencils and school notebooks among stones, sea-smooth fragments of glass, large, rusty nails. Gerard picked up a first-grade notebook and opened it to the first page. From the top left corner to the bottom right, the letters crushed together without spaces, was written ABCDE FGHIJKLMNOPQRSTUVWXYZ, over and over, with no space even between the end of one alphabet and the beginning of the next. Gerard repeated to himself, over and over, A B C D E F G H I J K L M N O P Q R S T U V W X Y Z. He closed the notebook and pushed it back among the strange assortment of objects on the table, a bottle cap, a stone embedded with mica, an empty spool for thread, part of Harry's collection, and after sitting still for a long moment he rose from his cramped position on the chair and left the room, leaving the door open.

Peggy was in the kitchen. He kissed her, lightly, on the lips.

Peggy said, "You're a little late this evening."

"When I got home, I went up to Harry's room."

A wince wrinkled the corners of her eyes. "I didn't hear."

"I was quiet."

Gerard walked away from her, to the end of the kitchen, where the door to the backyard was open; he stepped out, and from under a yellow maple tree he looked at Peggy take a roasted chicken from the oven. With two large forks, she lifted the carcass of the chicken out of the roasting pan and placed it on a platter, then she picked up the platter.

"Are you ready to eat?" she called.

He came in, but stayed near the door to watch her go from the kitchen into the dining room, and through the doorway to the dining room he saw her place the chicken on the table set with a clean white cloth and white napkins. He pressed his thumb and index finger into his eyes. Two silver candlesticks were on the table, on either side of the chicken.

As they ate, he asked, "Have you ever wondered why the alphabet is set up the way it is?"

"What do you mean?"

"Well, why does it start with *A B C* and not *F D Q*? Who arranged it the way it is, and when?"

"Why do you want to know that?"

"It just occurred to me."

"I've never thought about it."

"I'd like to know if the very first alphabet is known, and if it's arranged *A B C,* as ours is. And if so I'd like to know why. It's the first thing we learn, but I've never heard anyone ask why it's arranged the way it is. Why, do you think?"

"No one has ever asked, I think, because no one has ever wondered."

"That's odd, isn't it, that no one has?" Gerard said. "Well, maybe someone has."

"You should be able to find someone at the college you can ask."

"The different disciplines at the college are so departmentalized, I wouldn't know where to begin."

"You could find out."

"Yes, I could," he said, but as he said this he felt too low to find out anything.

Peggy must have sensed how low he was, because she tried to keep up his interest. She asked, "How are the ABCs arranged in Latin?"

"Arranged? I'm not sure, unless they're arranged according to the Greek alphabet."

"All I remember of the Greek alphabet," Peggy said, "are letters from fraternity and sorority houses when I was in college."

"Alpha, beta, gamma, delta, epsilon, zita," Gerard recited.

"Zita doesn't sound right."

"Alpha, beta, gamma, delta, epsilon, are right, though."

"Except that gamma could be a *G*."

"It's close enough to *C*."

"Close enough," she said. He knew that she was keeping up his interest when she added, "Was there an earlier alphabet that the Greek alphabet was based on? I know that the Hebrew alphabet begins with Aleph. Didn't the Hebrews come before the Greeks?"

"The Phoenicians did."

"Did they arrange the alphabet the way it is?"

"I don't know, Peggy. How can I know? I don't know anything. I couldn't even recognize the Sanskrit alphabet."

"I'm sorry, I'm just trying to keep up the talk."

"I'm aware that you are, and I'm very grateful."

"Shall I stop?"

"No, please don't stop."

She lowered her head, then raised it to ask, "Who came before the Phoenicians?"

"The Egyptians."

"They had hieroglyphics, though, not letters."

"Yes."

"You should look into it, Gerard. You should try to find out."

"I'm sure there isn't an answer."

"Maybe not, but even so it'd be interesting to try to find out. Who knows what you'd come up with?"

"I don't know if it matters," Gerard said.

"It matters. You should find out."

"No," he said, "it doesn't matter. Not really."

"Yes it does," she said.

He helped her clear the table and wash the dishes, and this they did in silence. After, she went upstairs to get ready to go out, as she did now every evening, to visit her old friend Henrietta, in whom she found more comfort than she found staying with him. He didn't understand what the comfort was that she got from Henrietta, but he accepted her needing it; and, he thought, he preferred staying alone after the strain of having dinner together and trying to sustain interest in some subject neither wanted much to talk about. The fact was, he wasn't interested in anything, and least of all in his work as a professor of French at a small liberal-arts college in Manchester, New Hampshire. When Peggy came down, she called him from the entry hall, and he went to her. Her hair was brushed out and her face appeared fresh in its simplicity.

"Yes?" he asked.

She said, "You left the door to Harry's room open."

"I did," he said.

"Did you do that on purpose?"

He hadn't, but he said, "I did."

"Oh, Gerard," she exclaimed, and, her arms out, she rushed to him. He pressed her to him, his head on her shoulder.

Drawing back, her cheeks now wet with tears, she said, "I won't be late," as if she did not want to leave him, but she must.

He let his arms hang loose and stood still after she left. He looked about the entry hall, up the staircase with its dark wooden railing, at the stained-glass window at the top through which the late sun cast different colors down the stairs, and, down the stairs, on the little Turkish rug.

Against the wall below the stairs was a bookcase, and on the bookcase were objects that, it occurred to him, made up something of a collection as strange as Harry's, for they did not appear to connect in any way that would make anyone assume they were a collection: a Persian puppet held up by a stand; an old wooden carpenter's plane; a Chinese-export porcelain plate with a crack in it; a Murano glass vase; a toy bear on wheels with a patch on its haunch; a fragment of a stone rosette from a Gothic arch; an oval, dented, and scratched candy tin with roses pictured on its lid; a big teacup. Within the context of his life before he met Peggy, within the context of her life before she met him, and within the context of their lives together, these all meant something; but as he stared at them, stared with a concentration that made him feel he was going into something of a trance, he had the sense that they were connected in ways that had nothing to do with Peggy and him and their lives, but with something else that they, between themselves, were aware of, and that he couldn't himself connect with, as if the connection remained just outside his ability to grasp it.

In the bookcase was kept a miscellany of books. On the bottom shelf, lying on its side because it was too tall to fit into the shelf, was an old Webster's dictionary.

Gerard reached down and, a little cloud of dust coming off it, he drew it out. It was very heavy, and he almost stumbled forward hefting it up into his arms. He brought it into the living room and, sitting in the middle of the sofa, placed it on the coffee table. The cover was brownish, very scuffed, and held to the thick spine by bands of clear tape. Within a gold circle, placed within a gold wreath at the top of the circle, was the letter *W* in fancy cursive, and below that, in capitals, was: *WEBSTER'S INTERNATIONAL DICTIONARY.* Part of the binding was torn, and a strip of brown cloth dangled from the bottom edge.

The dictionary had belonged to Gerard's grandfather, who once explained to him how the top and bottom stain of the pages of the enormous book had been made: by colored oils that were floated on water and swirled about lightly with a feather, a process he was told about because, his grandfather said, it was no longer used, had ceased to be used long, long before Gerard's birth. The bottom stain was of pale blue and pink swirls, faded. Gerard opened the cover to the brown endpapers and the signature of his grandfather, in ink, in large, awkward letters.

That his grandfather had owned such a dictionary should have been a surprise to Gerard, because his grandfather had not been educated beyond primary school; it was not a surprise because of course someone who was so uneducated would want to possess, simply by possessing one book, all of knowledge.

The first pages of the dictionary were very wrinkled, some folded on themselves. Among them were black-and-white photographs of the editors and the specialists who supplied definitions to specialized subjects: Anthropology, Catholicism, Mineralogy, Accounting, Chemistry, Wines, Gems and Jewelry, Zoology, Athletic Sports, Weights and Measures.

On an impulse, Gerard stuck his index finger, arbitrarily, into one of the little indentations on the side of the dictionary, each with a black tab with a letter of the alphabet, and he opened the book. The part he lifted was heavy and began to fall sideways when Gerard raised it to a standing point, so the book seemed to take on a momentum of its own and to slam open with a thud. It opened on the letter *K*.

Gerard turned the pages, thin and foxed here and there, until he stopped, not with any intention, and began to read down a list of entries. He felt he was still in that slight trance, that of sensing connections all about him that he himself couldn't connect with, as if they crisscrossed in invisible lines through the very air, bouncing from a ceramic bowl on the coffee table to the shade of a floor lamp to a pillow on the sofa to a framed watercolor of trees against a sunset, creating a pattern too complicated for him even to imagine, and in their midst he read down the list of entries, and was surprised by the number of different worlds and the languages of these worlds that were listed, one very close to the other, as if the letter *K* were particularly evocative of them:

**Khar'i·a** (kŭr'ĭ·à), *n.* A member of an animistic tribe in western Bengal; also, their Munda language. See AUSTROASIATIC **d.**

**Kha'ri·jite** (kä'rĭ·jīt), *n*; *pl.* KHAWARIJ (kä·wä'rĭj). [Arabic *khāriji* dissenter.] A member of the oldest religious sect in Islam. The modern representatives are the Abadites.

**Kha·rosh'thi** (kà·rōsh·tē), *n.* [Sanskrit *kharoshthī*.] A script of Aramaic origin used in northwestern India, Afghanistan, and Turkestan, about 300 B.C. to A.D. 200.

**Khar·war'** (kàr·wär'), *n. sing. & pl.* One of a people in Bengal speaking a Munda language.

**Kha'si** (kä'sē), *n.* **a.** A member of a group of Mongoloid tribes of the Khasi and Jaintia Hills, Assam. **b.** Their language. See AUSTROASIATIC **b.**

**Khas'·ku'ra** (käs'koŏr'ä), *n.* The Pahari dialect of Nepal. See KHA, 1; PAHARI; cf. GORKHALI, NEPALI, PARBATE.

**Khat'ti** (kăt'tē), *n.* **a.** The cuneiform var. of HITTITE. **b.** One of an ancient non-Indo-European people of Asia Minor, sometimes called proto-Hittites.

**Kha·zar'** (kä·zär'), *n; pl.* KHAZAR, KHAZARS (-zärz'), or KHAZARES (-zā·rēz'). Also **Cha·zar'.** One of a nation powerful from about A.D. 200 to 950, at first in the Caucasus region, later in southeastern Russia. In the 7th century many of them embraced the Jewish religion. They were finally overcome by the Russians. It is not certain if they were a Turkish or Georgian race.—**Kha·za'ri·an, Cha·za'ri·an** (kä·zä'rĭ·ăn), *adj.*

**Khond** (kŏnd), *n.* **a.** One of a mixed Dravidian Kui-speaking group of tribes of Orissa, India. Called also Kandh. **b.** Their language. See KUI, 2.

**Kho'war** (kō'wär), *n.* The language of Chitral, northwestern India. See DARD LANGUAGES.

**Khu'zi** (ko͞o'zē), *n.* **a.** One of a tribe in western Persia, which became extinct during the 11th century. They were descendants of the ancient Elamites and their name is preserved in the name of the province Khuzistan. **b.** The language of the Khuzi.

**ki'a o'ra** (kē'ä ō'rä). [Maori.] Be well; be happy; —used in toasts. *Australasia.*

It seemed to Gerard that the trance he was in raised him above himself, so that he saw himself as if from a higher level, leaning closer and closer to read the book as the room became dim; saw himself and saw the room and saw the other rooms of the house, then saw the house from outside; he saw the roofs of neighboring houses, saw the streetlights go on along the streets lined with dark maple trees, saw the lights of the downtown of Manchester go on, saw the river reflecting the lights. And while on that level Gerard saw to the great circle of the horizon, still pale on the west with the light of the falling sun and becoming pale to the east with the light of the rising moon, on the lower level of himself hunched over the dictionary, squinting to see, he was concentrating on the entries he read as he had never before concentrated. It seemed to him that the invisible lines he was sure zigzagged about the room, connecting the disparate objects in the room, were zigzagging not only from entry to entry on the page, but through the pages, connecting rugs, clothes, food from all over the world, and, more, connecting the tribes, civilizations, races which the rugs, clothes, food, were the products of—tribes, civilizations, races that spoke Khuzi, Khowar, Khond, spoke Khaskura and Kharia, spoke Maori. On the level of himself reading, hardly able to see, he was absolutely certain that every entry in the dictionary, over three thousand pages of them in tiny print, connected with every other. And on the level of himself now looking down at the whole, revolving Earth, he was absolutely certain that everything in all the world interconnected.

It was too late for him, too late to devote his life to philology, but it came to him with a sudden shock that this was all he was interested in. Nothing else interested him just now. Not his teaching, not his marriage, not even the death of his son.

He was just able to make out an entry:

**khir** (kēr), *n.* [Hindi, from Sanskrit *kṣīra* milk.] A porridge of millet or rice boiled in milk. *India.*

Peggy entered the room. Alarmed, she called, "Why are you sitting in the dark?"

"Am I sitting in the dark?"

She went quickly to the lamp on the table by the sofa and switched it on, then stood over him.

"You're looking up something in that old dictionary?"

"I don't know why; I got interested."

"Does it have anything to do with what we were talking about at dinner?"

"What were we talking about at dinner?"

"You don't remember?"

"I don't think I do."

"I thought it was interesting."

"What was it?"

Peggy sat in an armchair at an angle to the sofa. She put her hand to her forehead. "Maybe it wasn't that interesting," she said. She let her hand fall into her lap. "I came home early. I felt that I've been neglecting you wrongly, felt that, after all, we have our lives together."

"Did you decide that with Henrietta?"

"Please don't berate me for going to Henrietta. She's been a great support at a time when we both needed support from someone outside. I've wished that you'd find someone to go to."

"I'm not berating you. I'm grateful to Henrietta for supporting you." He looked at the page of the dictionary and, still more fixed on it than on Peggy, was able to read quickly:

**Kick'a·poo** (kĭk'à·pōō), *n*. An Indian of an Algonquian tribe, originally of southern Wisconsin. About 800 descendants live on reservations in Kansas, Oklahoma, and Chihuahua.

He didn't listen to Peggy say something, and not until she called him—"Gerard"—did he sit up and look at her. "I was trying to tell you something important." Half her face was lit from the lamp, half in shadow.

"Yes?" he asked.

"Are you listening?"

He didn't respond, but continued simply to look at her, and he thought for a moment that he didn't know who she was.

"Are you?" she asked.

He nodded.

"When I told Henrietta that I found the door to Harry's room open, that you had gone into the room and left it open when you left, she said she thought that was meaningful."

"Meaningful in what way?"

"That something has changed in you about Harry."

"What's the change?"

"That you no longer feel you have to understand why our son died, the way you have up to now been obsessed with trying to."

"Was I obsessed with trying to understand why Harry died?"

"Gerard, Gerard. One of the reasons why I went so often to Henrietta's was because you were making *me* obsessed. You honestly don't remember that?"

"I don't."

"You see, you have changed. I'm amazed, I have to say, that you've changed so much that you can't remember your being as obsessed as you were. It was so unlike you, you sometimes frightened me."

"I frightened you?"

"I felt I'd lost you, didn't know where you had gone, and that frightened me. Mostly, you made me very sad, sad because I knew, I know, there's no reason for Harry's death."

Gerard lowered his head, and as he did he tried to catch a glimpse of the page of the dictionary he had been reading. The distraction—which, he thought, was all it was—was wrong now, and he must be attentive to Peggy. She was right: what she had to tell him was important. But he was aware that he sounded as if he hadn't been listening when he said, flatly, "No, no reason," and, unable to hold himself back, he leaned over the page to read another entry. Before he was able to focus, Peggy, wiping her cheek with her fingers, said, "Gerard, are you with me?"

He had to look up. "Where else could I be?"

"I hoped, coming home early, that we would be together in a way we haven't been in—" But she choked up and wasn't able to continue before swallowing hard. "I so pray that you've changed. That would help me change. And I need to change, Gerard. I need to believe that we can go on with our lives, not as before, but maybe in a closer way."

"You don't believe that now?"

"It's everything I need to believe."

"And it depends on me?"

"It does, Gerard, it does." Her voice high, she asked, "You have changed, Gerard, haven't you? You may not have known the meaning of it, but you can see now, can't you, that leaving the door to Harry's room open means a change?"

He smiled at her, a tender smile because he felt such tenderness towards her for her simplicity, for her obviousness. "Yes," he said softly, "I have changed."

At that, she gave in to sobs, and he, smiling his tender smile, watched her, her breasts heaving, her face contorted in spasms. With a last heave of all her body, she became still, the bodice of her blouse soaked with tears.

Even more softly, he said, "Go up to bed now."

As she rose from her chair, she lurched to the side, too weak to stand, and was about to fall. Gerard jumped up to support her by holding one of her arms, and when she got her balance she leaned towards him, expecting him, he knew, to take her in his arms, but he said again, whispering, "Go up to bed."

"You'll come too?"

"I'll come."

She was so unsteady in her walk that he felt he must go with her, and he realized that everything she had been through was worse than what he had been through, that she had suffered, and was suffering, more than he. As she left the room, he took a step to go with her, but then he drew back, he told himself, to turn off the lamp. His hand on the switch, he turned to look at the dictionary open on the table, and that trance-like state came over him, came over him with the recognition that it had for a while vanished and had now come back, and he was aware of it expanding about him, aware of it separating him from himself, so he was there, standing over the dictionary with all his concentration converging to a point that made it possible for him to see, even at a distance,

> **Khal'di·an** (kăl'dĭ·ăn), *adj.* Of or pertaining to ancient Khaldia (or Uratu), or its inhabitants, or their language; Urataean; Vannic.

He was there, and he was also somewhere else. He sat before the dictionary.

As though the dictionary were itself drawing his concentration, with greater and greater acuteness, he found himself reading:

> **Khal'kha** (käl'kȧ), *n.* Also **Khal'ka, Kal'ka. a.** One of a tribe of the eastern Mongols, subject to China. See Mongol. **b.** Their language. See Ural-Altaic Languages.
>
> **Kham'ti** (käm'tē), *n. sing. & pl.* One of a group of tribes in northeastern Assam and Burma. Also, their language. See Indo-Chinese Languages.

Gerard sat back into the sofa and put both his hands over his head, unable, suddenly, to stand the concentration that was being demanded of him, as if what was being demanded of him were not only to be more attentive than he had ever before been in his life, but to bring together, in an all-inclusive figure so complicated it could not be devised, everything he was being made so amazingly attentive to. He couldn't do it. No one could do it. To do it would be to try to have everything, and everything could only ever be an idea, because everything all together was impossible. He pressed his hands down hard on his head and closed his eyes.

With a deep breath, he lowered his hands and opened his eyes and, feeling that he was being impelled and that there was nothing for him to do but give in to the impulse, either because it was too great for him to resist or because he was too weak to resist it, he once again leaned over the dictionary.

No, he thought, he must go up to Peggy, he must.

And he closed the dictionary, which, at the point when the heavy thickness of pages he lifted began to fall, seemed to him to shut itself and, giving up on him as easily as it had held him in thrall, suddenly exclude him from it. But he didn't leave. He placed a hand on it and for a long time sat without moving.

Maybe his hand rose of itself, he couldn't be sure, and moved to the side of the book, where the black tabs with the letters of the alphabet indented the marbled pages; and, though he couldn't be sure, maybe his index finger of itself inserted itself into the indentation for the letter *A,* and maybe his hand lifted the pages and opened the book to the first page of that letter. His hand slowly turning the following pages, all Gerard was aware of in what was happening was that the word "alphabet" was being looked for. In the gutters of the book were a toothpick, a short length of gold string, tiny seeds. At the turning of a page, he saw, revealed before him, this:

Showing the Name of the Letter (for the Hebrew, Arabic, and Greek), the Roman Transliteration (used in the Etymologies in this Dictionary), and, in parentheses, the Websterian Phonetic Symbol.

### HEBREW[1]

- א aleph ' (')
- ב beth b, bh (b)
- ג gimel g, gh (g)
- ד daleth d, dh (d)
- ה he h (h)
- ו vau w, v (w)
- ז zayin z (z)
- ח cheth ḥ (ḳ)
- ט teth ṭ (t)
- י yodh y (y)
- כ caph k, kh (k)
- ל lamedh l (l)
- מ mem m (m)
- נ nun n (n)
- ס samekh s (s)
- ע ayin ' (')
- פ pe p, ph (p)
- צ sadhe ts (s sharp)
- ק koph q (k)
- ר resh r (r)
- שׂ sin ś (s)
- שׁ shin sh (sh)
- ת tav t, th (t)

### ARABIC[2]

- ا alif ' (?) (ʻ)
- ب bāʼ b (b)
- ت tāʼ t (t)
- ث thāʼ th (th)
- ج jīm j (j)
- ح ḥāʼ ḥ (h)
- خ khāʼ kh (ḳ)
- د dāl d (d)
- ذ dhāl dh (th)
- ر rāʼ r (r)
- ز zāy z (z)
- س sīn s (s)
- ش shīn sh (sh)
- ص ṣād ṣ (s)
- ض ḍād ḍ (th)
- ط ṭāʼ ṭ (t)
- ظ ẓāʼ ẓ (z)
- ع ʻayn ʻ (ʻ)
- غ ghayn gh (ḳ)
- ف fāʼ f (f)
- ق qāf q (k)
- ك kāf k (k)
- ل lām l (l)
- م mīm m (m)
- ن nūn n (n)
- ه hāʼ h (h)
- و wāw w (w)
- ي yāʼ y (y)

### GREEK[6]

- A α alpha a (ä)
- B β beta b (b)
- Γ γ gamma g (g)
- Δ δ delta d (d)
- E ε epsilon e (ĕ)
- Z ζ zeta z (z)
- H η eta ē (ä)
- Θ θ theta th (th)[7]
- I ι iota i (ē)
- K κ kappa k (k)
- Λ λ lambda l (l)
- M μ mu m (m)
- N ν nu n (n)
- Ξ ξ xi x (ks)
- O o omicron o (ŏ)
- Π π pi p (p)
- P ρ rho r, rh (r)
- Σ σ ς sigma s (s)
- T τ tau t (t)
- Υ υ upsilon y, u (ü, oo)
- Φ φ phi ph (f)[8]
- X χ chi ch (k, ḳ)[9]
- Ψ ψ psi ps (ps)
- Ω ω omega ō (ŏ)

### RUSSIAN[10]

- А а a (ä)
- Б б b (b, p)
- В в v (v, f)
- Г г g (g, k)
- Д д d (d)
- Е е e (yä, ä, yŏ, yŏ, yĕ, ĕ)
- Ж ж zh (zh, sh)
- З з z (z)
- И и Й й i, ĭ (ē, y)
- I i[10] i (ē)
- К к k (k)
- Л л l (l)
- М м m (m)
- Н н n (n)
- О о o (ŏ, ŏ)
- П п p (p)
- Р р r (r)
- С с s (s)
- Т т t (t)
- У у u (oo)
- Ф ф f (f)
- Х х kh (ḳ)
- Ц ц ts (ts)
- Ч ч ch (ch, tsh)
- Ш ш sh (sh)
- Щ щ shch (shch)
- Ъ ъ[10] *
- Ы ы y (wē, üē, ĭ)
- Ь ь e, —, ʻ† (ĕ, —)
- Ѣ ѣ[10] ye (yĕ, ĕ)
- Э э[10] e (ĕ)
- Ю ю yu (yoo [ü])
- Я я ya (yä, yä, ĕ)
- Ѳ ѳ[10] f (f)
- V v[10] y (ē)

\* marks nonpalatalization
† marks palatalization

### GERMAN

- A a (ä)
- Ä ä (â, ĕ)
- B b (b, p)
- C c (k, ts, s)
- Ch ch (ḳ)
- D d (d, t)
- E e (ā, ĕ)
- F f (f)
- G g (g, k, k)
- H h (h)
- I i (ē, ĭ)
- J j (y)
- K k (k)
- L l (l)
- M m (m)
- N n (n)
- O o (ō, ŏ, ŏ)
- Ö ö (û)
- P p (p)
- Q q (k) Only in qu pron. kv
- R r (r)
- S ſ (z, s)
- Sch ſch (sh)
- T t (t)
- U u (oo, oo)
- Ü ü (ü)
- V v (f, v)
- W w (v)
- X x (ks)
- Y y
- Z z (ts)

### SANSKRIT[11]

- अ a (ă or ŭ)
- आ ā (ä)
- इ i (ĭ)
- ई ī (ē)
- उ u (oo)
- ऊ ū (oo)
- ऋ ṛ ('r or rī)
- ऌ ḷ ('l or lī)
- ए e (ā)
- ओ o (ō)
- क k (k)
- ख kh (kh)[12]
- ग g (g)
- घ gh (gh)[12]
- ङ ṅ (ng)
- च c (ch)
- छ ch (chh)[12]
- ज j (j)
- झ jh (jh)[12]
- ञ ñ (n)[13]
- ट ṭ (t)[14]
- ठ ṭh (th)[12, 14]
- ड ḍ (d)[14]
- ढ ḍh (dh)[12, 14]
- ण ṇ (n)[14]
- त t (t)
- थ th (th)[12]
- द d (d)
- ध dh (dh)[12]
- न n (n)
- प p (p)
- फ ph (ph)[12]
- ब b (b)
- भ bh (bh)[12]
- म m (m)
- य y (y)
- र r (r)
- ल l (l)
- व v (v)
- श ś (sh or s)
- ष ṣ (sh)[14]
- स s (s)
- ह h (h)
- ं ṁ[15]
- ः ḥ[16]

1. See HEBREW ALPHABET and ALEPH, BETH, etc., in Vocab. 2. In the names of the Arabic letters ā, ī, and ū respectively are pronounced like a in *father*, i in *machine*, u in *rude*. 3. When initial, or hamza; otherwise represented by a macron. 4. Like the Greek smooth breathing. See ALIF, in Vocab. 5. A deep guttural, or glottal sound. 6. See ALPHA, BETA, GAMMA, etc., in Vocab. 7, 8, 9. In classic Greek, about like th, ph, kh, in *hothouse, uphill, inkhorn*. 10. In the reformed orthography of Russia, ѣ is replaced by e, э partly by e, i and v by и, ѳ by ф, and the sign ъ by ʻ in the middle of words (omitted at the end of words). 11. The alphabet shown here is the Devanagari. The characters for the long vowels (ā, ī, ū, ṛ) and diphthongs (ai, au) resemble those for the corresponding short. When vowels are combined with preceding consonants they are indicated by various strokes or hooks instead of by the signs here given, or, in the case of short a, not written at all. There are also many compound characters representing combinations of two or more consonants. 12. See ASPIRATE. 13. As in *inch*. 14. See CEREBRAL. 15. See ANUSVARA. 16. See VISARGA.

(74)

In minuscule letters at the bottom of the page, he read some of the footnotes as indicated by numbers placed here and there along the lists of letters:

1. See HEBREW ALPHABET and ALEPH, BETH, etc. 4. See ALIF. 6. See ALPHA, BETA, GAMMA, etc. 11. The alphabet shown here is the DEVANAGARI. 12. See ASPIRATE. 14. See CEREBRAL. 15. See ANUSVARA. 16. See VISARGA.

For him to find out anything substantial about the alphabet, if only in terms of this dictionary, he would exhaust the entire diction-ary in cross-references, the definitions of "*Anusvara*" and "*Visarga,*" whatever these were, referring him to other words, which would refer him to other words. And this is exactly what he wanted to do, turn the pages backward and forward searching for cross-references, until everything connected; this was what he was drawn to doing, right now, though he knew Peggy was waiting for him in their bed.

But, for all the cross-references he did make, nothing explained why the alphabet was arranged the way it was.

Even the definition of **al'pha·bet** itself, which contained more information than he had ever known about his ABCs, only made him wonder more about the arrangement because it brought the arrangement so far back in time, further back than he would have imagined, further back, he thought, than any existing explanation. And yet, someone, somewhere, must have set out the letters in an order that survived up until now, survived and was so much taken for granted that he had never met anyone who had expressed any wonder, as he did now, about the order.

**al'pha·bet** (ăl'fà·bĕt *or, esp Brit.,* -bĭt), n. [Latin *alphabetum,* from Greek *alpha* + *bēta,* the first two Greek letters.] **1.** The letters of a language arranged in the customary order; a series or set of letters or signs which form the elements of a written language; a collection of the signs for the sounds of a language. Cf. IDEOGRAM, SYLLABARY.

And there followed a small table:

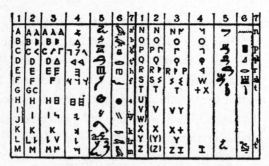

**Table showing descent of English Alphabet.**

**1.** Present English.

**2.** Early Latin (which did not adopt Y and Z until the 1st century B.C.).

**3.** Western Greek.

**4.** Phoenician.

**5.** Egyptian hieratic.

**6.** Egyptian hieroglyphic.

**7.** Probable phonetic value of the hieroglyphics: "a" standing for a weak breathing; the 1st "k," for a sort of k or g; the "4," for a guttural aspirate; and the last "t," for a sort of t or z.

And then he read this more detailed account of where the alphabet came from:

The letters of the English alphabet are derived from the corresponding forms in the Latin alphabet, the early forms of which in turn came from the Western Greek (Chalcidian) alphabet, and the Greek letters from the Phoenician. It is now held probable that the Phoenician letters were ultimately derived from the Egyptian hieroglyphs through the Sinaitic letters. Although, as appears from the table, some of the Egyptian signs had come to be used as letters, Egyptian writing was not strictly alphabetical (See HIEROGLYPHIC; cf. PICTOGRAPH). The use of an alphabet on a strictly phonetic basis seems to have been due to a Semitic people of the early part of the 2nd millennium B.C. which left a few inscriptions recently found in the Sinaitic peninsula and deciphered. A number of the characters in these inscriptions are intermediate between certain Egyptian hieroglyphs and letters of the Phoenician alphabet, thus apparently bridging the gap between them. The Western Greek and Phoenician alphabets are not here given entire, those letters being omitted which were not adopted in writing Latin. The ordinary Greek alphabet, afterwards generally adopted, is an Eastern Greek alphabet, differing slightly in its form from the Western Greek. The parent of the Latin alphabet was a form of the Western Greek alphabet brought to Italy in early times by Greek colonists. See ANGLO-SAXON ALPHABET, LATIN ALPHABET, A, B, C, etc. **2.** The simplest rudiments; elements; A B C.

The dictionary he had was the 1923 edition, and surely much more had been found out about the alphabet in the seventy years since then, seventy years exactly up to the present. He should have been a philologist, except that his interest was not really scientific, it was in making connections that could not be supported by science but that he needed to make, that he was compelled to make, that he sensed obsessing him, he had no idea why. And he couldn't hope for Peggy to understand why—Peggy who, he was sure, was lying awake, worried about him.

Peggy was concerned about him; he was not concerned about himself.

# FOUR

s Gerard drove along the highway, the windshield was covered more and more thickly with a sparkling scrim of snow that was wiped away again and again. He kept telling himself that he must turn back, that the snow would deepen so much he would probably not be able to turn back once he got off the highway and onto the country roads through the snowbound woods, but his warnings seemed to be made not to himself but to some person apart from him who had nothing to do with him, someone who had a reason for going to the abandoned house where the accident had occurred, a reason that Gerard himself didn't have, wasn't even interested in. He had a sense of someone else beside him, and he at flashing moments glanced to the side to give that sense a visible body; but at those moments the sensed presence shifted behind him, or to the other side in the narrow space between him and the door, or outside in the snow. Gerard didn't know, but that someone else knew what to expect in the house. What that was might have nothing to do with Harry, might have nothing to do with anything Gerard could imagine, might have to do with a banality so insignificant it would never have entered Gerard's imagination, and yet it would make a vital connection. Though that someone else knew what to expect in the house, Gerard sensed no anticipation in him, no suspense, as if he was so sure of what would happen that there was nothing to anticipate, nothing to be in suspense about. And yet it was that presence that made Gerard leave the slushy highway and turn off into a small, clapboard town and drive past it, through fields of snow and broken stubble, and into woods along a road that no car had entered recently, the impacted snow squeaking under the heavy, deep-tread tires of his high-suspension vehicle. The winter-bare woods, narrowing on either side, were filled with falling snow that sometimes, in small gusts of wind, did form into presences that quickly disappeared.

Gerard parked where he usually parked in the summer at what was called the camp. He trod through snow knee deep to the back door of their vacation house. The door was unlocked, and gave way, with a cracking of ice around it, when he pressed against it. It hadn't been shut tightly, and, inside, he found that the windows had not been closed, and snow had drifted in on the wooden floor. Summer clothes were thrown about, among them Harry's.

But the someone who had come along with Gerard, the someone whose presence he sensed but couldn't see or hear or reach out and touch, wasn't interested in Harry's clothes, wasn't interested in the house, which was colder inside than outside. Gerard's breath steamed so it filled the air. Hanging on a wall were snowshoes—snowshoes that Gerard and Peggy had used when, in the past, they came to the camp in the winter to walk through the snowbound woods and even out onto the frozen, snow-covered lake. The fur-lined moccasins needed for the snowshoes were hanging from nails next to them. They were stiff with cold, but Gerard, taking off his boots, put them on with a shock of cold that ran through him so that he shivered; then he unhooked the snowshoes and went back outside to the stoop where he inserted his feet into the straps and buckled them. Here and there, as if they belonged to another world that was hardly remembered, were patches of dry pine needles and brown oak and maple leaves. Gerard put on his snow glasses, raised the hood of his parka over his head, and drew on his heavy gloves and stepped out onto the snow. The someone else hovered around Gerard as he went down to the lake, the shore buried under the snow stretching out without an edge onto the large, white expanse, and, hesitating for a moment, Gerard seemed to float on his snowshoes onto that expanse, the someone else with him. He had come early enough that he had hours of daylight before him.

He hadn't asked Peggy to come with him, hadn't even told her he was going. He felt badly about this, and it wasn't exactly that he thought she wouldn't understand his coming that had kept him from telling her, because she would have said she did understand that he was driven more and more to get over the death of their son, and returning to the site of his death would help him do this. But she didn't understand. He wasn't on his way to the house where Harry died to get over his death and return to Peggy and their lives together, perhaps even to have another child, or children. He wasn't sure his going to the house where Harry died had to do with Harry, but with something more overwhelming than that, something that the *house itself* must reveal to him.

Out on the wide, flat, white plane, the only marks apart from the tracks behind him were long, soft lines where, under the snow, the ice had cracked.

Maybe he wouldn't go back to Peggy, or maybe he would go back to her only to tell her he had to go off on his own somewhere, he didn't know for how long. Maybe the difference between Peggy and himself that divided them so that he could not see them coming together again, the biggest, disconnecting difference between himself and Peggy, was that she never, ever sat—as she said jokingly about him—"moodily" in silence and stillness. In the past, he'd been glad when she'd snapped him out of his "moodiness"; now he did not want to be snapped out of it. The mood had made him drive out into the country, put on snowshoes, and walk across the snow-covered, frozen lake to a house that he might have been attracted to not because of anything he might find, but only because of the mood he was helpless to resist. He had not told Peggy he was coming. She did not know about helplessness; he did. She did not know that it was with a kind of gratitude that he was rendered helpless. She had no sense, none at all, of anything larger than herself to be given in to. Sure, sure, she was a more reasonable person than he was for not having this sense, because the sense was, really, *nothing* but a mood. But he had given in to that sense, that mood, and he had given in helplessly—the sense that there existed around him and above him and below him something larger than himself, and this something larger pulled at him, pulled at his body as if to disembody him; the mood that of a spirit that extended beyond all his thoughts and feelings, and made them, out there, thoughts he had never had and maybe would never have, filled with more frightening possibility than he himself was capable of. His helplessness came to him as a great, a spiritual, and a physical relief, as though spirit and body had become one, and both were eager for the freedom of total helplessness. Peggy could never, ever understand this, and he could never, ever try to explain, because she was the better person for not understanding, the person who believed in devoting herself to the helpless, devoting herself to them to make them capable of helping themselves, but he—

He?

He saw the broken dock ahead, embedded in the ice and snow. Stopping by it, his toes numb with cold, his face smarting from the snow, he did wonder if he should go on, go all the way and make himself, with no chance of turning away, totally helpless. The house was visible through the bare trees, blocked only by the large pine with the bell; through branches of scrub oak and maple and thin birch the house appeared to rise up higher than he remembered, with its large fieldstone chimney. Gerard felt the someone else behind him, pushing at him with a windy thrust, and he thought, Yes, all right, and, first knocking the sides of his snowshoes against a post of the old dock that jutted above the ice to shake off the impacted snow, he slowly climbed the incline to the house. As Gerard climbed, he heard the wind through the woods around him, and this sound seemed to him to be in itself a vast mood, the wind the thoughts and feelings of that mood, so far beyond his thoughts and feelings. He paused at the rope that dangled from the clapper of the bell, which was encased in a bell of snow, and he left it to its silence and stillness, and continued. As he did, he was sure that other presences emerged, maybe from the very snow, to join the someone who had been urging him on since he'd left Manchester—urging him on, or just watching what he did, perhaps with no more intention to make Gerard act than an attentive witness would, but making Gerard act so that that someone, with wide, lidless eyes, would have something to witness. As he neared the house, he felt attentiveness all around him, the attentiveness of more and more presences emerging from the snow, watching him with lidless eyes. The snow-covered area before the house was delicately marked by animals' paws and birds' feet, and the shadows of trees were beginning to slant across it. Traversing the lake had taken more time than Gerard had thought. He was cold, but he knew that there was no way he would be able to warm himself in the house, not even, it occurred to him, by lighting a fire in the fireplace, as he had stupidly forgotten matches. Lifting his snowshoes high, as if not to leave marks on the snow, he approached the house, and as he did those presences gathered closely about him, attentive, watching. Icicles hung from the eaves of the house, and the screens of the porch sagged with ice and snow. Inside the porch, where the concrete was black, Gerard removed his snowshoes and propped them against the side of the house, near the door, which was ajar. He pressed a hand against it until it was open enough for him to see into the room. There, at the back, was the old bicycle. He stepped inside, into a chill that was like a block of ice, all the broken furniture standing as if frozen into the ice.

He picked up from the floor an old, torn summer dress, the cloth partly rotted, and as he examined it he felt the presences examining him in turn, waiting, maybe, for a reaction from him. This dress filled him with horror. Dragging the dress behind him, he crossed the room to the fireplace to see if there remained any sheets of paper with script on them, but a fire had been lit in the fireplace and in the ashes were nothing but the shards of broken bottles, and it seemed to him the reason he had come—the reason he hadn't been able to admit because it really was naïve—was to have found more writing, maybe more than an alphabet in a script he didn't understand, but words and sentences. The reason was now lost. He again held up the dress to examine it, and horror struck him with a force that made him feel he would not get out of the house alive, and that he could not leave. He was sure that the girl who had worn this dress had been tortured and killed. He had not come for this—he had come for something altogether different, something that reduced horror to a banality, something all the invisible presences around him now were aware of, which was not horror. The invisible presences, their lidless eyes bulging, waited for what he would do, now that he had no reason for being in the house.

He knew who they were, these invisible but acutely sensed presences—they were the dead, and all they could do, in their helplessness, was watch, was be attentive. Everything that had happened in the house wasn't horrible to them, because they knew what the living did to the living. These dead, they had seen worse, much worse, and nothing they saw shocked them. It came to Gerard that the dead around him were not even shocked by Harry's death, which they saw had not been an accident, but had been intended by the living so that anyone who stepped into that room would fall through the floor and die. The dead expected that from the living. Maybe they had been the victims of horrors, horrors committed not only in this house but, more, in houses all over the world, cellars, attics, closets, cells, alleys, sheds, cars, woods, all over the world, and they gathered here to watch what the living did to one another. Gerard found himself clutching the dress to his chest, and he dropped it.

He felt all those dead surround him closely when he went into the room, still empty, through the floor of which Harry had fallen to his death, and Gerard almost to his. He trod about the hole in the floor and, around it, the loose boards that had been arranged so that they would give way to anyone stepping on them. Below, because a wall of the house had been pulled down to get him and Harry out on stretchers, there was a snowdrift, and, leaning a little forward, he thought of falling, not onto concrete, but into that snowdrift and lying there and sleeping. He really was very tired, and his knee, the one that had been shattered, was hurting him badly. The dead formed a circle around the hole to stare down into it with him.

Beyond the room, which at one time must have been a dining room, was a door to what must have been the kitchen. The dead were at Gerard's back, they were crowding against Gerard's back, as he entered the wrecked kitchen, through the windows of which shone a dim snow light. And they followed him into the room, where, written on a wall with, maybe, a stick of wood burnt to charcoal, were the letters

# A B C

Gerard fell to his knees and pressed his forehead to the floor, and rocking back and forth he wept, with relief, helplessly.

# FIVE

When he got up, the light in the house appeared dimmer, and in that dimness Gerard was sure that traps had been set throughout the house to kill. And yet, he didn't leave. He went down a corridor that brought him to the bottom of the flight of stairs.

Some of the treads were broken, and some still had tacked to them parts of a torn linoleum runner. Off the landing was the bedroom with the wallpaper patterned with sailboats. The very emptiness of the room, for the possibility of what had occurred in such emptiness, horrified him.

On the floor was a piece of paper with writing on it that he recognized as Sanskrit, and he picked it up to study it. The letters appeared to make up words, the words a sentence. The paper had been torn from a notebook. This was everything he had come for. He folded the paper and inserted it into his glove, against a palm.

When he got back down to the porch and was putting on his snowshoes, the snow had stopped, and late winter sunlight, breaking through the dark clouds in long, sharp, arctic beams, illuminated the lake and penetrated the pines and bare trees along the shore, exposing, here and there, cabins, and, grouped together at angles under the trees, a trailer camp. Some of the windows of the long trailers had lights lit, smoke rising from narrow chimneys.

The people who had the most impermanent of homes were the people who lived on the lake all year long.

Out on the ice, Gerard walked, always with that sensation of floating, towards the trailer camp. They made up a world of their own, those people who lived in the trailers or mobile homes, some of them immobilized on cinder blocks. It was a world, seen from the distance Gerard and Peggy kept from them during the summer, of people about whom he had ideas as general as, say, his ideas about people in a village in India or Mexico or China. The people in the trailer camp might have spoken their own language. As he approached the trailer camp from the frozen, snow-covered lake, he told himself that whatever general idea he had of the people who lived there was not only wrong, it was unfair, because his most general idea was that they were all, in one way or another, criminal, or they took criminality for granted, as if it formed their culture. During the summer, it was not uncommon to see a police car, sometimes two, parked in the scruffy camp, the doors open. And the summer people stayed away from the public beach, a stretch of ragged shore, where the trailer people congregated, and where, especially, the adolescents from the trailer families lit fires at night and raved. They were the people who had ravaged the abandoned house; they were the people who used the house as a crack house; they were the people who went to the house for grotesque sex; and it was among those people that a group existed who had arranged floorboards as a trap that would kill. This was, he again told himself, unfair to them, the baseless accusation was out of his character, he who always tried to be fair-minded. But the general idea became fixed in the irrational certainty—he *knew* it was irrational—that some of the people living here were so innately evil that they would kill, that they had set up a trap that would kill *anyone*. With the sweaty heat that rose out of his closely encased body, a rage came over him: he would find them, he would find those people who, for no reason but to kill, killed. His exuding sweat, damp in his groin, armpits, in the roots of his hair, increased the rage, the irrational, physical rage, to find those people and—

And? And what?

Kill them? Nothing of that impulse was in him. Then, confront them, confront them and stare at them and demand that they tell him why they'd done what they'd done? That would be the expression of his rage: to confront them, or just one of them, and press him against a tree trunk, Gerard's invisible, silent entourage close about him, and shout, *WHY?*, the question as violent an attack as a beating. And while he was attacking, Gerard must try not to weep.

He walked up onto the shore, the crusted snow cracking in large, slanting sheets under his snowshoes so he at moments almost lost balance.

The horizontal rays of sunlight shone against the light of the window of a trailer, the wide rectangle of the inside light blunted by the sharp outside light. There were no footsteps in the snow to the door at the side of the window. There were, Gerard noted, no marks anywhere of people having left or entered any trailers, most of them dark, with snowdrifts blown against them. The only movement was of the high branches of pine trees, from which, in small, twanging gusts of wind, snow dropped in soft thuds about him.

No, Gerard told himself, there was no more answer here than there was rage in him to command an answer. He would turn back, cross the lake at a diagonal to his summer cabin, and leave.

But he felt he was kept, against his will, where he was. A figure appeared in the lighted window of the trailer, that of a woman, who, as if she were looking in a mirror, lifted her long hair from the sides of her head with both hands, then let her hair fall; then she began to pull a flower-patterned curtain over the window, but stopped and looked out, Gerard knew, at him, standing still. Gerard raised a gloved hand to her. She didn't move, evidently trying to identify him. Gerard dropped his hand and the woman pulled the curtain across the window. He did turn away, but, his back to the trailer, he heard its door open, cracking the ice that sealed it, and a woman call, "Hey there," and he turned back. Her head was in a cloud of her steaming breath.

He was incapable of rage. It was not rage he felt, not rage that had impelled him to come to this trailer camp to find the killers, or just the killer: it was longing.

He walked slowly towards the woman, who held the door open.

"You lost?" she asked.

"No," he said. "I just came up from the city to see what it's like here in the country in the winter, the way I do from time to time."

"You one of the summer people?"

Gerard pointed vaguely in the direction of his—no, Peggy's—house, though it was hidden from view by winter woods. "I've got a place."

She appeared to stare at him through her steaming breath. "I recognize you. You come into my grocery in the summer."

And he recognized her. She had a grocery store in the run-down clapboard, country town, where the only well-maintained house, the biggest and fanciest, with an awning out to the potholed street, was the funeral parlor. He even knew her name: Claudette.

She said, "You're Gerard."

He nodded.

Opening the door wider, she said, "It's cold out there."

"Yes, cold," he said.

She opened the door wider. Gerard knocked the frozen snow from the straps of his snowshoes so he could remove them, and, in his thick moccasins, he climbed the steps into the trailer, past her. She shut the door.

She had a broken nose, and the brutal face of a woman who had been beaten up enough not to consider it abnormal. But her long, bleached-blond hair was glossy, and swung heavily when she, looking at Gerard, tilted her head back with a little jerk.

Bluntly, she said, "So there you are, there."

She repeated "there" in the way he remembered his grandfather had, translating the often repeated *là* of the Canuck French also spoken by his grandfather. She probably thought he was a Yankee.

He smiled. "Here I am," he said, as if he had a reason for being there he would leave to her to figure out.

She apparently knew the reason. "I heard about the accident," she said, "the accident in the old house, there."

"My son was killed," he said flatly.

"I heard." Again she swung her hair.

"He fell through the floor. Somebody arranged boards on a floor so that anyone stepping on them would fall through and be killed."

"A lot of kids play in that house."

"Is that who you think did it, kids?"

"Kids don't know what they're doing, there, when they set traps. They don't think anyone is really going to get killed."

"You have any idea who those kids are?"

She bit her upper lip so her jaw stuck out, as if she were considering his question. "No, I don't. And the police don't neither. They came around, questioned people, questioned some of the kids in the camp. And maybe they wasn't kids anyway, because if they was, my son would know them, there, and my son he would never do anything like that, set a trap that would kill anyone."

"I'm sure your son wouldn't. But who would do such a thing?"

"There are people out there in the world, there, who do all kinds of things like that."

"Why do they do them?"

Her voice remained blunt, as if it had no modulations even though she wanted to speak more softly. "People just do. They done it to me enough, I can tell you. And when I asked, 'Why are you doing this to me?' that just made it all worse, their not being able to answer the question just made it all worse. Why not try to answer the question, why do some people live in a dump of a trailer camp and try to live on selling canned beans from a grocery no one goes to anymore except the summer people? Why are there poor people and rich people? Why do people get together and get married and have children? Why do people sit around a table and eat? Why do people go to school, go into the army, some even into the priesthood? Why do people live and why do people die? Do you know why?"

"No," Gerard said softly.

"Come on, I'll make you a cup of tea."

"Thanks," Gerard said, taking off his gloves, and the folded sheet of paper fell to the floor; he reached down to pick it up, and, standing again, he unfolded it, as if to read it.

"What's that?" Claudette asked.

"Writing."

"A message?"

"A message? I don't know. I didn't think of it that way when I found it."

"Where did you find it?"

"I found it in the house."

"The house where the accident happened?"

"That house."

"We call it the Wreck. You went to the Wreck, there?"

"I went, yes."

"You wanted to see it again, the way people want to see again the place where something bad happened to them?"

"I guess I had some idea of coming and finding out who set that trap."

"All by yourself?"

"All by myself."

"You really thought you could do it?"

"I thought I could try."

"So what's on that paper?" Claudette narrowed her eyes and held out a hand, eager, Gerard thought, to read the writing; and though he suspected she was eager because she was suddenly worried that the writing revealed information she didn't want revealed, he didn't care what that worry revealed about her, was too low to care. He gave her the paper.

"What kind of writing is this?" she asked.

"It's Sanskrit."

"What's Sanskrit?"

"An old Indian language."

"American Indian?"

"Indian from India."

"And you can read it?"

"I can't read it, no, but not even many Indians can read it, the way not many people can read Latin. It's the old language of the religion of the Hindus."

"How come you know it's that language if you can't read it?" It was as if all the suspicion he should have felt towards her suddenly shifted and became transformed into her suspicion of him. "How come?" she insisted.

He gave in to her suspicion of him, making him vulnerable not only to suspicion but, maybe, accusation; he was too low not to. "I recognize the letters," he said flatly.

"And how come you recognize the letters?"

Weak with fatigue, he said, "Can I sit down?"

"Sit, sit," she said, and with the piece of paper indicated a built-in divan.

He lowered the hood of his parka so his sweating head was exposed and he slumped back into the cushions. She would not, he knew, offer him the cup of tea until he satisfied her interrogation. As hot as he was, he felt a little shiver pass through him. "Last summer," he said, "when my wife and I went into the house with Harry, I found a sheet of paper in the fireplace with strange script on it, and I kept it, and later someone told me that it was Sanskrit letters, the Sanskrit alphabet, written over and over."

Claudette stretched the torn piece of paper between her hands to study it, as if she could read it, and she frowned.

Gerard said, "I wonder why someone—I guess, some Indian—goes to that house to practice Sanskrit."

"That house is used for all kinds of reasons."

"I'm sure it is, but to go to write Sanskrit is a strange reason."

"There are stranger reasons," Claudette said matter-of-factly, and she again studied the piece of paper and frowned for a long moment before she let her arms fall, the paper still stretched taut between her hands, and, raising her chin, suddenly called out, "Pierre."

Startled, Gerard sat up.

Again she called out, in a louder voice, "Pierre."

A narrow door at the end of the narrow room opened, and a boy came in. He was wearing a sweat suit, and his feet were bare. His delicate face was pale, his hair long, loose black curls. Seeing Gerard, he stopped at a distance. The sight of Gerard seemed to frighten the boy, as if he was suspicious in his own way of why this outsider was in the trailer, which was his home, but where, no doubt, strangers often came, and among these sometimes the police. Gerard recognized him from past summers: he was Claudette's son. The father was as absent as his family name.

No, no, Gerard thought, it wasn't possible that someone as young and delicate as this boy could have been involved in setting up a killer trap—and if he had been, he and his gang couldn't have meant the trap to kill, not really, but only as some fantasy that would never be realized in fact. And yet, where did that fantasy originate from? From where in this boy whose eyes were large with helplessness? If Gerard had been able to work himself up enough to get the boy to admit he had set the trap that killed Harry— if Gerard had been able to find the strength to press the boy to admit it—Gerard would have felt not revenge but defeat in the admission, in the boy crying, "I didn't mean it, I didn't mean it." And no further pressing of the boy to explain why he had done it, why he had had the fantasy of doing what he hadn't meant to end in anyone's death, would have explained anything. Gerard had a moment of pity for the boy, for his inability to explain, for his helplessness, and, because of his helplessness, for his innocence— innocence even if he had been involved in setting the trap, even if he had killed.

The boy's wide eyes were indication enough of the apprehension he felt for the way his mother had called him, and he turned to her when, holding the piece of paper out to him, she commanded, "Does Anjuli go to the Wreck?"

"The Wreck," the boy repeated.

"So," Claudette interrogated her son, "does Anjuli go there?"

"Why are you asking me if Anjuli goes to the Wreck?"

"Because I want to know."

Pierre shrugged his narrow shoulders. "Who doesn't go to the Wreck?"

"So Anjuli goes."

"Yeah, she goes."

"Did you take her there?"

The boy's voice rose. "Come on, why do you want to know if I took Anjuli to the Wreck?"

"Because I want to know if you did, because if her father finds out she goes to the Wreck and that you took her there, he'll kill you."

"I wasn't the only one who took her."

"So all of you, there, all you little wreckers, you took Anjuli to the Wreck without her father knowing."

"She wanted to come."

"And you said sure, even though you knew her father would kill her and all of you, there, if he found out."

"She wanted to be one of us."

"Right, she wanted to be one of you, a bunch of little wreckers."

The boy became defensive. "Anyway, what makes you think Anjuli came to the Wreck?"

His mother thrust the paper at him. "This."

He took it and, as if he too could read it, he studied the writing. He frowned deeply.

Gerard said to him, "I found it in the Wreck. Just now, I crossed the lake and went to the Wreck, there where my son, Harry, was killed, to look around, and I found that piece of writing. Who's Anjuli?"

Pierre let his shoulders slump. "A friend."

Claudette answered, "Her father's an Indian from India. He left his wife behind and brought his daughter to the States. His name's Ramesh, and he's living with someone here in the trailer camp, some slut of a woman who was born and brought up around here. I don't know how he got to living with her, with that slut, in the camp, but there he is, there, with his daughter, Anjuli. All I know is that he's so strict with her he almost won't let her go to school. I've heard him speak some strange language with her. Is that the language on the piece of paper?"

"I don't think so," Gerard said, and, not wanting to make her resent him for showing off his knowledge, he almost whispered, "He probably speaks Hindi to her."

"Whatever he speaks to her, he don't like her mixing, I think, even enough for her to speak English."

Pierre said, "She thinks she should be free."

"Sure, free the way you all are, free like real Americans."

Gerard asked Pierre, "Do you all go back to that house—the Wreck—since my son was killed there?"

The boy lowered his head so his spine appeared at the base of his nape beneath the curls.

"Do you?" Gerard asked again.

"Answer him," Claudette shouted.

His head still lowered, the boy said, "Sometimes."

"And what do you do there?"

"What do you think they do?" Claudette said to Gerard. "They draw dirty pictures on whatever walls there are left, they smoke dope, they fuck, and they do some more wrecking." She confronted her son. "Isn't that right?"

His head swaying a little from side to side, he said, "We use it like a kind of clubhouse."

"A clubhouse?" his mother said. "That's the first I ever heard of that, of a club made up of weird little wreckers. What do you do besides draw dirty pictures, there, smoke dope, and fuck, and wreck?"

Pierre swung his head more and said, "We just get together and talk."

"Sure you do, sure. And what do you talk about?"

"We just talk."

"If you or any of the other kids get Anjuli knocked up, you know what will happen to her? Her father *will* kill her."

Gerard asked the boy, "Do you ever talk about what's happened in that house?"

"We talk about a lot of things."

"And what does Anjuli talk about?" Claudette asked.

"She tells us about her religion."

Claudette shouted, "In that place, in that place where you commit every sin that was ever invented, and even some that were invented there, she tells you about her religion?"

Pierre swung his head so low that his heavy black curls fell forward and almost hid his face.

"Does she teach you the Sanskrit alphabet?" Gerard asked.

Raising his head so his curls fell back and exposed his fine, palely glowing face, Pierre said to Gerard, "She tries to, but it's too hard."

So, he thought, they had been using the house as a clubhouse at the time Harry was killed. If they hadn't set the trap, they would have known about it—would have known about it and, maybe, even liked knowing that if someone who wasn't a member of their club went into the house, the trap would deal with the intruder. Did the police, who were supposed to have investigated the case, know this? Gerard could have pressed now, he could have found in his very despair the strength to get the boy to admit he at least knew about the trap. But more overwhelming to that strength than before was: what would his knowing do for him, because knowing was not an explanation?

Gerard stood, and in the narrow space the boy stood back from him. Pointing to the paper in the boy's hand, he asked, "Can you find out from Anjuli what that means?"

"Now?"

"Yes, now."

"I don't know if I can now, not if she's with her father."

"You can always get to see her when you want, even if she's with her father," his mother said, "so what's stopping you from going for her now?"

"All I want," Gerard said, "is to know what's written on that piece of paper. That's all."

"That's all?" the boy asked.

"That's all."

But the boy squinted. "Why do you want to know?"

"Haven't you ever wanted to understand something just because you want to, because something makes you want to?"

"Something makes you want to?"

"You've never felt that?"

Pierre kept still, as if trying to think if he had ever felt that. Gerard realized he could not be more precise about it, because he himself didn't know why he so wanted to understand the writing on the piece of paper.

After a moment, the boy said, "I'll go see if I can find her." He went back into the rear of the trailer, into his room, which Gerard could not imagine.

"You want that cup of tea?" Claudette asked Gerard.

"Just a glass of water."

He was left alone when Claudette went into the opposite end of the trailer, and while she was away he stared at a picture hanging over the built-in sofa of birch woods in the snow, and beyond the birch woods a frozen lake and the setting sun reflected on the ice. She came back with a glass of cold water, which he, his throat parched, gulped down.

He asked her, "Who owns the Wreck House?"

"I don't know, and I don't know anyone who knows. It's been empty since I can remember. I used to go there, I used to draw disgusting pictures on the walls, I used to smoke dope there, I had my first fuck there, and I did some wrecking there. Everybody from around here did."

Pierre emerged, the only difference in what he was wearing outsized, heavy-duty boots, as if they were all he needed to go out into the winter cold. He was still carrying the piece of paper.

"Do you have some kind of signal to get her attention if she's with her father, some signal that he doesn't know about?" Gerard asked him.

Without answering, the boy went out into the cold.

"This Ramesh, how did he get from India to here?" Gerard asked Claudette.

"Who knows? They come, there, from God knows what places in the world, most of them, I guess, illegal, and how they end up shacked up with some slut in a dump of a trailer camp is just another one of your questions. Was his life in India worse than his life here? I doubt it."

"Do you ever talk with him?"

"I try not to."

There seemed to be nothing more for her to say, and she left him to go into her part of the trailer, where she shut the door. Gerard waited, and though he was waiting a little jolt went through him when the door to the outside opened. It was Pierre.

"She's outside," he said.

Apprehensive, Gerard felt cold sweat under his parka when he stepped out, the long shadows on the snow now appearing to fill the air in thin stripes, and standing among those stripes was someone wrapped completely in a blanket, which hooded even the head. One pale brown hand was extended through the folds in the blanket, and it was holding the piece of paper with the Sanskrit script. Pierre led Gerard to Anjuli, whose face was in the shadow of the blanket.

"I can't stay long," she said.

The blue blanket had a pattern of white flowers.

Her voice was very matter-of-fact. "It's from the Bhagavad Gita," she said. "Do you know what that is?"

Gerard nodded.

"It's a quotation by Krishna."

"Yes," Gerard said, nodding again.

The girl said, "Krishna says, 'Of sounds, I am the first sound, A.' " And she held the paper out for Gerard to take.

He took it, but he closed his eyes, and, in the darkness behind his closed eyes, it seemed to him that everything that had meaning in his life came together, and he knew, with greater concentration than he had ever known anything else in all his life, what he must dedicate himself to. For so much of his life, he thought, for maybe all his life, he had longed for something, but nothing, not even the religion he was brought up in, had centered that longing; it was only now, now when he did sense all the longing both pull inwardly to a center and beam out from it, that he realized that he had always known the center would one day occur to him. The dead moved around him in a slow, shifting dance, as slow and as shifting as light winds.

When Gerard opened his eyes, he saw that the girl, the blanket wrapped around her trailing a corner on the snow, was walking away from him. And Pierre too was gone. Gerard stared at the script to try to make out the letter *A* in Sanskrit. He folded the paper and shoved it into an inside pocket of his parka.

He went into the trailer, where no one met him, to get his gloves, then back outside, where he put on his snowshoes and raised his hood over his head, and the dead accompanied him out onto the snow-covered lake, leading him, he thought, through the dusk deepening to dark to Peggy's house and his car, all of them still dancing lightly around him, and—unless it was the sounds of nature during the winter—faintly but resonantly clapping.

As he entered Manchester, they abandoned him, and he felt more alone than he had ever felt as he opened the door to his house. Peggy was in the living room, off the entrance hall, waiting for him; though she didn't say she'd been waiting, he knew, from the way she quickly rose from a chair, that she had been.

# SIX

The main street of the city of Manchester did not go anywhere, but terminated at one end in a wooded hill, and at
the other end at huge, ice-age granite rocks. On one of the downtown side streets off the main street was a secondhand-book store,
where Gerard often went for books that publishers in the past
devoted themselves to for their moral more than their commercial
value and now for whatever books he could find on the origins of
the alphabet. The owner of the store was a Franco, Roger Lambert,
with whom Gerard spoke in French. It amused both Gerard and
Lambert that a Franco should be so cultured as to have a bookstore
that stocked books in high-grade French, as if there were a Franco
reading public in the city that demanded books in an elevated language they assumed to be their native language, and not low-grade
Canuck French. Lambert made the little money he did selling
books, in low-grade English, that Gerard condemned as commercial, though he was aware, with a self-deprecating irony, of the
always vague generality of his superior moral vision. He liked talking with Lambert for his own sense of irony. Lambert was in his
sixties, with a short, pointed, gray-and-black beard and a bony

Adam's apple, and he wore, as always, a black crewneck sweater that sagged about his thin body.

*"Tu n'as pas un bouquin sur les origines de nôtre alphabet?"* Gerard asked.

*"C'est à dire, l'alphabet franco-canuck?"* Lambert joked.

He did have a book, so old he remembered it because it was old, not specifically on the origins of the Franco-Canuck or any other Latin-based alphabet, but on many different ways of inscribing, on sticks and bones, animal skins, clay tablets, papyrus, in runes, pictograms, incised dots and dashes, glyphs, and, yes, letters, accounts, laws, memorials, missives, and poetry. It was called *Histoire de L'Ecriture*. It had been published in Paris, and the typeface was that of an old typewriter with uneven—sometimes light and sometimes dark and not always consistent—type. The illustrations were clearly hand drawn. Lambert had been looking through it just a few days before, telling himself what an interesting subject it was, the history of writing; he should read the book. He had put it aside, under the counter, to take it home with him and begin studying. Odd, Lambert said, the way you suddenly become interested in a subject and you think you're the only one to be so suddenly interested, and then you find someone else is interested in the same subject, and then someone else is, and then everyone is. How did it get around that everyone should be interested in a subject you thought originated with you, all at once, for no reason outside its just coming to you as a bright idea?

It was odd, Gerard said.

Lambert asked Gerard if he knew of anyone else who was interested in the history of the alphabet, and Gerard said no, not until now, not until he came into the store and asked for a book on the subject and found that Lambert himself was interested.

Reaching under the counter, Lambert brought up the book and placed it before Gerard. It was a large paperback book, the paper cover rough and brownish, the title in dark blue, and below the title there was a yellow upright rectangle in which were drawn, in dark blue lines, two men with shoulder-length hair, beards and earrings and Semitic noses and long robes, who were writing, one on what appeared to be a sheet of paper and the other on a tablet.

*"Le voilà,"* Lambert said.

Gerard didn't touch it, as if he must first be given permission.

He asked who the men were, and Lambert answered that he wasn't sure, he hadn't been able to get enough into the book to have learned much, really, but he thought they were ancient Syrians.

Gerard wondered if the alphabet was invented by one person.

*"On se demande,"* Lambert said.

Yes, Gerard said, one did wonder.

Both men looked at the book, Lambert now not seeming able to bring himself to touch it either, as if with Gerard's interest it ceased to be his, though Gerard knew it wasn't his either, no matter how interested he was in it. It appeared not to belong to anybody, not even to have been written by anybody, but to have come about by itself.

Lambert shook Gerard a little and said, *"Mais c'est le tien, tu sais, si tu le veux."* He was all at once offering the book to Gerard.

Mine? Gerard asked.

As you're so interested, Lambert said.

But so are you.

Oh, in a way, in a way. Lambert was interested in so much, he explained, had so many books he had put under the counter because the subject was fascinating to him, and most of them he had only read into here and there, content enough with an impression, which, in any case, was what any book he in fact finished left him with—an impression.

Gerard asked him what he meant, an impression.

Lambert raised a hand and made a loose gesture. He didn't have ideas, but only impressions. He read, or partly read, history, science, philosophy, even theology, but, knowing that if he read the whole of the book he wouldn't remember anything he'd be capable of explaining to anyone else, the way a teacher would to a pupil, he'd long before decided that impressions were enough for him.

Gerard said he still didn't understand.

No, Lambert said, he wouldn't understand, Gerard being a teacher who had to be able to explain to pupils.

Explain?

Well, wasn't that what he did as a teacher?

Gerard wasn't sure. He wouldn't be able to explain to his pupils why the alphabet is arranged the way it is.

The way the alphabet is arranged? The way *A* is followed by *B* and *B* is followed by *C*? No one can explain that.

No, no one, no one yet.

Was that Gerard's intention, to find out why and explain?

Gerard laughed.

He would never find out, Lambert said. He picked up the book, opened it at random, looked at a page, and, with one hand holding the book splayed open against his chest, with his other hand he pointed at an illustration with a long dirty fingernail:

With a lilting tone of enjoying such talk, Lambert admonished Gerard to explain *that*—to explain why someone at some time wrote, in a script evolved from God knew where, *This is Nasum. She loves Dhou-Taym*. Something had to have happened to inspire Nasum to put into letters that she loved Dhou-Taym. Something had to have happened at some time, maybe in just a second of time, to inspire some person to make marks that still had meaning. But no one would ever understand how this happened. You could say it was wonderful, it was phenomenal, it was miraculous, but that didn't explain anything. That was just being impressed.

Gerard said he wasn't going to try to go that far, he only wanted to find out why the alphabet was arranged the way it was.

Lambert challenged him. He couldn't find out. That knowledge was too lost in time.

Oh yes he could.

Even if he devoted his whole life to finding out, he wouldn't.

Gerard would devote his whole life to finding out, would begin now and would find out.

Begin here? Being in this secondhand-book store with a book Lambert couldn't remember acquiring?

Turning the pages of the book, Gerard thought it had been written by an amateur, as he himself was an amateur.

He shut the book and placed it on the counter.

Why, Gerard asked, were he and Lambert, Francos themselves, so self-deprecating? Why did they see any intellectual activity among Francos, including their own, as pretentious?

Ah, Lambert said, *he* accepted the pretensions as liberating. *He* allowed himself to be as pretentious as he wanted, because it was only in being pretentious that he'd been able to expand his world beyond the small Franco world he was born into. Francos *had* to be pretentious.

Yes, Gerard said quietly.

He'd never do it, Lambert said, Gerard would never find out why the alphabet was set up the way it was, but, sure, he had to try, he had to try just because it was pretentious. Lambert's voice rose, and he announced to the world, Yes, pretentious. *He* knew about being pretentious. A Franco considered anybody who went to France to be pretentious, as if a Franco were a provincial who should know he had no right to be in the capital. Well, he, Lambert, had gone to Paris in the 1960s, had lived in Paris to claim his right to be French, and he wanted everyone back in the Franco world of Manchester to know he'd been and come back overblown with the pretensions of the capital, such as his beard, such as a black crewneck sweater *and* a beret. If the small-minded Francos of Manchester had even enough knowledge of the capital to be aware that he had made himself into a parody, he gave them some credit, though most didn't know. Most didn't know he *wanted* to be pretentious. Well, that's what he was—pretentious, a total phony, and being a phony made it possible for him to have a philosophy, as unoriginal, as derivative, as banal as it was, which philosophy was based in the belief that there were no explanations, but only impressions, some vivid and some not so vivid, but always ultimately vague. *"C'est que nous sommes toujours dans le vague,"* he said, *"toujours."*

Submissively, Gerard said, *"Tu as raison."*

Lambert said, *"Etrange expression—'avoir raison.' "*

Gerard admitted it was strange, and didn't really have an English equivalent, because *to have reason* was not the same as *to be right.*

A vague cloud of unknowing seemed to be suspended over the two men.

Lambert had made the bookstore so old-fashioned that a little bell, attached to the architrave above the front door, rang when the door was opened, as it was now by a girl with long, slack hair and a long, slack skirt. Lambert looked at her advance, then quickly looked at Gerard with an expression of *And here we have a beautiful work of pretension!* then back to the girl, who, before Lambert could offer to help her, asked for whatever number of copies of the Bhagavad Gita he had.

Smiling, Lambert said, "All of them?"

The girl didn't smile, but shook her head so her long hair swung. "All of them."

"A lot of youngsters have been coming in asking for that book, but no one, so far, has asked for all of them. Everyone seems to be asking for it."

"You think I'm just anyone?" The girl frowned.

"I didn't say that, not that you're just anyone"—still smiling, Lambert paused, portentously—"but everyone." He held the girl still by portent, but then his smile broadened, and after a while the girl smiled, and Gerard understood that she imagined Lambert was in some profoundly philosophical way being complimentary when, really, he was playing with her. "I've got some left," he said, and turned away to go down a narrow corridor lined with warped shelves of books.

Gerard asked the girl, "What will you do with more than one copy?"

Again, the girl shook her head to swing her hair away from her face, as though she did not allow herself, for some religious belief, to touch her hair. "I buy as many copies as I can and give them away," the girl said.

Gerard said, "I thought I must be among the very few people interested in reading that book, and now I find you give copies away."

"Whenever I give a copy of the book to someone, he'll say, 'I've been interested in reading this for a long time. How did you know?' "

"How *do* you know?"

The girl shook her head.

"Do you believe in it as a religious book?" Gerard asked.

"I believe in it as a book of the most important questions ever asked by any religion."

Gerard laughed, but he knew it was a forced laugh. "I wonder why I'm interested in it, then, because it doesn't at all interest me as a religious book."

"Why does it interest you, then?"

Again, Gerard laughed, or tried to, his laugh more forced. "I can't say, because, really, I don't know anything about it, haven't ever read it."

Lambert came back with a pile of paperbacks, five of them, and he spread them out on the counter. They looked as if they had been soaked in water, the covers creased, the pages swollen. He said he'd sell them to the girl for a dollar each, and from a pocket in her long skirt she took out a small money purse and held out a five-dollar bill to Lambert, who took it. She didn't pick up the books immediately, but first *Histoire de L'Ecriture,* and she thumbed through this as if suddenly considering buying it too.

Gerard wanted to tell her that that was his book, but he watched her look at the line drawings illustrating the scripts, and he was struck by how beautiful she was, her face smooth and bright in her concentration, and he asked, "Are you interested in the history of writing?" as if he were about to offer the book to her.

She looked up at him and asked, "Isn't everyone?"

"There again," Gerard said, "I assumed I was the only one."

She handed the book over to him, seeming to know that it was his, then she picked up one of the copies of the Bhagavad Gita and handed this to him. "Please take this," she said.

"I hope you don't imagine it's going to convert me," he said.

"I only imagine it inspiring you to ask some questions," she said, and, thanking Lambert, whose look of playful irony left his eyes as he stared after her, she turned away without saying goodbye to either man.

They continued in English, which, as a matter of fact, they spoke less self-consciously than they spoke French, which they always spoke jokingly.

After the little bell rang with the departure of the girl, Gerard asked, holding up the copy of the Bhagavad Gita in one hand, "Do you know anything about this book?" He held *Histoire de L'Ecriture* in the crook of his other arm.

"Not a thing," Lambert said flatly. "But, you know, I realized some time ago that I don't know anything about any other religion than the Catholic religion I was born and brought up in, and have now mostly forgotten. I once went to a Jewish wedding, and all I remember was the groom or the bride, I can't remember which, stepping on a glass and breaking it. As for what Hindus, Muslims, Buddhists, Taoists, do when they get married, I don't know."

"I guess I don't know either," Gerard said.

"I wouldn't know the first thing to do when going into a Hindu temple."

Gerard repeated, "I wouldn't either."

Again, a cloud seemed to hang over the men, and they were silent for a while.

"But I'm not interested, I'm really not interested in any religion. Why I'm interested in this, this Bhagavad Gita, is just a short, very short passage I came across from the book that made me think it had something to do with the beginning of the alphabet."

"Like, 'I am the Alpha and the Omega'?"

"Yes," Gerard said slowly, "yes, like that."

Lambert now reverted to French, telling Gerard to give him ten dollars for *Histoire de L'Ecriture* and to go, go and devote his life-long pretensions to finding out about the alphabet. After Gerard paid him, Lambert reached his hand across the old, scratched, and scuffed wooden counter to shake hands, and Gerard clasped Lambert's hand with a laugh.

"And keep on laughing," Lambert said in English.

As he was leaving with the Bhagavad Gita in one hand and *Histoire de L'Ecriture* under his arm, Gerard asked Lambert, "Where did you say this book comes from?"

"You mean the history, not the holy book?"

"The history."

"Maybe it just appeared, just appeared from nowhere, especially for you."

Gerard laughed lightly.

When he was in his car, he opened, not the history of writing, which he put on the seat beside him, but, not able to wait any longer, the old, damp-smelling copy of the Bhagavad Gita. He tried to find the quotation translated for him by the girl, Anjuli, in the trailer camp, still thinking, yes, yes, of course, it was so similar to the Christian God who defined Himself as the Alpha and the Omega. And wasn't He the Old Testament God, which meant he was the Jewish God too, Yahweh? And alpha and omega were Greek letters, so there was the possibility, wasn't there, of some ancient Greek god defining himself as the beginning and end of all by using the letters of the alphabet? Meaning that as far back as then, as ancient Greece, alpha was set as the first in the series of letters and omega was the last. Or was he, in his excitement, making presumptions that were so far off historically that they just showed his total ignorance? He admitted his ignorance, but he excused it with his enthusiasm. And if he was wrong now, he would, driven by his enthusiasm, eventually correct himself, and get it all right. But he knew nothing about other religions. How could he find out if the god of every religion defined himself in terms of the first, if not also the last, letter of the alphabet? Where could he begin to find out?

Almost pulling the damp, already loose pages from the spine in his eagerness to find that quotation, Gerard read here and there; then, all at once, a few lines appeared to stand out from the others and make him focus on them, as if these lines and not the ones he had been searching for presented themselves to him as just the lines he wanted to read:

*What power is it, Krishna, that drives man to act sinfully, even, as if powerlessly, unwillingly?*

He was arrested by and impressed by something in the lines for a long moment before he understood what they meant. He read the quotation again and again as if the impression it created was so much stronger than his understanding. He thought, Lambert was right. But when he did understand, the question appeared to him unoriginal, derivative, banal, as pretentious as any Lambert would have claimed for himself; and yet here it was, made a holy question because of its place within a holy book.

He sat motionless in the driver's seat of his car, and, staring out, he stared at a blankness, and his mind too was blank—but blank, he sensed, in preparation for something about to occur to him. It was when he noted drops of rain falling on the windshield, as if this small particular suddenly expanded into the vast general, that that something prepared for did occur. The rain fell in a downpour, and beyond the shimmering sheet of flowing water, which the glass itself appeared to become, he saw, distorted, a vision that opened up to a depth as deep as time, right back to the first sin that no power or will could stop, right back to the jagged stone smeared with blood and skin and hair, right back to the question: Why?

In his awareness of the powerlessness of the world against sin even when the world swore not to sin, Gerard was overcome by a great sense of the innocence of the world, and he felt in his heaving soul that he was weeping for this innocent world.

When he got back to the house, he called out, not for Peggy or Peg, as he always had, but for Margaret, as he had lately become used to. She called back that she was upstairs, and he went up. She was not in their bedroom, nor in the guest room, but at the end of the hallway, in Harry's room, and she was packing away his clothes in a cardboard carton, taking them from the bureau with its drawers open, and the closet, its door open. She didn't offer any explanation of what she was doing, and he didn't expect one from her. For some time, she had stopped asking him where he'd been, as if she'd allowed him to go as far, emotionally as well as physically, as he wanted, with, maybe, the hope that he would return from such distances. But now, seeing her on her knees folding Harry's clothes and placing them in the box, he had the keen feeling from her that she knew he had gone so far he wouldn't return. She was right, and the pain he was causing her was easily included among the sins of the world. He did not want to cause her pain, and that he did caused an equal pain in him, but he couldn't help himself. All he could think to say was, "Do you want me to help you?" She looked up at him, and he dropped to his knees by her side and put his arms around her and held her tightly, but she didn't, as if now she couldn't, put her arms around him, and when he gently let her go she simply resumed taking some folded clothes from the pile on the floor and placing them in the box. Gerard stood and walked about the room. There were two empty cardboard cartons, the flaps open, on the floor, and he began to pick up Harry's toys to pack them away. He wouldn't ask Margaret what she intended to do with all of Harry's belongings, and he wondered if it was worth packing away his boy's collection of incongruous bits and pieces—the burnt-out vacuum tube from an old, old radio, the crystal prism from a chandelier, a rusted latchkey, a bunch of gulls' feathers tied together with red thread, among so many other objects that had meaning known only to him—because the collection wouldn't have any meaning to whomever else Margaret intended all his belongings to go to. Gerard left them aside for her to decide. Then he picked up Harry's school exercise book and while slowly turning the pages to examine the rows of ABCs he said, "This is all I want."

"Then take it."

He asked, "What will you do with all the rest?" and she

answered, "Give everything away that can be of use to someone else."

"Do you have someone in mind?"

"Henrietta is pregnant with a boy, and she'll need Harry's clothes and toys when the boy gets older."

"Henrietta isn't married."

"No. Should she be?"

"I was just wondering."

"She didn't want to be married, but to be a single mother. The father is a donor who'll never know his son."

"Oh."

When Margaret went out again to see Henrietta, leaving him to prepare a meal for himself, he went into the living room and, first removing a basket of dried flowers from the hearth, placed Harry's notebook in the fireplace and set it on fire. He stood back to watch it burn.

# SEVEN

He began to read *Histoire de L'Ecriture* in a room called the office by Margaret's grandfather, who had acted as an agent for one of the big corporations that owned the textile mill, whose board of directors and most of its stockholders were in Boston. From her grandfather it passed on to her father; as the mills had already closed when he would have been ready to take over his father's position as agent, her father went into banking. And now it was Gerard's, whose grandparents had come down from French Canada as children to work in the mills. Usually, he left the door open, but now he shut it, even though he knew that Margaret was not in the house and would not in any case have disturbed him.

He sat at an old rolltop desk, on a wooden desk chair, and he read in the light of a desk lamp with a green glass shade.

With a flash of recognition as if it was so obvious that he himself should have thought of it, he read that objects in certain combinations communicated meaning—so, a tribe may send to an enemy tribe a stick with notches, a feather, the burnt end of a firebrand, and a fish, and this combination would be interpreted as: the number in their fighting force, that they would be as swift in their attack as a bird, that they would burn the attacked village to the ground, and that they would drown the surviving populace.

Just a short way into the book, Gerard closed it to imagine objects familiar to him communicating a message when assembled. Since his boyhood, he had had the vivid sense of objects having meaning—the more useless the object, strangely, the more meaningful to him—and a still more vivid sense that there was a message to be read in his collection of objects.

Harry too must have had that sense. Gerard regretted, keenly, that Harry's collection no longer existed for him to lay it out, to configure it, and in different combinations try to read it. But Margaret, as if to deprive him of just this attempt to find meaning where she insisted there was none, had gotten rid of Harry's collection, Gerard didn't know how.

His own collection from when he was a boy had meant something, of course it had, and the meaning, he was now positive, was greater than any defined by his personal and esoteric attraction to the objects. He recalled the shoebox in which he kept his collection; recalled opening the cover with priestly ceremony to look inside; recalled that there beamed up from the seemingly incongruous bits and pieces—the carved wooden handle of a knife popped into his mind, and the brass casing of a bullet, and a smooth lump of lead— a strong impression that, all together, they had a meaning, and that the meaning was not for him, but for— No, he didn't know whom it was for. Not for him, not for anyone in particular, but for those whose awareness was wider and deeper than his.

Now, in the greenish light of the desk lamp, he opened various little drawers below the row of pigeonholes. In them were objects left by Margaret's grandfather and father, objects that Gerard, never thinking whether or not there was a reason for doing so, had kept as he'd found them. He took some of them out and placed them haphazardly on the desktop: the briar bowl of a pipe, a bunch of pipe cleaners, an old red airmail stamp with a propeller plane on it, a matchbox with a drawing of slick-haired pugilists threatening each other with boxing gloves, a copper penny. There was nothing odd about the objects, they were familiar, and yet a meaning had to be implied by them, however haphazardly they were placed.

He would be accused of being psychotic if he said to anyone that he was sure there was a message to be read in the objects if they were arranged in a way that would reveal it. Certainly Margaret would have accused him had she known just how far he'd gone in this belief; but if she did find out and did accuse him of being psychotic, he would say, yes, he was, but not dangerously so. Psychotic or not, he felt that those objects, even in disarray, already gave off the impression of a latent meaning, an impression, not reducible to a statement, at least not by him, but which was all the more compelling for being irreducible, for being latent. He stared at the objects for a long while, until they appeared to increase in size and become isolated in themselves.

Gerard sat back and closed his eyes. He *was* being psychotic. He was losing touch with this reality. Turning away from the desk in the swivel chair, his eyes still closed, he sat for a moment, then opened his eyes, stood, and went to the door of the office and opened it wide.

The house was dark beyond. It hadn't occurred to him that he'd been in the office, the door closed, for so long that the rest of the house had gone dark with nightfall, as if night had fallen only in the office. Out on the landing, he switched on a ceiling light, and then, as if to bring himself back into the real world, from the top of the stairs he switched on the light at the bottom of the stairs, and he went down. He switched on the light in the entry hall, switched on the lights in the living room on one side of the entrance hall and, on the other side, the light hanging in a multicolored glass shade over the dining table. He lit lights in the kitchen, in the pantry, in the back entry, where there was a jumble of dusty rubber overshoes, including, in the jumble, some that had been Harry's, which Margaret hadn't gotten rid of. Back in the living room, he sat in an armchair, and an unaccountable flash of fear went through him—unaccountable because there was nothing in the brightly lit house to be frightened of.

The silence and stillness seemed to Gerard to become a space within the space of the room, within the space of the house, within the space of the world, and in that space he felt himself pull away from himself to stand and see himself, alone, listening for some sound, apprehensive about some movement in the air. But the silence and stillness remained.

He went upstairs to the office.

The furniture was exactly as it had been, and the brown velvet curtains on the one window were drawn as they had been. But the objects on the desk were arranged in a row: the penny, the stamp, the matchbox, the bowl of a pipe, and under these, as though to make of the objects a coherent whole, were the pipe cleaners lined up end to end.

He sat to study this arrangement. But the portent was always greater than any interpretation, however long he studied, so long that he felt his head throb.

Even in bed, alone because Margaret, without having telephoned to let him know she would be away, had not returned for the night, his head throbbed with trying to make connections that *had* to be there but that left him with only the unbearable *impression* of connections.

# EIGHT

Though summer had begun and he was not obliged to teach, which meant he could devote himself to *Histoire de L'Ecriture,* he read the book haphazardly, imagining that the answer to the central question he wanted answered would occur to him on the turning of a page. And yet, he didn't want it to occur, but wanted a question to remain. His not wanting the answer, his wanting the unanswered question to remain dominantly central, was much stronger than his desire for the answer. The unanswered question *was* more imaginatively potent.

In the library in Manchester, he took down a few books that had to do with writing, but, really, wasn't up to more than searching through the indexes for references to the origins of writing, and he read, here and there, paragraphs, and he was reassured that not one even raised the question of the arrangement of the alphabet. It was his question, it had occurred to him and to no one else. And as long as it didn't have an answer, it was an obsession—an obsession, however, that demanded an answer.

He felt guilty leaving the chores, such as shopping and cooking and doing the dishes, to Margaret, but she never reproached him;

and when she came in from he wasn't sure where, for she spent more and more time out, she climbed the stairs quietly to the landing off which was his office and simply glanced in without saying anything and passed by. Each time she appeared, he half rose from his desk chair to go to her, at least to ask her how she was, but each time he saw something in the book that made him sit again, his elbows on either side of the book and his fists on his temples, to study. She began to bring him a sandwich and a glass of milk for lunch, but he insisted on going down to the dining room for dinner, because to expect her to bring a plate up to his office for that meal really would be going too far, would be presuming so much on her indulging his obsession that he would be insulting her. She didn't understand—and he didn't expect her to understand—but she allowed him his obsession, or he thought she did until, coming into his office one morning after a solitary breakfast in the kitchen, he saw that the space the book had occupied was empty, a hollow among the scattered papers that appeared to him to be deeper than the surface of the desk, and to be darker. After a moment of bewilderment, a chilling bewilderment as extreme as it would have been had the book disappeared before his eyes, the certainty came to him: Margaret had taken it away, Margaret had all along resented his obsession, Margaret was letting him know that she would no longer tolerate his selfish fixation on an old yellowing book to the detriment of their married life. The thought did flicker into his mind that she considered their married life more important than the book, that she was, in having removed the book, trying to save their married life, but the thought, which he knew to be sane, was overwhelmed by rage, rage he knew to be insane. She was in the house—he heard her in their bedroom, on the other side of the landing—and he went to the door of his office, no farther, as if to go to her were to submit to the sanity of her trying to save their marriage. He shouted her name only once, commandingly, "Margaret!"

She came immediately, frowning, a little hunched as she approached him.

He heard his voice as though it came from someone else, someone who frightened him as much as his voice frightened Margaret. "What did you do with my book?"

Her mouth hung open for a long moment, and she frowned more deeply. "Your book?"

"You know. You know. I know you know."

"I don't know."

"Yes, you do."

"But I don't."

And now, in the midst of his rage, he felt a fool, as if he were suddenly reduced by her to a little boy who had to explain that a toy he wanted to play with was missing, he didn't know where to, and it wasn't his fault it was missing, it was hers. The sense of being a fool enraged him all the more. "The book I kept on my desk, the history of writing."

"You never told me you had a book on the history of writing."

"What do you think I've been doing, sitting at my desk, hour after hour, day after day?"

His rage, he saw, cowed her so that she stepped back, though she tried to defend herself. "I have no idea what you've been doing. You never told me."

She was right. He never had told her, and he hadn't because he was too embarrassed to, too embarrassed to because, again, he knew that his obsession was that of a boy obsessed by a toy, even a fantasy toy.

It was sheer insanity that made him shout, "It doesn't matter whether or not you know what I've been studying, it's enough that you knew I was studying something, something so important to me you couldn't stand the importance it had, it *has*. You looked in on me often enough when you brought me something to eat to see that I was studying a book. Is that why you brought me the sandwiches, to see what I was up to? It was, it was. Where is my book?"

She stepped back farther. "I didn't take a book from your office."

"Who could have taken it?"

"Maybe the cleaning lady."

"An illiterate Mexican woman who can only speak Spanish? What would she have done with an old battered book in French? Of course she didn't take it."

"Maybe she put it somewhere else in your office to dust your desk and didn't replace it."

He turned back into his office with that possibility, and Margaret, cowed and yet agitated by an accusation that she must clear herself of, joined him, frantically, to search the little room, though, he knew, she had no idea what to search for, and he thought, drawing back and looking at her for a moment, No, she doesn't know what happened to it. But there was no one else whom he could accuse, and when, finally, she simply looked around into space, he said, staring at her, "It's gone," and he said this severely enough that she still felt he was accusing her, for her body jerked a little. He was accusing her of something she had not done, but he couldn't help himself. She turned and rushed out of the room.

Gerard sat at his desk, his face in his hands, his breath heaving.

Did I, he asked himself, throw the book out? Am I made helpless, so helpless?

He thought it would be best for Margaret if he left the house and went to Boston for the day without telling her.

The bus was empty but for him.

He walked from the bus station in Boston and out into streets that took him, through a green Chinese gateway with golden Chinese characters inscribed along its high, wide arch, into Chinatown. Here, his attention shifted from a store window filled with ceramic figures of laughing men with elongated earlobes and open robes revealing rounded tummies to a delivery van with large Chinese characters on its side to a Chinese clothing store with an old Chinese woman smoking a jeweled pipe standing in the doorway.

Gerard came out on a corner of the Boston Common, and as he was walking along the crowded sidewalk bordering Tremont Street, the air about him agitated by the movements of the other pedestrians, he noted for the first time, across the street, a cemetery behind an iron picket fence. He crossed, through traffic, to the Central Burying Ground, according to an old plaque by the gate, of 1756. The ground was uneven, as if the bodies below had, over the centuries, tried to push up against the earth. Above the old, worn, slate stones, listing with the efforts of the buried to rise up, were spread the branches of big oak trees in bright spring-green leaf, themselves a leafy sky, and above the trees was a sky of thin, vaporous clouds, and above the clouds the pale blue of another sky. The burying ground appeared so contained within itself it might have had nothing to do with Tremont Street or the Common, even to have its own air. Before he looked at any of the gravestones, his attention, as various as when he was walking through Chinatown, was drawn together and centered on a woman standing at the far side of the burying ground, where the fence separated her from the Common, looking down at a gravestone isolated from the rest. She was turned towards him enough for him to see that she was Asian—a slender woman in a light summer coat, her dark, stiff hair cut short and revealing a thin white neck as she bowed her head to read the inscription on the stone; her eyes had delicately hooded lids, and her nose and mouth were delicate too. She appeared to gather about herself the stillness within the fenced-off burying ground. Gerard stood back to watch her in her stillness for a long moment before she turned towards him, and, without glancing at him, walked with a gliding step past him over the uneven grassy and mossy ground, and out by the gate into Tremont Street. Alone, he was drawn to look at the stone the woman had studied.

The carving at the top, the lines of it whitish against the dark slate, was of a winged skull, and the inscription read:

*In Memory of Susan L. Whipple*
*daughter of*
*Ben & Catherine Whipple*
*who died March 4 1800*
*aged 18 years old*

What, Gerard wondered, attracted an Asian woman—a woman who could have come from Chinatown a few streets away—to study, excluding, it seemed to him, all others, this gravestone, which he could not imagine having anything to do with her world? When he looked to see in which direction she was headed beyond the pickets of the black iron fence, he was surprised that she was not going towards Chinatown, but towards the Back Bay center of Boston. Maybe, he thought, she was a Chinese tourist, in Boston to see in Yankee America a world that had nothing to do with hers. Surely, she would have known that Boston had had, with its clipper ships, commercial relations with China that significantly financed

Yankee America. If she had already been, she would have seen the old evidence of China in America in the Museum of Fine Arts, glass case after glass case containing Chinese vases, scrolls, furniture. But it could have been that she wanted contact, however historical the objects of that contact, with a world that was essentially Occidental—for no other reason than that it was different from her Oriental world. Certainly, in his travels outside of America— which went only as far as Europe, though he did as a college student go to Mexico—he had always looked for differences. Now examining, here and there, other gravestones, some broken, the inscriptions illegible, he asked himself why he should have always looked for differences when he traveled to unfamiliar places. Why differences and not similarities? He stopped at a stone on which all he was able to read was: WHOSE MORTAL REMAINS SLEEP BENEATH THE SHADOW OF THIS STONE. Seeing similarities, he thought, would have given him a greater sense of one united world, which he believed was how the world must be in its consciousness of itself; but he had looked for differences, and he had done so, he told himself, because— Surprised, he wasn't able to say why he had always looked for differences, the question itself never having come to his mind before. He thought he had always looked for connections. At another stone, this one carved at its top with an urn and weeping willows on either side, the name and date of death were undecipherable, but the inscription read: LEGIONS OF ANGELS CAN'T CONFINE ME HERE. Wouldn't a legion of angels have done everything to free this person, body and soul, from the confines of the grave? Gerard left the burying ground asking himself, again, why he had always looked for differences, as he imagined that Chinese woman, if she was Chinese, was looking for differences. Why was difference such an attraction to him? Then the thought came to him—perhaps he looked for connections just because he looked for differences.

Boston was familiar to Gerard, and yet as he continued his way along Boylston Street to Copley Square, he found himself noting details he hadn't noted before, details that stood out for being, well, odd in Yankee Boston: a man wearing cowboy boots and a Stetson hat; a woman wearing a Hawaiian muumuu walking with a man in a Hawaiian sports shirt, both the muumuu and the shirt patterned with large red flowers; a fat man with a beard just around his mouth and a greasy ponytail, wearing a black leather jacket with a star made of metal studs on the back. They were, Gerard supposed, all Americans.

Across Copley Square, he faced the broad, grand granite Italianate façade of the public library and its deep steps, and he climbed slowly, as if holding back on an imminent discovery to be made just by opening one of the library doors and entering. He passed the guard and went into the lobby, holding back on the discovery he was about to make. He stopped to read an announcement of an exhibition called "Faces and Places." He read it as though this were the reason for his coming to the library, as though the other reason must be put off because he knew the discovery would not be made, and the disappointment must be put off—put off precisely in order for it to *seem* to remain imminent.

He suddenly wasn't quite sure why he had come to the library.

He entered the exhibition room, in which freestanding panels were arranged at angles with large photographs and maps hung on them. The large photographs were all of young people, and next to them were blown-up reproductions of old maps of where their ancestors had come from: China, Jamaica, Haiti, Cape Verde, the Dominican Republic, Italy, England, Ireland. Gerard was sure there would not be a Franco represented, and he went through the exhibition hoping there would not be. There wasn't. And this pleased him in some way, because the assumption was that the French in Boston were too different to have contributed to the shaping of the culture of Boston. As a Franco, he had not shaped or defined any culture, not even a Franco culture. And that was fine with him, just fine. The difference he was drawn to was a difference so great it couldn't even be included in "diversity," from which, in any case, he was left out. The difference he yearned to identify with, not yet knowing what, really, it was, was so great that he wondered if it was ethnically classifiable at all. With a degree of resentment as well as relief that Francos were not seen to have helped shape and define the culture of Boston, the capital city of New England, he told himself, more emphatically, that the difference he must finally identify himself with was not yet known by anyone, but he would find it, even though that meant he was entirely alone in his difference. And that, maybe, was what he wanted: to be entirely alone in his difference.

Leaving the exhibition, he was pleased with himself. He was pleased with himself both because the exhibition had made him feel left out and, because he had been left out, proud to be different from anyone else.

Gerard climbed the stairs to the second floor and went up to a long desk with inset wooden panels. Behind it stood an elderly woman whose glasses hung on her flat bosom by a gold chain, leaning forward to talk to a woman standing before the desk, her back to Gerard. As he approached, he saw the Chinese woman—or he presumed Chinese—he had seen in the Central Burying Ground. He heard her say to the librarian, with fine articulation, "I would like to find out about the alphabet."

The librarian asked, to clarify, "You mean the history of the alphabet?"

Gerard had expected her to be asking about the alphabet.

The librarian took a plan of the second floor from the desktop and, fixing her glasses to the tip of her nose so the gold chain swung, she placed the plan before the Chinese woman and drew a circle around the letters of stacks where, she said, dictionaries of many languages were to be found and where, no doubt, would also be found reference books on the history of the alphabet.

Merely to inform her, Gerard said, "That's what I came for."

The Chinese woman looked at him. She frowned delicately, but her delicacy appeared to be edged with sharp severity in the angles of her face.

"Then you'll want to look through the same stacks as this lady," the librarian said, and she held out the plan, on which she had drawn a large circle.

The Chinese woman immediately reached for it and went on ahead to the doorway of a large, stark room, but she stopped at the jamb and turned to Gerard, held the plan out, and matter-of-factly asked, "Do you understand this?"

"I think I do," he answered.

"Will you take it then?"

She was abrupt, almost impersonal, in her politeness, and this almost impersonal abruptness reassured Gerard. She was not interested in him, not any more than he was in her.

He took the plan and held out an arm to indicate that she should go into the room first. They walked side by side among the open metal stacks, and he was for a while disoriented and, though he referred often to the plan with its circle around the stacks they wanted, he led her in the wrong direction. In open spaces among the stacks were simple tables with piles of books left on them, and only here and there a person reading behind a pile of books. He stopped to examine the plan once again to orient himself. She stopped with him.

"I'm sorry," he said, "we're going in the wrong direction."

She held out a hand for the plan, and he gave it to her. While she studied it, he told himself he was disoriented because he was with this woman who was looking for exactly what he'd come for. She said, "This way," showing the way with the plan, and he followed her to a stack, the long rows of books too many for him to take in.

What they found were mostly dictionaries, bilingual dictionaries, which, as they came across them, they took out to place on a table nearby to look through them for hints of information about the alphabet; and the more exotic the languages, the more they imagined there might be information, as if exoticism itself promised revelations. Going back and forth from the shelves to the table, they began to enjoy, to the point of light-spiritedness, the exoticism of languages doubled up with English, such as Basque-English/English-Basque. That Basque was an Iberian language more ancient than Latin and unrelated to any other known language from which Latin was derived made it irrelevant to their research, but they were in no way ready to focus their research, with all languages now open to their unfocused curiosity. The Basque word for "alphabet" was *agaka*.

They sat side by side, the piles of books before them. They *were* light-spirited in what they shared, and would, from time to time, laugh quietly at the intriguing oddities.

The word for "alphabet" in Turkish was *alfabe.*

The word for "alphabet" in Ukrainian was *alfávit.*

The word for "alphabet" in Estonian was *tähestik.*

The word for "alphabet" in Azerbaijani was *älifba.*

The word for "alphabet" in Ibo, one of the eight major languages in the Benue-Congo group of African languages—two others being Hausa and Yoruba—was *abd.*

The phrase meaning "alphabet" in Vietnamese was *bảng chữ cái, bảng chữ.*

The phrase meaning "alphabet" in Xhosa was *uluklu loonobumba abalandelelanayo.*

The word for "alphabet" in Tagalog was *abakáda; baybayin.*

The word for "alphabet" in Pulaar—a dialect of Fula, and spoken in Mauritania, Senegal, and Gambia—was *alkule; limto (ngo).*

The phrase meaning "alphabet" in Swahili was *herufi za lugha zilizo—pangwa katika taratibu ya kawaida, yanni.*

The word for "alphabet" in Yoeme—a language of the Yaqui tribe of the American Southwest and northern Mexico—was *hiohtei.*

They could go no further, she now laughing with a hand over her mouth, he with the back of his hand pressed to his lips, and they left the table with the books scattered on it. There was a notice that the books must not be replaced by the readers, but by the staff, no doubt because the readers would put them out of order.

When, in an open-air courtyard with a pool and the statue of a slender dancing nymph dripping with water at its center, the woman stopped to look, Gerard stopped with her, waiting for her to determine what he would do next, because it was all up to her.

The courtyard contained a block of bright sunlight. Around the square pool, against the stone walls of the library, were chairs, only two occupied—by a young couple sitting close to each other and holding hands. Gerard continued to wait. He felt that not only what he would do next, but the course of his entire life was determined at the moment the woman asked, "Shall we sit?"

# NINE

Her finely hooded eyes half closed, she scrutinized him as if to decide something about him before speaking to him, which, once decided, she did directly. She said, "I saw you back in the Central Burying Ground on the Common."

"I know," he said. "I saw you."

"And here we are."

She left it to him to continue.

The image came to Gerard of the gravestone with a winged skull carved at its top, and the inscription, whitish against the dark slate:

*In Memory of Susan L. Whipple*
*daughter of*
*Ben & Catherine Whipple*
*who died March 4 1800*
*aged 18 years old*

He said, "You had a daughter, Susan, who died."

"Yes."

He added, "She died a terrible death."

"Yes."

"And this changed your life."

"Yes," the woman said. She looked at the water in the pool, then at Gerard, and she said, "Someone very close to you died."

"Yes."

"Who?"

"My son."

"And his death was terrible."

"It was terrible."

"And it changed your life."

"It changed my life," Gerard said.

They leaned towards each other.

The woman said, "My name is Catherine, not a Chinese name, though I was born in Shanghai of Chinese parents. I married an American from Boston, Benjamin Whipple. What's in the coincidence that the name of that Susan Whipple's father should be the same as our Susan's father, Ben, and that the name of that Susan's mother should be the same as my name, Catherine?"

"Are you asking me if there is some meaning in coincidence?"

"No, no, no," Catherine Whipple insisted, to answer herself, "none."

"None," Gerard repeated.

Catherine Whipple said, "I came to Boston from London to see the grave of the girl our daughter was named after, Susan Whipple, the most remote ancestral Whipple grave Ben knew of."

"Do you know how the ancestor Susan died?"

"I don't, but I have the impression that she killed herself."

"Is that what your Susan did?"

"Yes, she killed herself."

"I'm sorry, I'm so sorry."

Catherine Whipple rocked a little in her chair, then stopped and said, "Susan overdosed on heroin while she was an undergraduate at King's College, Cambridge. Ben couldn't bear her death. I believe he believed there was no way out of his grief for him but to die."

"He killed himself?"

"Ben couldn't bear her death, but, more, he couldn't bear living in a world in which people sell death to young people. He kept asking, Why? Why? Why? Why? That they do it for profit wasn't enough of an answer for him. I didn't have another answer. Ben drowned himself."

Gerard almost sang, "Why? Why? Why? Why?"

Catherine's face was so deeply expressionless, it could only have been kept so by her willing it.

"Shall we go?" she asked.

He stood, and she stood, and he let her go ahead of him out of the courtyard and out of the library into Boston.

Silent, they walked side by side across Copley Square, neither, he was sure, knowing where they were headed. He was aware of his arms swinging and sometimes brushing hers.

This was the least of what he wanted to say, but he wanted to say something, so he asked, "Is there an alphabet in Chinese?"

As slowly as they were walking, he saw that they were almost across the square.

"No," she answered.

"If there is no alphabet in Chinese, how can you look up a word in a dictionary?"

"With difficulty."

"Do they even exist, Chinese dictionaries?"

"They do, and they have since the year A.D. 121. That dictionary contained some nine thousand characters classified into five hundred and forty groups. In 1716, the number of the groups were reduced to two hundred and fourteen. Under communism, the groups were radically reduced."

"I don't understand."

"Do you honestly want me to explain?"

"I do."

"Say there are nine thousand different characters in Chinese, each originating from a picture, a graphic representation of an object—"

"Like a hieroglyphic?"

"I suppose, though I don't know anything about hieroglyphics."

"Neither do I. But I don't know much of anything."

"Many of these characters have in them similar strokes. These strokes are called radicals, and all the characters that share these radicals are grouped together. To find the character in a dictionary, you have to know its radical to look up what group it's in."

"And how many radicals are there?"

"Under communism, I don't know how many. But I know pre-Communist Chinese, which post-Communist Chinese in China can't read. I know as many of the two hundred fourteen radicals of the 1716 dictionary as I could possibly memorize."

"So you must have a good memory."

"My memory is good."

"I'd be hopeless."

She laughed.

They were across the square.

"So," he said, "no alphabet in Chinese."

"None," she said.

He stopped walking, and she with him.

"Then what made you wonder about the arrangement of"—he laughed lightly—"I was going to say, of our alphabet?"

She too laughed lightly. "Susan was reading philology at King's, and one day she asked me, 'Do you have any idea why the alphabet is arranged the way it is?' At the time, I wasn't interested, and answered, as if rejecting her interest, that what she wanted to know was unknowable. And since she died—"

"You think it can be known?"

"To make up, perhaps, for my telling her it couldn't be."

Reluctantly, Gerard thought, she continued to walk, and after remaining still for a moment with the expectation that she would turn back to him, he continued with her.

# TEN

Just before they got to brown, many-pillared Trinity Church on the other side of Copley Square, Gerard suddenly felt that in the next moment everything would be either lost or gained. Everything would be lost by his leaving Catherine, which there was no reason for not doing because nothing had been planned between them to keep them together. But everything would be gained by his going on with her. He would not have been able to say what this *everything* was, or what plan between them would have him go on with her and achieve it. Yet he did have a sense, an englobing sense, of *everything* simply being with her, and the moment they turned away from each other, which they were just about to do, that sense would cease to have a center, and he would, as before he met her, be isolated in it, isolated in it and lonely. He and Catherine stopped together before the church, and in a flash he had the idea of asking her if she had ever been inside and if not would she like to go in now to see the stained-glass windows? But before he could speak she said, "I know someone who can help with the alphabet," and he knew that in a flash an idea had occurred to her that would give them a reason for going on together. She'd spoken first because she was the more decisive person.

"Oh?" he asked.

"A philologist at King's will help," she said.

"Are you suggesting that I come to England with you?"

"I'm insisting."

The dead, as always around him, hysterically urged him to hurry to Manchester and, after leaving a note for Margaret, to return to Boston.

He had not known about himself that he could be so impulsive.

Catherine, whom he met in the lobby of the Ritz, had done all the organizing. She did not appear impelled.

A limousine service took them to the airport outside of Boston. Most of the trip across the Atlantic Catherine slept. At times he wondered what he was doing with this woman who appeared to him so totally a stranger she was not quite real. He had had the same sense of unreality come over him at the death of his son, the same sense of unreality when he'd jumped down into the cellar after his son and held him, dead, in his arms, the same sense of unreality when the airplane suddenly dropped as if out of the sky and with the thought *I'm going to die* came the simultaneous thought *This is just a dream.* The airplane did not drop out of the sky, he did not die, but he was still amazed to find himself alive next to a woman who woke from sleep and, unperturbed, read an article in the in-flight magazine. She appeared the least helpless person in the world.

A limousine met them at the airport outside of London, and Catherine's housekeeper, a Filipino woman named Anna, opened the front door of Catherine's large brick house in Hampstead.

Catherine's house appeared to have nothing Chinese in it. She was born in Shanghai of Chinese parents who were rich and Western-minded, who gave her a Western name, and, soon after she was born and before the Communist takeover, who left China for the West and emigrated to Brazil. There her father became even richer in flour mills. One of his pleasures was to pay to have one of the best players of the Chinese fine-stringed instrument the erhu come from China to give him lessons. Brought up in a Chinese household where the language was Chinese, Catherine was sent to a school where the languages were English and French, while all about her the language of the country was Portuguese. Because she was the third daughter of a family of no sons, when she was a girl her mother often told her, worthless daughter that she was, that she should have been left behind in Communist China. To spite her parents, Catherine herself wished she had been, and imagined being an avid Communist, active in the massively destructive Cultural Revolution. However, she knew that if she had in fact been left behind, she would have been shot. Ignored but allowed to do what she wanted, as soon as she was old enough she went to Europe, first to Paris, for a foundation course in fine arts at the Sorbonne, then to London, to concentrate her interest in the fine arts on a specific topic at the Courtauld Institute. As she knew both Chinese and Portuguese, she was advised to write on the Portuguese Jesuit influence on art in China, if she were able to persuade the keepers of the Jesuit archive in the Vatican to let her in, a difficult test of her seriousness. As mild as she appeared, she was as willful as she was serious, and she did get into the archives, where she copied out, by hand in Chinese and Portuguese, more information than she needed but took away with her information that her professor at the Courtauld was amazed to read for the revelations it contained about the depth of Jesuit influence in China. While writing her thesis, she met Benjamin Whipple, an American a year behind her at the Institute, and they fell in love and married, so she became Catherine Whipple, a name so un-Chinese that she was a surprise to people who hadn't met her and knew her only by her name. She liked, she said, to surprise people, especially liked being very different from what people expected a Chinese woman to be.

Gerard said, "I think I'm different from what an American is expected to be," and laughed. She did not ask him what he meant, maybe because she was too polite to ask, maybe because she was not interested, as though their private histories were not really interesting to either.

After dinner, Anna served them coffee in what Catherine called the drawing room.

On the table by the armchair Gerard sat in was laid an open case of juggling balls.

"Whose are those?" Gerard asked, to ask something.

To say something, Catherine answered, "They were Susan's."

Any association between juggling balls and a girl who had killed herself must be so far-fetched that nothing could be said about them that was less than absurd, so he said nothing.

But Catherine said, "She wanted to be a juggler."

Gerard had to take this absurdity seriously. "Did she have lessons?"

"She had lessons from the young man who supplied her with the heroin that killed her."

"Did you know that?"

"Yes."

"He was also taking heroin?"

"He was made to sell to Susan, to any number of other students at Cambridge, or he'd have his supply stopped."

"By?"

"By I don't know what network of dealing, a network that is, I feel, as widespread as the economic network of free-market trade in the world, and perhaps one with it, as I'm financially one with it. I'm not sure that any one person can be singled out and brought to justice for it, the evil is so interconnected among thousands and thousands and, oh, thousands."

"Isn't that true of all evil in the world?"

Catherine said, "That's just what Susan wrote in the letter she scribbled before she overdosed, overdosed to kill herself, and left on her bed in her room at King's. She saw everyone—even the leaders of the Colombian cartels—as victims of such overwhelming evil that every single person is a helpless victim of the evil. Susan was drawn, drawn as if to make love with each one, to people she considered to be victims. The more a victim she saw someone to be, the more she was drawn to that person, and she did, in fact, fall in love with, made love with, the most pathetic victim, a young helpless drug addict. She didn't think of saving him, no. She fell in love with him because he was a helpless addict, and the more helpless he became the more she fell in love with him. I imagined he roused in her a kind of compassion that was close to passion, sexual passion. Do you understand that?"

"Do I?"

Catherine said abruptly, "I refuse to understand any impulse so fatal to others, to oneself. I refuse to think of such an attraction to helplessness, and forgiveness of the worst weaknesses in helplessness, as anything but pathological. I refuse to accept that helplessness makes for innocence. And I especially refuse to believe that the very evil of the world, which no one can help, makes us all victims, and, as victims, innocent. A rage comes over me when I think of her, overdosing to kill herself, drawn to the most helpless of helplessness, feeling herself a princess fated by the helpless world to no other choice but to kill herself."

Gerard got up and stood over the case of juggling balls, different colors, rounded with a fine sheen. He couldn't touch them. He said, "But I understand, understand in some small way, in the way I understand death makes everyone, every single person no matter what evil he may have committed, an innocent."

Catherine lowered her head so far her long, thin neck stood out.

Turned away from her, Gerard lifted a juggling ball from the case. It felt solid and heavy, as if weighted to fall rather than to rise. He put it back and looked round at Catherine, who was now looking at him.

She said, "I bought those for her. I did everything I could for her. I even had her boyfriend to dinner, even for nights over to sleep with her in her bed. I thought I must not ever let her think she had anything but my support. However much I knew what was going on between them, I thought I'd lose her if I disapproved of him. In fact, I didn't disapprove of him. I liked him. He was also an undergraduate at King's, reading history, hoping to go into law. He played the piano for us, played beautifully and sensitively, Debussy, Fauré, Chausson, delicate pieces. He was, himself, delicate, and, yes, the most pathetically helpless person in the world in all his delicacy. She loved him *because* of that, and when he died, she went into a state of grief inconsolable in any other way but to die, to overdose, and kill herself."

Gerard sat again. Weakly, he said, "Surely she knew that you loved her."

He regretted having said it when, wiping the tears from her cheeks with her fingers, Catherine frowned, a sudden severe frown. "If that is meant to help me, thanks, but it isn't any help. However much she knew I was trying to do for her, however much she knew that I wanted their happiness, however much she knew that I loved her, none of that means anything to me, because she's dead."

"Yes," Gerard said, "yes."

"What she once might have known of my efforts to help her, of my so wanting her happiness, of my loving her, she no longer knows. What she might have once known means nothing to me now because she no longer knows and feels anything. She's dead, and everything she might have been, might have become, all of that, is dead too, and meaningless. You do understand that?"

He said, "I understand. And I understand how much you resent anyone trying to comfort you."

"I refuse to be comforted, I refuse."

"You have to know how much I understand."

"Understand that nothing can help, nothing?"

"I do, I do understand."

Her voice was low. "Understand that all the thoughts I have, all the feelings, are too much, occurring as they do, all together too much?"

"Such as, oh, guilt that we couldn't save them?"

Catherine groaned, a rough sound to come from such a refined woman. "No, not guilt. Shame. I remember being told stories of Chinese families who disowned sons or daughters by publishing in newspapers that they were no longer members of the family for much less than taking drugs. Even now, emancipated from all that as I insist I am, I have to fight the shame I feel at Susan dishonoring herself and me by killing herself, and also the shame I feel at that shame. Perhaps it's to save myself from shame that I tell myself I could have saved her just by willing her to be saved. Perhaps it's shame that makes me think I didn't do enough to help her. Though

I devoted myself to her, still I didn't do enough. I go over and over in my mind what more I could have done, and I can't think of any more, but there must have been something I could have done, just one act, that would have saved her. I sometimes think I could, if my will were strong enough, will her back to life, will her to enter this room, right now. I go into her room and I stare at her bed and I will her to be there, asleep and well and happy. But, dead, Susan defies my shame."

"You can't stand not having the will to bring her back to life."

"I can't bear it, I can't bear it."

"You can't."

"I think that if I don't change anything in the house, don't remove even the popcorn she left, the crime novels, her doll on the chimney piece, she will come back to find everything as it was. I can't change a thing."

"But you want to."

"I want to get rid of it all, including the furniture in her room, her bed especially. I want to be free of it all, free of her, because she has no right to possess me, she's dead."

"You're angry at her."

"Violently angry at her, violently. I want her to recognize that she's dead, that's all, and there is nothing to be done for her, and relieve me of my shame, relieve me of my anger towards her, which I don't want to have, because I loved her."

"And you still love her?"

Catherine sat upright and narrowed her eyes. "Love her? No. How can I love her? For me to love her she must know that I do. For me to love her I must know that she loves me. She can't love me, because she's dead, so I can't love her." She leaned far forward. "And yet I do love her, of course I love her." She sat upright, and, her voice low, said, "But if I love her, what do I love, because she's not here?"

Gerard rocked his head against the back of the armchair.

Gerard asked, "And jealousy, do you feel jealousy?"

"Jealousy?"

"Jealousy that they led lives apart from us that they kept from us, which my son was beginning to do. And jealousy of the life he would have led as he matured, jealousy of his developing independence to lead a life different from mine that he would have kept secret. I have dreams of him as, say, a nineteen-year-old, and in my dream I go into such a rage of jealousy at the life he has been leading apart from me in his different world, I try to beat him up, I try—"

Catherine said, "In my dreams about Susan, I try to kill her."

"Oh, I try to kill Harry in my dreams. I can't stand his appearing in my dreams. But he won't be killed."

"Susan won't be killed."

"She knows she can't be killed. She doesn't resist," Gerard said, "she simply looks at you and smiles."

"You know that."

"Whatever violence I act out on my son in my dreams, he simply looks at me and smiles. Whatever thoughts and feelings come to me in my grief, I see him, in the midst, looking at me and smiling."

Catherine whispered, "Looking and smiling."

"In the worst of my dreams," Gerard said, "Harry tells me he loved someone more than he loved me and this shocks me so much I wake up and for a while try to think what other person in his short life he could have loved more than he loved me—someone other than his mother, because I was never envious of his love for her, his love for her making me love her more than ever. In my dream, when Harry tells me he loved someone more than me, someone I didn't know, someone he kept his secret, I wake up and lie in bed for a while, sure that there was someone else he loved more. I even suspect he had a strange relationship with a man who warned him he had to keep a secret, a man he did love more than me. I tell myself, No, no, that's impossible, of course it's impossible, but the suspicion that he did goes on until I get up, but during the day the suspicion will come over me suddenly that he rejected me for that someone else. I know that this level of grief is base, and I know it has only to do with me, not with Harry, who is dead. I wish, I wish I could rise from above the baseness to another level."

"What possible level?"

"I don't know."

"There is no higher level. I try to keep all my thoughts and feelings to the most base level, about Susan, and about my husband. I refuse to allow thoughts and feelings to rise to any other level."

Gerard asked her, "Were you brought up with a religion?"

"None," she answered starkly, defiantly. "None."

# ELEVEN

She was sitting by him in the window seat of the train, and, looking out at the English countryside, he often shifted his eyes to glance at her, at the side of her slender face, just for a second before he looked out again at the countryside, greener than he had ever seen green, the green of trees and fields so saturated it appeared to run in rivulets in the narrow ditches alongside the tracks, to drip wetly down the rocky side of a cutting, to flow into small ponds, and seemed too about to precipitate in drenching rain from low clouds. Did she see this? He could not be sure what she saw.

In what way did she see the town of Cambridge, which a taxi from the station took them through?

As if the clouds had held it in until the moment they got out of the taxi onto the cobbles outside the great gateway of King's College, rain began to fall. They hurried past the open, heavy wooden doors for protection under the groined arch of the gateway. Gerard saw through the rain on the other side of the gateway an expansive green lawn and, beyond the lawn, a long, white, neoclassical building; he felt that it was only because of Catherine that he could be entering a place, enclosed within walls, where even the rain would be different from any rain he had ever experienced before. She asked him to wait under the arch while she went into the porter's lodge, and, standing on the worn flagstones and looking out at the rain, he sensed his reaction of strangeness modified by her matter-of-factness. He *did* feel the strangeness, and he felt it more when she came out of the porter's lodge holding out a key and said, with, it seemed, no sense of strangeness, "I asked if I could see Susan's room before our meeting with Charles. Because it's not term time, there are no undergraduates living in, so the rooms are empty."

She pointed the way to him with the key, into rain contained by the courtyard, rain that fell so heavily as they, with hunched shoulders, hurried along a paved path to the right, that it appeared to form a block of water they were submerged in. He saw her hair become wet, her dress become soaked, revealing her bra and clinging to her sharply angled shoulders, and, all around, the buildings were blurred by the water. He was just behind her, in step with her as she hurried ahead, eager, he was sure, to get them both inside. But she suddenly stopped, and he, advancing still, bumped into her. She turned round to him, strands of her black hair now stuck together and dripping, and she was blinking against the water that ran down her face. She was holding the key up. Her eyes, usually half closed, were wide open. In a voice he had never heard come from her—a deep voice as if from behind her voice that she herself didn't utter—he heard, "They're here." He became as motionless as she was. Here they were, here they were, the dead, coming out of the rain, emerging out of the water, to surround them. They were coming from neither of them would have been able to say where, a countless number that as they emerged from the rain also merged with it. Catherine was staring at him and, it appeared, past him at the same time; at him for his reaction and past him for what the dead would do. They would do nothing but simply watch, watch intently, because they knew that she was going to Susan's room, the room where her daughter Susan had died, and they had to witness whatever it was that occurred to her in that room. Now holding out the key in both hands as if for him to take it, she began to shiver. He did take it, and he assumed as much matter-of-factness as he was capable of by saying, "We must get inside."

Taking her by the arm, he pulled her, as if she were still transfixed and couldn't move herself, towards a neo-Gothic door, in a neo-Gothic building, and, opening the door, he more or less pushed her inside. The door closed of itself behind them. They were both streaming with water.

"Do you know where we are?" he asked.

She nodded.

"And how to get to Susan's room?"

She nodded again, but he could tell that she didn't know, and felt she must let on that she did.

With wet shoes, they went through what must have been the common room for the students, now empty, the stark booths of banquettes of red plastic around stained tables, on one table an empty pint glass and a blank sheet of dark paper.

The dead followed Catherine and Gerard not only through double doors from the common room opening onto a passage beyond, but right through the wooden doors when they closed behind Catherine and Gerard and, too, through stone walls. She opened a single door onto a flight of stone steps, the stone treads worn, and Gerard climbed behind her, the dead massively crowding about them.

On a landing was an old wooden chest, and on the chest a wooden tray with a dirty plate, crisscrossed by a dirty knife and fork, and a teacup and saucer, and, in their midst, a crumpled red rag. Gerard stood next to Catherine as she studied the objects on the tray, and, without asking, he was sure he could tell what was going on in her mind: she was asking herself what the meaning of the red rag was in the midst of the ordinary objects. The rag in itself was ordinary, but in conjunction with the plate and cutlery and cup and saucer it appeared as extraordinary in its meaning as it made the plate and cutlery and cup and saucer appear. Those who wondered about meaning needed the sympathy of others who also wondered.

He felt such tenderness towards her.

The stairs led up to another landing and a door. Catherine stood before the door, her eyes closed. She said, "I'm lost." Gerard opened the door onto a modern corridor, the floor covered in gray linoleum, on one side wide windows in metal frames against which the rain beat, on the other a row of metal doors. He held the door for Catherine to enter first.

"Do you have any idea where we are now?" he asked.

As if defeated, she said, "I'm sorry, I am lost."

Side by side, they walked along the corridor. Attached to the doors were little plastic-like notice boards, on which, Gerard assumed, students wrote messages that were wiped out once read; on some boards the writing remained in faint outline. On one legible enough for Gerard to read were the words DON'T YOU DARE.

The key clutched tightly in Gerard's hand hurt his palm.

When they came across the door to a toilet, Catherine told Gerard to go in to see if there was a towel to dry themselves. Having given in to her in every way, he thought, he did what she asked him to do and went in, and a moment later came out to say, yes, there was a towel roll, and she went in with him. But the towel roll gave out after one pull, and he took it upon himself to open a cupboard in which he found more. The key gripped between his lips, he unwound a length of towel and, holding the bolt end and unwinding it more and more as she needed it, watched her take the loose length to dry her hair, to pat the wet out of her thin summer dress, even to take her low-heeled pumps off to dry her bare feet, the loose length of the towel roll falling in a tangle about her. He said he would be able to take care of himself, and while she, at a mirror, combed out her still damp hair with her fingers, he wiped his head, his neck, unbuttoned his shirt to dry his chest, and took off his shoes and socks to dry his feet, put his shoes on over his bare feet and threw his socks into a rubbish bin. It was as though they were preparing for the event that the dead were waiting for.

Back out in the corridor, Catherine said Susan's room was in one similar, but not this one; when they came to double doors with small windows in them she looked through the glass out to a landing and another flight of stairs, and she said she thought Susan's room should be on the floor above.

They were on the top floor of the modern building, where the sound of rain was a constant hum.

As if suddenly panicked that it had been as lost as she was, Catherine asked Gerard, "You have the key?"

He opened his hand to show it to her in his palm, and just as he did she stopped, and he stopped with her, before the one door among all the doors on either side of the corridor that was ajar.

She said, "This was Susan's room."

The door was open just enough for water to flow out from the room onto the floor of the corridor.

Catherine cried, "I can't."

But Gerard, putting the key into a trouser pocket and side-stepping the flow of water, placed his hand on the door to push it open.

As he pushed the door, the sound of splashing water became louder. The small room was lit with summer light through rain, the rain splashing through the open window onto the floor, the narrow, built-in bed, the built-in, institutional-like desk and institutional-like chair, and forming a puddle that flowed out into the corridor where Catherine still stood.

If Gerard himself did not feel horror, he felt that the dead did, and in their shock they withdrew to a far distance, though from that distance they remained attentive.

Gerard shut the window, a wide pane in a metal frame, and the rain beat against it. He turned to Catherine and said, "There's nothing here."

Catherine was holding her hands to her cheeks. "Nothing?" she asked.

"Nothing."

Taking careful steps, Catherine entered the room. She stood in the middle and looked about, her hands on her cheeks. "There is something here," she said.

"What is it?" Gerard questioned, and he was aware that he questioned to keep himself at a distance from his own horror, though there was nothing here, now, to horrify.

Catherine pointed to a sheet of paper on the stark desk.

Gerard should have made a mockery of the scene, which struck him as out of a mystery novel he'd read when a boy, but he was incapable of mockery. He went to the paper. It was wet through, the row of crude figures drawn in thick lines with a black marker blurred. Catherine came to stand next to him to study the sheet, torn from a spiral notebook.

Touching the first figure, Catherine asked, "What do you make that out to be?"

"I think," Gerard answered, "the head of an animal with horns."

"A cow?"

"Or an ox."

"And the next figure?"

"A door?"

"It could be. And the next?" she persisted.

"An eye?"

"An eye."

"Yes, an eye. And the next is an axe head."

"Yes," Gerard said, "an axe head."

The dead, standing all about the room, as if pressed against the walls to keep their distance, seemed, all together, to draw together to surround her when Catherine peeled the sheet of paper from the desktop, folded it and tore it into shreds, then threw the shreds into a wastepaper basket under the desk.

Gerard all at once remembered burning his son's notebook, and he wondered on what impulse he had, as he now wondered what impelled Catherine to tear up her daughter's drawing.

"The rain has stopped," she said.

Weak sunlight was filling the room. The dead had disappeared with the rain, disappeared, maybe, because their anticipation of something occurring was disappointed. The dead could be badly let down by the living.

Catherine said, "We're late for our meeting with Charles. We'll have to say we were caught in the rain, which explains our being late and our being still wet."

She knew her way out.

Gerard admired her for the way she could abruptly arrest her feelings.

# TWELVE

She pushed her way past a wooden swing barrier with a notice attached to it stating that only members of the college were allowed past it.

On the stone lintel of black double doors were painted the names of dons; the don she had arranged to meet was Mr. Craig, all the other dons listed were professors.

"He isn't a professor?" Gerard asked.

Catherine reassured him: Charles Craig considered it better to be Mister, because this showed his research had been done for itself and not for a degree.

She said, "Believe me, if anyone is able to help us, he is."

Gerard opened one of the double doors for her, and followed her, now into an entrance paved with worn stones and, before them, an old, unpainted wooden staircase, its treads also worn, and, to the side, a door, half open, covered in green baize that was torn in places. Catherine knocked lightly on the inner door, and when a voice from inside called out, "Come in," she pushed it.

It opened onto a room crowded with tables—drop-leaf tables,

pedestal tables, gateleg tables, secretaries—on which were piled books. Where there were no books were objects—bowls and figurines in porcelain, beakers and plates in silver—and the walls were covered, heavy gilt frame abutting frame, with pictures. Across the room, standing by a fireplace, was a portly man wearing a burgundy-red velvet smoking jacket watching another portly man in a large green apron winding a clock on the mantel.

Mr. Craig said to Catherine, "I'll be with you in a moment, a brief moment, but I must now give all my attention to Mr. James, whom I always have to wind my clock, as he is a renowned expert in clock-winding, a talent—if I dare call it such, and why not? as it requires all the innate skill of the most accomplished artisan—sadly almost lost. Is that not so, Mr. James?"

"Afraid so, sir," said the clock-winder.

Catherine and Gerard held back, among the tables.

Mr. Craig raised his heavy chin and said, "My uncle had a clock-winder come to wind this very clock. Some in the family thought it odd, as this was his only clock. Some in the family thought it odd that he should have a librarian, as he did not have a library. I never thought it odd, no, not I." Mr. Craig's hair, thick and gray, appeared to be set into a solid, shining mass by brilliantine.

"I shouldn't think it odd," Mr. James said.

"Because, Mr. James, you are among the few who understand that what may appear to be an oddity is in fact the expression of a great need, and my uncle's need to have a young librarian, though he did not have a library, was indeed great. Some may think it odd of me to have you, Mr. James, come to wind my uncle's clock, but it is very precious to me, as it was given to me by my uncle, who loved me as much as I loved him, and as it was only ever wound by someone such as you, expert on winding clocks as you are, to wind it myself would be too great a risk, for I could easily do something irreparably wrong. I am capable of that, Mr. James."

"I'm sure not, sir," Mr. James said.

Gerard, frowning a little, was certain that a parody, even a mockery, of a scene in which Mr. Craig and Mr. James were characters was being acted out, and he was also certain that, whereas Mr. Craig did not think he was enacting a parody, even a mockery, Mr. James did, and he was amused.

Mr. James gave a last turn to the key inserted into the face of the clock, paused as if a moment of silence and stillness were essential to the enacting of the scene, during which moment Mr. Craig also remained silent and still, then Mr. James extracted the key, delicately touched the pendulum below the clock face so it began to swing, closed the glass over the gilt case that contained the now ticking clock, and handed the key to Mr. Craig. The don thanked him and said, "You'll send me your bill," and the clock-winder said, "As usual," and, bowing a little to Catherine and Gerard as he maneuvered around the tables to pass them and leave the room, he smiled a wide, knowing smile.

The don opened a drawer in a little table—a sewing table from beneath which hung, like a pouch, an embroidered bag—and carefully placed the key in it, and slowly closed the drawer. Turning to Catherine and Gerard, he said, "One must always know where one keeps what one will need, a very important principle in doing research." He indicated with a grandly accommodating gesture a wide doorway, the door open, and he said, "Do come into my study." Making their way around the tables, Catherine and Gerard went into the study, and Mr. Craig came behind them, gesturing again, in a grandly accommodating way, to the chairs they were to sit in before his large desk.

But Catherine didn't sit, so Gerard didn't. She said, "Charles," and held out her arms to Mr. Craig, and the big don went to her and embraced her as she embraced him, pressing a rough, red cheek against hers. When he drew away, he pulled from the sleeve of his smoking jacket a white handkerchief and, astonishing Gerard, he wiped tears from his eyes, blew his nose, and stuffed the handkerchief back into his sleeve.

Though he was at a remove, Gerard blushed with embarrassment for Catherine, but she seemed not at all to be embarrassed. She said, quietly, "Thank you, Charles," and apologized for their being late, due to the rain. The don waved off any inconvenience to him. Turning to Gerard, Catherine introduced him to the don, who held Gerard's hand tightly and stared into his eyes with the same intensity with which he'd stared into Catherine's. He said, "If I may be so bold, Catherine has told me about your suffering, as great as hers, and I can only repeat what I just said to her, that as unbearable as my feeling of commiseration is to me, the pain you feel must be much more unbearable."

Gerard felt his face flush. He said, "Thank you."

"May I call you Gerard?" the don asked.

"Of course," Gerard said, though perspiration broke out on his forehead.

"Then you must call me Charles." He made another gesture for Catherine and Gerard to sit, and he went behind his desk and sat as well. All the wall space, up to the high, ornamented ceiling, was filled bookshelves, the shelves jammed with books, and there were stacks of books on the desk, on chairs, on the floor, and on a table before a window. The high, wide, many-paned window gave onto a view of a field and cows.

When Gerard crossed his legs, he saw that Charles Craig spotted his bare ankles, and he uncrossed his legs. His embarrassment—embarrassment at Charles Craig's manners compounded by his own bare ankles, though it was embarrassment that neither Charles Craig nor Catherine felt—made him shift about in his chair.

He kept looking out the window at the field and the cows as Mr. Craig carefully inserted a cigarette into an amber holder, lit it, inhaled and exhaled smoke, and said, through an ever-expanding cloud of smoke, "As for the business at hand, I do think it is essential to inform you both that, by I can only imagine coincidence—because, surely, it could not have been planned—a gentleman will soon arrive—I asked him to come after your own arrival to prepare you both for his appearing, which, due to the rain's delaying you as well as wetting you, will be imminent—as I say, a gentleman will arrive—a Greek, he told me, a certain Mr. David Sasson, a very un-Greek name, but, given our days of the prominence of what are called ethnic minorities—horrible expression, but I hasten to say I am all in favor of the attention such minorities are demanding, for to the degree that they disappear for lack of attention so too do their languages—one can never be sure of anyone's national identity, not even, Greek though Mr. Sasson says he is, that Mr. Sasson is Christian, for David is, in the Mediterranean countries, a Jewish name—as the saying is, Jewish Christian name, meaning Christian to those people who assume everyone with a first name is Christian, as distinct from a Jewish family name—and Sasson is decidedly a Jewish family name."

Gerard had imagined that the name David, or pretty much any

name, was too common to connote and specify identity anywhere, and he wondered what identity his own name connoted. But he was too intimidated by Charles Craig's showing off so elaborately to ask.

"A minority in Greece," Charles Craig went on, "though once, in Salonika, as Thessaloníki is familiarly known to the Greeks, there was a large and populous and prosperous Jewish community, exterminated by the German Nazi occupiers. Greek Jews are now, however, recognized as a minority—as, I must happily say, those Turkish Muslims who remained in Greece after the exchange of the Turkish and Greek populations in 1923 are also recognized as a minority by the Greek state—though I am not at all pleased to say the Macedonian, Pomak, Vlach, Roma, and Arvanite minorities, each with its linguistic peculiarities, are in no way recognized—he, Mr. David Sasson, is, as both of you indicate to me you are, fixed on the alphabet as an historical construct, and he begged me to receive him, though I must say you and he will all leave disappointed. But be that as it may"—he removed the only partially consumed cigarette, inserted another into the holder, lit it, and continued—"be that as it may, I did want, dear Catherine, to see you under any pretext." He looked at Gerard through the smoke. "You will please excuse me, Gerard, for concentrating on Catherine, for, though I am fully aware that your suffering is in no way less than hers for the loss of your son, I knew her daughter, Susan."

That Catherine had told Charles Craig about his loss, which he had only been able to tell her as an exchange of confidences, annoyed Gerard. He shifted again in his chair and said, "Sure," telling himself this was colloquial and unaffected.

"Tell me, Catherine, tell me how you are bearing up."

She answered, "I know you don't want me to keep up appearances, Charles."

This surprised Gerard even more than he'd been surprised by her lack of embarrassment, surprised him for the way she was able to confide in this man whom Gerard found ridiculous. But then he wondered if he was wrong to find him ridiculous, if what he found ridiculous in the don he did only because of his own limited sense of what was insincere and what sincere. Catherine, with other values, spoke to the old don with a simple sincerity she clearly expected him to reciprocate.

He said, "No, no, never. You know how I hate put-on appearances, hate them, as I hate all pretense. You must tell me exactly how you are."

"Hopeless."

"As you have every reason to be." Startling Gerard, Charles Craig was stopped from talking and smoking by a short, heaving breath. He became motionless to compose himself, then he said, "You must never deny such a feeling, neither to yourself nor to others. Those English who do, who deny their feelings to themselves and to others, keeping their upper lips stiff in public as well as in private, are parodies of some principle they have of being English. I have had to endure that denial in my very family, the only exception being my dear uncle. They, those people, have no idea how ridiculous they appear, how *affected,* and how inhuman in their affectation." He sighed softly. "My uncle, my dear uncle, wept so much when his librarian died—as peculiar as it was to the rest of the family that he had a librarian, for he had no library—wept hopelessly, and I wept with him, wept so he must try to console *me*, must hold me in his arms where I wept all the more because his great consolation was to allow *me* to weep, to weep as I had believed no one is allowed to. You see, he loved his young librarian, I knew he loved him, and I knew that should I ever in my life fall in love as he had and lose the one I loved, I should weep and never stop, weep privately and publicly."

He drew into himself, and when he spoke again he addressed Catherine with, "Forgive me, my dear, for presuming to ask you something that has always fascinated me about you," and Gerard, imagining that the don would embarrass himself more deeply, cringed.

But Catherine did not cringe. "Anything."

"What is, as is said, your maiden name?"

"Tang."

"Shanghai."

"Yes, Shanghai."

"And you, Gerard, you—?"

But before he could finish, a distant knock made the don stand.

"You will, please, excuse me. I don't want to keep my guest waiting, lest he think I was not as prompt in welcoming him as he is in arriving." Leaving the study quickly, he hit his shoulder against the door jamb and rebounded a little, then went through.

Gerard smiled at Catherine to reassure her that he was amused by Charles Craig, but she didn't smile back.

She said, "Susan came to him, more than to us, for help. He did love her, and she loved him."

Gerard looked up to see Mr. Sasson, followed by Charles Craig, enter the study, a tall, thin, taut, blond man with thinning hair, in a black pin-striped suit and plain silvery-gray tie, his shirt cuffs revealing large cuff links, intaglios fixed in heavy gold.

Shaking the hand of Catherine, who remained sitting, and the hand of Gerard, who stood, he appeared to have stopped for only a second on his way to some other, more important business than meeting them, though he said, in perfect English, and with not so much an accent as a nasal tone—though, Gerard wondered, what standard of pronunciation determined accents?—"Mr. Craig has told me you are both here for the same reason I am," and he turned to the don as if with the expectation to get down to business right away. The don responded, "We'll come to that," to take an upper hand in the matter of the business, and Gerard guessed that Charles Craig was not, as he himself might have said, favorably impressed by the Greek gentleman. But he offered him a chair, on the side of Catherine opposite Gerard, and he took his place at his desk. "If I may be so forward," Charles Craig said to him, "I do wonder about the derivation of your name."

His knees and elbows jerking, eager to get up and go on to his next appointment, Mr. Sasson was in a hurry. He said, "My ancestors were Sephardic Jews from Spain."

"Surely," the don said, "your history goes much more deeply into the past."

"No doubt you would know."

"I can bring you at least as far back as ancient Syria, when, if you don't mind my saying so, the Sassons were a nomadic tribe."

"I think we still are."

"Oh, I like that. And you spoke a form of ancient Hebrew."

"I'm afraid, for me, that was lost a long time ago."

"You speak no Hebrew?"

"Only that 'Sasson' is said to mean 'joy' in Hebrew."

"And I do hope that is true of you."

David Sasson simply bowed his head a little.

"But you speak Ladino?" the don asked.

"Ladino was my parents' first language."

"And is it yours?"

"If the language of one's parents is one's first language, yes, it is, though, my parents being dead and my having no living relatives, I never speak it. I was married to an Armenian, whose first language was Armenian, which I don't speak."

"Greek being your lingua franca?"

"English."

"Though you live in—?"

"Athens. My wife and I lived in Athens, where I still live. She has died."

"I am sorry," Charles Craig said, and clearly not to presume to ask about the death of Mr. Sasson's wife, but, as if out of gracious commiseration, to give him a context that would make him feel he was being welcomed into the unfamiliar world he now found himself in, he said, "You no doubt know that our national poet Siegfried Sassoon was of a distinguished Sephardic Jewish family."

"I did know that."

"And that he was an undergraduate here in Cambridge."

"Clare College," Mr. Sasson said.

"You do know."

"I was at Cambridge myself."

"What college?"

"Jesus."

"Well, well."

Charles Craig seemed not to know how to carry on from this, and after a pause to consider how, he lowered his chin and recited:

I stood with the Dead, so forsaken and still: / When dawn was gray
I stood with the Dead. / And my slow heart said, "You must kill: /
Soldier, soldier, morning is red." / On the shapes of the slain in
their crumpled disgrace / I stared for a while through the thin cold
rain . . . / "O lad that I loved, there is rain on your face, / And your
eyes are blurred and sick like the plain." / I stood with the Dead . . .
They were dead; they were dead . . .

Overcome, the don stopped, and Gerard felt that David Sasson's
body loosened and appeared to give way, itself, to its own indwell-
ing and inevitable fate.

Charles Craig said, "For someone who loved tennis and riding
and hunting, a product of all the old social graces, our poet knew
such horrors."

And it seemed to Gerard that a sense of fatality, immanent and
inevitable for the three of them, deepened among them.

Charles Craig raised his chin and said, "You will, I hope, have
tea," and he picked up the receiver of a large old black Bakelite telephone on his desk to order the tea.

Catherine said to David Sasson, "You're wearing such beautiful
cuff links. Where are the intaglios from?"

"They are ancient Assyrian," he answered.

Gerard got up and asked, "Can I see them too?" and, as David
Sasson thrust his shirt cuffs out farther from the sleeves of his jacket
to show him the links, Gerard leaned forward to examine them.
The indentations represented lions with wings. "Where did you get
them?" Gerard asked.

"Where, originally, the intaglios would have come from—Iraq,
Baghdad."

Gerard returned to his seat, thinking, Baghdad? A place that, to him, no one could possibly visit to buy cuff links.

Once again agitated, David Sasson said to Charles Craig, "I've come from Athens expressly to see you."

"And I'm honored that you should have come, though, I must say, the honor you do me you will find undue." He raised a hand to stop David Sasson, who was clearly impatient, from taking over. "Of course I understand your fascination with the alphabet, a fascination that inspired the very course of my life when I, a mere adolescent, read, in the first-century-A.D. Annals of Tacitus his account of the evolution of the alphabet—the Annals brilliantly translated by my dead friend Michael Grant, which, to save anyone here from the shame of not knowing Latin, I shall test my memory by trying to quote as accurately as possible. Tacitus records that the first people to represent thoughts graphically were the Egyptians, in animal-pictures, which could be seen engraved on stone. According to the Egyptians, they claimed to have discovered the alphabet and taught it to the Phoenicians, who, controlling the seas, introduced it to Greece. The story—and stories are themselves of the greatest fascination, no one knows why—is that Cadmus, the son of the king of Phoenicia, the same young man, if I may digress, who slew the dragon that guarded the fountain of Dirce, sowed the teeth from which an army of men rose intent on killing him, for no other reason, one assumes, than that soldiers do kill, but Athena herself advised him to throw a jewel in their midst, and they killed one another fighting over it, all but five who helped Cadmus build the city of Thebes. This same Cadmus, arriving in Greece with a Phoenician fleet, taught the uncivilized Greeks how to write. According to other accounts, Cerops of Athens, or Linus of Thebes, or Palamedes of Argos in the Trojan War, invented sixteen letters, the rest being introduced later, notably by Simonides of Ceos. The Roman emperor Claudius, himself fascinated by the alphabet, added three, but these became obsolete, still to be seen in Tacitus' time on bronze plaques in public squares and temples. What is of particular interest is that the alphabet, from so early on, was thought to be the product of one man."

David Sasson waved a hand to dismiss all this talk, and, to get right down to business, he said, "Interesting, yes, but—"

"But what, Mr. Sasson?"

David Sasson jerked a knee. "Fascination, from however far back, is not proof of anything."

"And you have come to me with proof of something?"

"I'm sorry." David Sasson stopped jerking his knee. "I've come to ask you if something I have thought about—something from even deeper in the past than Tacitus—may be a little more scientific than fascination."

"You are testing me, Mr. Sasson, and I think you fortunate that I like to be tested. However, you must not put fascination below science, but above it, and a necessary inspiration to it. Now go on, test me."

"You of course know Plato's dialogue *The Cratylus.*"

"Indeed." The don rose, went to a shelf of his library, and, about to take down a volume, turned and asked, "Do you, Catherine and Gerard, know Greek?"

Catherine said some, but Gerard had to admit he didn't.

"Then we'll look into the English," and the don went to another shelf to pull out a volume. Back at his desk, he laid the book down, inserted a cigarette into a holder and lit it, then gave his studied attention to David Sasson. "I'm keen to know what you have to say about *The Cratylus.*"

"Where, in the dialogue, Cratylus talks to Socrates about the letters of the alphabet—"

"Ah, but our tea has arrived."

Charles, Gerard thought, must have seen David Sasson as a caricature—as Gerard saw Charles—as someone not to be taken seriously but to be politely mocked.

The tea, on a large wooden butler's tray, was carried in by a big-hipped girl in a red sweat suit, who, smiling, placed the tray on the don's desk. He said, "Thank you, my dear Illaria," and she, smiling more, swung her hips from side to side and said, "Any time," and left. Pouring out the tea into heavy cups, the don said, "One would hardly know, but she's Italian, from Lucca, Tuscany, where Illaria is a common name. She learned her English, and her manners, in San Francisco, where there is a colony of Italo-Americans from Lucca." Without ceremony, he handed the cups and saucers across his desk and each of his guests rose for one, the don saying, vaguely, that they must help themselves to milk and sugar. He then handed across a small plate of a few plain tea biscuits.

"There really is no need," Mr. Sasson said.

Charles Craig's voice rose in pitch as he said, "But I cannot allow you to leave with the impression that we English are without our culture," the last word almost sung out.

As impatient as he was, Mr. Sasson showed himself equal to the don, which seemed to be his intention, by saying, "No other culture that I know of, Mr. Craig, is as delightfully expressive of itself as is English culture with the importance it gives to tea."

This surprised Charles Craig, whose eyebrows did rise; but, however surprised, he was not going to give Mr. Sasson the upper hand.

"I would go so far as to say the English ceremony of tea—but it's a ceremony that is rapidly ceasing to exist, as English culture, whatever that can mean, is rapidly ceasing to exist, to be replaced by what? Not, for a moment, that you should imagine I regret the changes. I anticipate the replacement, I do, whatever it may be."

The tea, Gerard noted, was tepid and rough with tanning, and the biscuits were stale.

David Sasson took a sip from his cup, winced, and placed his cup on the edge of Charles Craig's desk.

"But we were about to look into *The Cratylus,*" Charles Craig said, and he, not drinking tea, put down his cigarette and opened the book placed squarely before him. "I know just the passage," he said, and said with the very authority David Sasson, and Catherine and Gerard too, had come for, "I shall read it." And no one told him not to.

David Sasson pulled at his fingers.

"We'll start with Cratylus speaking," Charles Craig said, and he read dryly: "Cratylus: 'Representing by likeness the thing represented is absolutely and entirely superior to representation by chance signs.'" First taking a puff of his cigarette, the don looked from one to the other of the three sitting before him and said, "A fascinating but difficult observation on the part of the young man. Shall we try to understand it?"

No one spoke, David Sasson now pulling at his cuffs.

"No?" the don asked, and with a "very well" continued to read: "Socrates: 'You are right. Then if the name is like the thing, the letters of which the primary names are to be formed must be by their very nature like the things, must they not?'" The don read to himself, murmuring a little, then said to all present, "As I think I know what your interest is, I'll skip, though what I skip is of great fascination, to Socrates asking Cratylus: 'Do you think I am right in saying that *rho* is expressive of speed, motion, and hardness . . . ? And *lambda* is like smoothness, softness—?' Am I right to skip?"

"You are," David Sasson said.

The don turned some pages. "Let us hear dear old Socrates: 'I myself prefer the theory that names are, so far as possible, like the things named; but really this attractive force of likeness is a poor thing, and we are compelled to employ in addition this commonplace expedient, convention, to establish the correctness of names.'" The don raised his eyes to David Sasson and said, "Socrates prefers names to be like the thing named, but, you see, he has to defer to convention. What position do you take?"

David Sasson said, "I of course believe that convention determines the meanings of words, as I believe that convention determines, or determined, the way the alphabet is arranged. What interests me is the possibility that in preferring the theory that names are based on likenesses, Socrates, without knowing, was referring to some long past characterization of the letters that originally *were* based on likeness."

"Possible, possible," Charles Craig said, closing the book. "I see, Mr. Sasson, that you are eager to tell us what you make of the possibility."

"I would like to know what you make of it."

"Let us use the Socratic method. I am interested in *your* interpretation of the passage we have all just heard and pondered."

But, shifting towards them in his chair, Mr. Sasson seemed to address Catherine and Gerard more than the don.

"I've wondered," he said, "if Socrates was referring to some letters that had survived in Greek from, let's say, the Phoenician, or from the Egyptian, or even from Sanskrit—survived in the same way there survived in the Greek pantheon some folk gods from far before the fifth century B.C., such as Hestia, Orthros, Kerberos, whose names *are* found in Sanskrit, and could date from Indo-European times. My question is, is it possible that some meaning of the letters of the alphabet existed long before Socrates that he had only the vaguest, distant, say, *impression* of, some meaning that could have been extended beyond the meaning of the individual letters to include the entire alphabet?"

"Are you asking my other guests, or are you asking me?" Charles Craig asked.

David Sasson, turning to him, was suddenly deferential. "Of course, you."

The don accepted the deference. "I apologize, Mr. Sasson, for seeming to have been rude. I did not intend to be so. We are all amateurs, myself most of all, and I hope I have preserved that approach to my research, which, had I another fifty years ahead of me, I should think I had not yet begun. You are right to wonder about the implication in *The Cratylus* about the alphabet, right to wonder if Socrates' designating a character to certain letters suggests some long-past association of character with each letter, an association so long past that Socrates was, without knowing himself, using only one or two examples of a vision of the alphabet that once was the prototype of all Indo-European alphabets. I repeat, how can one condemn your interpretation as impossible? It is entirely possible. It is entirely possible that Mesopotamian ideas reached the Aegean through Greek colonies in Asia Minor, that the so-called Phoenician secret books, now lost, inspired the very early Ionian Greek philosophers."

Charles Craig addressed the three before him, all of them, Gerard sensed, anticipating with relief what was now possible, what the philologist made possible.

"I must leave it to you, however, to continue your investigations on your own, as I myself have no knowledge to back up your interpretation. I thought I would have to disappoint you all, and I did not want to do that, so I shall not disappoint you. I don't doubt that you have all already done considerable research, and know that it is known that originally—whatever 'originally' can mean—the letter *A* meant an ox, or, rather, the letter *A* was originally a pictogram for an ox head, the letter *B* a house—"

Catherine's arms jutted out and her fingers spread open.

"What is that?" she asked.

"You didn't know?"

"I know nothing."

The don looked from one to the other. "Surely one of you knows?" But no one answered. "Well, well, perhaps you haven't done as much research as I thought you might have before coming to me."

"Please, Charles," Catherine said, "please tell us what the letters meant."

Pulling in his chin, Charles said, "I think I should send you all out to look up the information for yourselves."

"Please."

"You are desperate to know."

With a sudden flash of urgency, David Sasson pleaded, "Desperate."

"How can I not give in to your desperation, then, Mr. Sasson, although I don't understand why the desperation." He stuck out his chin and, as if reciting, began, "The letter *C* was originally a pictogram for a throwing stick, the letter *D* a door or gate, the letter *E* possibly a window, the letter *F* possibly a nail, the letter *G* improbably a symbol of the division of day and night—"

David Sasson interrupted the don by saying, "I hope, Mr. Craig, you don't mind my taking notes," and, without waiting for a reply, took from the inside pocket of his jacket a slim leather notebook and extracted a slim gold pen from loops at the side and began to record what the don had already recounted.

"I'm not sure I have a choice," Charles Craig said.

"Please," David Sasson said.

The don again recited, now quickly, as if to speak more quickly than David Sasson could write. "*H* could have been a fence originally, or, rather amusingly, could have been a stick figure with its arms held out calling hello. *I* was depicted as an arm and hand, and *K* the palm of a hand. *L* was an ox goad, *M* water, *N* a fish, which places them as near to each other figuratively as phonetically. *O* was an eye and *P* was a mouth, so the two appear to have made something of a face. *R* was a head and *S* a tooth, which seem to relate figuratively to *O* and *P*. *Q* comes between them as a monkey, so perhaps they all combine into a monkey face. *T* was simply a mark, though there was another form of *T*, somewhere between *H* and *I*, which meant a wheel, and which in fact looked like a wheel, a circle with cross spokes. There you have it: each letter of that particular alphabet, we can suppose, did originally have a meaning, however improbable our interpretations. In this, you can't be disappointed."

Raising his pen as if to ask permission to speak, David asked, "Can we possibly assume that the order in which you've given us the original meanings of the letters is an order imposed later, say by the Latin alphabet?"

Gerard, who'd been wondering if David Sasson was being pretentious, had to admit he asked questions that he, Gerard, would have asked if he were not embarrassed at appearing pretentious.

The don answered, "As for the order, what can I say? The Phoenician languages, with their different alphabets, were spread throughout the Mediterranean, especially the ports of trade, and continued to be used in the time of Alexander the Great. Phoenician, with all its variations, was a Semitic language, in that it originated in what is now Syria, Lebanon, Israel, Palestine, in ancient times centered on the cities of Byblos—the meaning of which I hope I don't have to explain to anyone, though it does occur to me, Mr. Sasson, and forgive me for singling you out, that in using that word for 'book,' the Greeks must identify the Bible as *Agia Grafis,* which in some way I should know came into English usage as 'Holy Writ'—and the cities of Sidon and Tyre. I digress. Older than the Phoenician is the Canaanite, also Semitic. During most of my life it was assumed that the Canaanite alphabet was the oldest. There is, however, no evidence left us of any particular order of the Canaanite letters." Charles Craig became aware that his cigarette had burnt out without his smoking, and he lit another and for a full minute inhaled on it and hardly exhaled. He said, finally releasing a vague cloud of smoke, "Well, within most of my life, as I've said, it was assumed that the Canaanite alphabet was the oldest, derived, it was thought—and as Socrates also thought all writing was derived—from Egyptian, a kind of hieratic cursive Egyptian—'hieratic' coming, as you, Mr. Sasson, must know, from the word for 'sacred' in Greek—an assumption too out of date, you may be grateful to hear, for me to go into detail about it. The fact is, the assumption was wrong. In recent years—too recent for me, old as I am, to take in the full implications—I must confess that as I get older the more I consider my position at King's (I being the only living-in bachelor don left, all others married and living out) as that of a fraud—inscriptions were found in Egypt, northwest of ancient Thebes, now Luxor, far out in the desert, in a valley of steep, sheer rock face along an ancient caravan or military route, the valley called the Wadi el-Hel, meaning, appropriately, the Valley of Terror—inscriptions, among Egyptian inscriptions pleading, most of them, for the protection of certain gods in that valley, that are not Egyptian ideograms, which represent the thing itself, such as a haunch of beef, and which we can presume Socrates would have preferred all letters to do, but, though derived from Egyptian ideograms—you see how complex it becomes, with all the crossing-over of one culture into another—are in fact individual letters, each sign representing an individual sound. In those inscriptions appears the ox head, representing *A,* appears the wavy vertical line representing *M,* appears the stick figure with raised arms who may be calling out *H.* As far as I know, the inscriptions have not been deciphered completely, but words have. For instance, the letters represented by box, eyes, cane, cross, spell out the Semitic *baalt,* or 'lady'—though what kind of lady we can't quite say, perhaps a goddess—Semitic because we know the word from later Semitic languages. You could ask, how was the word deciphered? By luck, but I leave that to your imaginations. You could ask, who wrote the inscriptions, if they were not Egyptian? It is thought that they were carved into the rock face by Semitic mercenaries in the Egyptian army. But who, in historical fact, were they, or who was he? He would have, as a non-Egyptian, been called by the Egyptians *Amu,* meaning 'Asiatic.' Who was this foreigner in the land of the pharaohs—the word 'pharaoh,' as, again, you, Mr. Sasson, may know, being the Greek way of saying the ancient Egyptian for 'great house' or 'royal palace,' which you may not know was *per-aa*—who took preexisting Egyptian figures, probably from the Egyptian army he was a mercenary in, and made each represent a letter? I can only leave that also to your imaginations. The inscriptions, you will like to know, date from 2000 B.C."

The three sat forward.

Charles Craig lit another cigarette, lit it so carefully that he had to have done so not only for authority, but for suspense. "To return to the alphabet, as you are so intent on my doing—if you have come to me to explain *why* an ox head, then a dwelling, then a throwing stick, then a door or gate, then a window, then a nail, then the division of night and day, *why* such an arrangement, which you may believe, with some justification, originally comprised, all together, a meaning, as do the words of a sentence, I must tell you that I have no idea *why*."

The three sat back simultaneously.

"We all might wonder, with awe, that what every schoolchild, whether trained to use the Cyrillic, Latin, Greek, Hebrew, Arabic, or Sanskrit alphabet, takes entirely for granted unites us now with the historical evolution of a culture some four thousand years old. We know that certainly since the eighth century B.C., the order of the Greek alphabet was fixed, as we see from craters and vases of that time inscribed with the letters in their present order. And we know that in Rome as in Greece students were exercised in recitations of the alphabet, sometimes in the set order, sometimes in reverse. But, I repeat, I can be of no help to you in your need to find out why *A B C*." The don held out his arms. "And there you are."

"There we are," Catherine said flatly.

Charles said after a moment, "You *are* all disappointed, as I was afraid you would be. I would rather not go on to try to relieve you of your disappointment, but I shall. I must admit that there has been some speculation about the order of the letters, based on the Pythagorean use of letters as numbers—as of course was common among the Greeks and Jews—but in the Pythagorean case to relate those numbers to the zodiac, the twenty-four letters of the Greek alphabet being twice the number of the twelve signs of the zodiac. Also, the seven vowels symbolized the seven known planets. But this brings us into the realm of mysticism. Again, who is to say that the mystical veneration of the alphabet by Greeks and by Jews, especially in the Kabbalah, and by Muslims—Shiite Muslims attribute to a certain Ali two books, the Djafir and the Djamia, in which letters are utilized mystically to predict the future—as do, I can add, some heretical sects of Islam, especially the Pure Brotherhood at Basra of the tenth century, in which the doctrine contains Neoplatonist mystical elements—not to mention—except, of course, that I do mention, a fifteenth-century sect founded by Fazil Allah, whom the conquering Mongol Tamerlane had executed in 1401, in which sect letters were the very source of mystical visions—and as for Christians, think of the number 666 in the Apocalypse of Saint John, which number has taunted interpreters for centuries for its mystical significance in terms of letters the numbers represent, as they surely do represent letters, for we know of lost concordances used to interpret the numbers back into letters, and, to complicate matters, letters used to represent other letters to form secret, sacred codes—who is to say, as I started out by asking, that all of these mystical uses of the alphabet do not refer back to some originating mystical arrangement of the letters? If you are drawn to this approach, I can only advise you to remain totally impersonal in your research, for any personal involvement can only lead you into—" He stopped.

"Into what?" Catherine asked.

"At best, daring yourself to go where embarrassment warns you not to go."

Glancing at one another, the three sitting before Charles Craig understood, more from one another than from the don, that they must leave. Together, they stood.

"I am sorry," Charles Craig said.

"No, you have been a help," Catherine said.

"Have I?"

"You've brought Gerard and me together with David Sasson."

"And I'm happy for that," the don said, but, as if together they represented a group that could only ever be wrong in trying to realize the need they shared, a group he had, perhaps himself wrongly, indulged as much as he could without making a total fool of himself as a philologist, a group that he was sending on its wrongheaded way, he couldn't, it seemed, rise to see them on that way. He said, "You'll find your way out."

When they reached the doorway, he called out, "I do understand deep bereavement, I do. My dear uncle died, did himself in, out of inconsolable sorrow on the death of his beloved librarian. I, all of seventeen years of age, was in a fit of inconsolable sorrow at my uncle's death. His beloved young librarian died in the trenches of the Great War, and could have been, Mr. Sasson, one of those commemorated by your, in a manner of speaking, compatriot, Siegfried Sassoon. I am always amazed at how everything connects, and connects more and more the older I become." Catherine went back to him and, sidling along the front of his desk, kissed him on his cheek.

"Thank you," he said.

But he had not concluded the meeting, for before his guests could leave, he asked Gerard, "Do remind me of your family name."

"Chauvin."

"French, obviously. But you are American."

"From New England."

"Then a New Englander by way of French Canada."

"We call ourselves French Canuck Americans."

"Fascinating, I must say."

"You think so?"

"Oh, more fascinating than you can imagine. I assume you take your name for granted, as people of course do, being unaware of the histories connoted by them. And do you know your history? When did your family leave France to go to Quebec?"

"I don't know."

"I would hazard from the province of Aunis, perhaps from near La Rochelle—which was, as surely you know, a center of trade with la Nouvelle France, now consisting of all of Canada and most of the United States of America, taken over, I must humbly excuse myself for the British having done so, for the historical sins of this island are great, by defeating the French who had already established themselves in cities, towns, villages, garrisons, as in Detroit, Des Moines, the very state of Maine named after la Duchesse de Maine—and I say *near* La Rochelle because the name Chauvin suggests a Catholic family, not Huguenot, and La Rochelle was Huguenot. Huguenots, as of course you know, were not allowed into la Nouvelle France, but only Catholics, leaving Huguenots to go, finally, to the British colonies, as did your—dare I say, your compatriot? for he did help to defeat the British—Paul Revere, a great American patriot, or so it is assumed by most Americans, though perhaps not by you."

"I'm sorry to say, I didn't know."

"And sorry you should be, my dear boy, for your history is deep."

And Gerard felt himself blush.

# THIRTEEN

The three stood on the cobbles before the gate into the college. Gerard had the same sense he had had when, in Boston, he'd stood with Catherine before the church in Copley Square—the sense of not wanting to leave the others but having no reason to stay together beyond the shared impulse to find out something insignificant about the alphabet that Charles Craig had just exposed as having no possible conclusion. David Sasson kept turning from side to side, as though anxious that he'd be late for his next appointment, and he even took a step or two away, but he always turned back to Catherine and Gerard, who stood together, already helplessly resolved to stay together. A woman, a lady don Gerard assumed because she wore a black academic gown, passed them to go through the gateway into the college.

Gerard tried to remember: Was "gate" the original meaning of the letter *D*? Or, as Gerard wasn't able to remember exactly, did the letter originally mean "door"? Gate? Door? An entrance, or an exit?

David had written down all the meanings. Motionless together, Gerard and Catherine were waiting for David to decide, on his own, if he *couldn't help* but join them in the search for what couldn't be found. Why, Gerard asked himself, couldn't they simply ask him to give them a copy of the meanings he had written? Why did they have to leave it to him to give in—yes, *give in*—to joining them? Was it because they knew that by joining them he would be giving in to some fatality, a dark circle he would then never be able to draw back from? He seemed to walk round the circle, then, suddenly confronting them, the muscles of his tensed face softening and his intensely concentrated blue eyes appearing to go a little out of focus, he said, "The tea in Mr. Craig's rooms was disgusting. I think we need to reassure ourselves that England hasn't altogether lost its standards and go to a tea shop. Do you both have time?"

Catherine spoke for Gerard, and he liked that she did. "We do."

David suggested, across from King's, the Copper Kettle, where he used to go as an undergraduate, a rather scruffy place, he said, but he remembered that the standards were kept for tea. But the tea, which he brought on a tray to a small table in a corner where Catherine and Gerard sat, was brewed in bags in a metal pot with a flip lid attached and no better than the tea served in Charles Craig's study.

David asked, "What, I wonder, will replace tea as English?"

And yet they remained at the wooden table, the insides of the unfinished cups of tea ringed with tanning.

"My wife was murdered," David said. "She was murdered by a terrorist group that, on a certain fixed date of a certain month, but not every year, murders someone, in most cases a diplomat, but also bank managers and professors, or simply guards at embassies. And they hit in places that are, it seems, as arbitrary as the people they murder, in Psychiko, in Kolonaki, in Piraeus. You remember that an English diplomat was murdered, shot in his car, some years ago.

Efforts are made to try to make out a pattern, but the group works against any pattern. After every murder, promises by the Greek government are made that the members of the group *will* be found and all of them brought to justice. Rumors are rife that the group has a wide network, national and international. And there are of course rumors that the government is implicated, and also that America is implicated, and who can say there is never anything in rumors? I hate the politicians more than I hate the members of the terrorist gang, but as much as I do hate them, and I hate them with passion, with passion, I would vote into power the most extreme right-wing government that would take all the measures needed to wipe out the terrorist gang. I know that by voting in such a government I would be doing just what the terrorists want me to do—help to create an age of government terror more violent than any terror the terrorists themselves can perpetrate, a government-led terror meant to protect the world from terror. The terrorists want the government in power to be a terrorist government, in name an antiterrorist government, so the people would finally rebel against the official terror, the interrogations, the torture, the executions. Once that occurred, the terrorists would rise up with the support of all those people who suffered the terror and take over, and impose their own government. And it will all happen so easily, as easily and as suddenly as my wife was murdered, which I had never, ever thought could in fact happen, however much I heard about the murders of the gang, but which *did* happen." He hit his chin. "It will happen, it will."

Catherine sighed, a deep sigh.

She asked David, "Are you going back to London?"

"I am."

"By train?"

"By train."

"So are we."

"What train?"

Gerard took from the pocket of his still slightly damp shirt a timetable. "There is one in half an hour."

"We could walk to the station," Catherine said. "It's a beautiful day."

"Yes," David said, "a beautiful day."

"Will you come with us?"

"If you would allow that."

Catherine simply rose from her chair, and the men rose too.

On the way to the station, they sometimes walked three abreast along the wide pavement and talked about incidentals, but incidentals that seemed to be filled with as yet unrealized incident, and sometimes they walked each behind the other when the pavement was narrow, and said nothing, as though following someone who led them to where the incidentals would become one overwhelming incident—or, perhaps, not. Gerard's sockless feet sweated in his shoes.

The station was at the end of a long tree-lined road, and from a distance its wide glass windows shone in the slanting early-evening sunlight.

While David was buying his ticket, Catherine asked Gerard, "Why did I destroy those crude drawings we found on the desk in Susan's room? Why?"

"You didn't want to know what they meant."

"No, I didn't want to know what they meant. And now—" She hesitated. "David wrote down the letters the figures represent."

"And you would like him to tell you what they are."

"As you said, maybe I don't want to know."

"Still, you do want to know."

Catherine looked down as David came towards them with his ticket.

On the train, Catherine and Gerard sat across a narrow table from David, who was in the window seat. The sunlight, slanting through the countryside in beams, broke through the deep green trees and became, itself, green. The beams rather than the train appeared to change directions and, shining through the diffusing dust on the window, would now strike the faces of Catherine and Gerard, now the face of David, and, blinking, they would shade their eyes with their hands.

David said, "My wife's Armenian name was Dirouhi, her family name Gazarian—names which I imagine would give Mr. Craig a lot of fun. Her grandfather went to Thessaloníki from Tokat in what she insisted on calling Anatolia instead of Turkey, as Greeks too do. That was at the end of the nineteenth century, when Thessaloniki was still under Ottoman rule. She came from a rich, old family, and though her father allowed his many children, including his daughters, to be educated abroad, in Berlin, in Paris, in London, in New York, they were as Armenians in Thessaloníki a very self-enclosed family, spoke Greek, German, French, English, Russian, some Arabic, no Turkish, but only Armenian to one another, and saw only other Armenians. I met her in London, where she was studying art history at the Courtauld—"

Catherine said, "I was at the Courtauld."

"When?"

"From 1967 to 1969."

"That was just when Dirouhi was there."

"We could have possibly met."

"You could have, possibly," David said, and he sank back as if to reflect on the meaning of Catherine and his wife's having met.

"What was her concentration?" Catherine asked.

"Armenian church architecture."

"I think perhaps I did meet her, just met her, because I do remember a conversation with a woman about Armenia."

"You met Dirouhi?"

"I don't know if it was your wife, but whoever she was she made me want to go to Armenia, a country I had never thought of, as strange to me as—" She hesitated. "As strange to me as America, where Gerard comes from."

"We are all so strange to one another," David said.

"Are we?" Catherine asked.

Gerard asked David, "How did you meet your wife?"

"I was a friend of her brother Arsen, also at Jesus College in Cambridge, and he introduced us. It used to annoy me that when the three of us were together, they spoke to each other in Armenian. And when, in Greece, I visited her and her family in Salonika, they all spoke to one another in Armenian, making me feel very left out. But I got back at her. When she visited me and my parents in Athens, I insisted on speaking Ladino with my parents, to make her feel left out. Well, both of us being, in our different ways, left out—left out, I suppose, by Greeks—we got together and married."

"You were brought up, a non-Christian, in a Christian country," Catherine said, "as I was. Do you have any religion?"

"As a Jew? I hardly knew I was one when I was growing up. Even during the Nazi occupation of Greece, when Jews, especially from the large Salonika ghetto, were being transported to death camps in Poland, my parents, in Athens, had no trouble, maybe because they looked like true Aryans, tall and blond and blue-eyed, the way the Germans imagined ancient Greeks to look. I have to say, present-day Greeks do not at all resemble the Aryan ideal, but then, present-day mainland Greeks are mostly Albanian. Greeks from Constantinople and Alexandria and from the islands are, in their ways, different. Added to his ancient Greek looks, my father spoke perfect German. They got through the Nazi occupation pretty well. I was born after, not knowing really that I was a Jew because my parents never observed any of the rites or holy days and never identified themselves as Jews. Brought up with Greek Christians—almost a tautology—I used to kiss the hands of priests the way my friends did, until one day my mother, seeing me kiss the hairy hand of a fat and greasy priest, told me I didn't have to do that. 'Oh?' I asked. She said, 'You're not Orthodox,' which meant, of course, Orthodox Christian. 'What am I?' I asked, and she answered, 'You're a Jew.' That meant I not only didn't have to kiss the hands of priests, I didn't have to hold my balls and spit three times whenever I saw a priest, as Greek men do, because priests threaten their masculinity, and my masculinity as a Jew wasn't threatened. My mother took me a few times to the Athens synagogue for Passover, but that was as much instruction in being Jewish as I got. And then, when I was doing my basic training in the army—and I'll interrupt myself to say that Greek Turks in the army, in my time, were not allowed rifles, and in my father's time were not allowed to have driving licenses—when I was doing my basic training, the first Sunday our commanding officer said we were all obliged to go to church, but I said I wouldn't go. 'Not go?' he shouted. 'What's your excuse for not going?' I said, 'I'm a Jew.' And he said, 'That's not allowed in the army.' But I refused to go, and, dismissed, I rang my father, who had his connections in the government, and apologies came from above right down to the commanding officer. I learned to use my being a Jew in a predominantly Christian country. And so did Dirouhi, Christian of another sect from the Greeks, use being an Armenian. One has to learn how to use one's difference."

"Why did you both go on living in Greece?" Gerard asked.

"Why? Because Greece was our country. Because I wasn't going to live in Spain, and I don't have and never have had any interest in Israel, except, somewhat, to go to see the Armenian Quarter in Jerusalem. Towards the end of his life, my father went back to Spain and bought a vineyard and its wine production. Perhaps he considered himself more Spanish, after all, than Greek. He and my mother were divorced by then. My mother lived in Paris, where, as a girl, she had been educated, and where she felt most at home, though it wasn't her home. Greece wasn't her home either, and Spain wasn't. She died shortly after my father. Well, Greece is the country where I was born and brought up, where I was educated, and so is it the country where Dirouhi was born and brought up. She was certainly not going to live in Armenia. We had no other country."

Catherine asked, "Why was she murdered?"

David shook his head violently from side to side. "I don't know, I don't know, I don't know. Why, as an Armenian art historian married to a Jew, she was murdered by a Greek gang—if they are Greek—I don't know, and no one I've begged some understanding of knows. Was she mistaken for someone else? Were they being totally arbitrary? My God, *did* she have connections with people she kept to herself, connections the investigators questioned me about in case, they said, such connections did exist, but which I had no idea of? She traveled often enough to Armenia, to Turkey, to Georgia, to Russia, and also to Syria, to Iran, to Iraq, always, I thought, doing research in art history. She was shot in her car, outside our house in Psychiko, just when she had parked. On the seat next to her was a large bouquet of her favorite flowers, lilies. They were splattered with her blood, with fragments of her skull, with bits of her brain, because her head fell on them. I saved the bouquet for a long time, simply spread it out on the dining-room table, until it began to rot. Even then, I couldn't throw it away, but brought it in a bag to the cemetery in Salonika where she is buried with her family, the inscription on the gravestone in Armenian." David hit his forehead.

"Are you staying in London?" Catherine asked.

"I'm staying in a hotel."

"Alone?"

"Alone."

"Will you join Gerard and me for supper in my house?"

"That's very generous of you."

"Oh, it's not a disinterested invitation," Catherine said. "You have to understand, as Gerard no doubt already does, that I'm not a sociable person, not interested in entertaining, and certainly not in being ingratiating."

"I used to be, but I myself am not up to being social now."

They went by taxi from King's Cross Station to Catherine's house in Hampstead, and while Anna made a simple supper in the kitchen they sat in the garden, where the evening light seemed to come not from a sun that was too low to be seen, but from the overspreading trees, which glowed green.

David Sasson said, "After she was killed—oh, weeks and weeks, months, after she was killed—I became obsessed with putting order in everything, starting with my desk, then going to her desk. I couldn't bear, honestly couldn't bear, seeing her handwriting, pages and pages of her handwriting, drafts of articles, or notes, I assumed, taken down during her research in Armenia, in Anatolia, in Russia, in Georgia, in Jerusalem. She liked to write by hand. I found it so unbearable to see her handwriting, her own distinctive handwriting, her very signature proof of her identity, that I had to stop myself from tearing up all the papers and throwing them away, burning them. You see, I couldn't read what she wrote because she wrote using the Armenian alphabet. I knew the Armenian alphabet—I'd asked her to teach me, thinking I should know at least that about her language—I could read the letters, I could read the words, even read them out loud. But though I could read the letters, could pronounce the words that the letters made up, I didn't understand. I never learned Armenian."

"Armenian isn't written in Latin letters?" Gerard asked, surprised.

"In ancient Armenian letters. Latin letters were imposed by Atatürk on Turkish in his determination to Westernize Turkey, so that Turkish in the old Arabic-derived script can't be read by generations since. But Armenia kept its alphabet. Dirouhi wrote in the cursive form of Armenian. I saw among her papers texts in that alphabet, and I realized that if she hadn't taught it to me, the letters would have just been marks on the page. I can voice them, but I don't understand the words the letters spell. I know from her that the ancient alphabet was made up of thirty-one consonants and five vowels, enough letters to be among the most phonetically precise alphabets there are. Twenty-two letters correspond exactly to Greek letters, and the fourteen others are non-Greek. Dirouhi told me a lot that I forgot, but I did remember this—that the invention of the Armenian alphabet and the Georgian alphabet, which it resembles, was traditionally meant to have been that of a certain Saint Mesrop, who died in A.D. 441. He had been the secretary— meaning a scribe—in the court of Armenian kings, where the language and writing were Persian, that is, Pahlavi, the language of the Zoroastrians. But he was a Christian, as Armenians had been for a century, and he left his post to devote himself to the Christian religious life. He met a Greek called, appropriately, Plato, who taught him the Greek alphabet, and the story is that out of the Greek he elaborated an Armenian alphabet according to a heavenly revelation, which led to his translating the New Testament into Armenian. Armenian was then made the official language and writing of Armenia by an Armenian king, who presumably got rid of Pahlavi, to unite and rule the country. The Greek letters can be accounted for, but what about the fourteen non-Greek letters, where do these come from—Pahlavi, the language of the Zoroastrians, or a more atavistic language? The alphabet was, clearly, based on older alphabets—as what alphabet isn't?—but, according to Dirouhi, the Armenian alphabet is distinctive in that, given the precision of it in accounting for pretty much all the sounds the human voice can make, and, more, given that the earliest known arrangement of the Armenian alphabet is so profoundly different from the known order of any other Indo-European alphabet, it must have been arranged by *someone,* perhaps by Saint Mesrop himself, and, if by him, arranged according to a divine revelation. The Armenians identify so with their alphabet that it's enshrined in their churches. Leave that aside. My point is, simply, that *someone* arranged the Armenian alphabet, and if someone arranged that alphabet, isn't it possible that someone arranged the alphabet as we know it, going even further back to those letters of 2000 B.C. found in the Valley of Terror? For what reason?"

"Your interest is purely historical?" Catherine asked.

"What is yours?"

"I don't know if I can say, but it reassures me that yours *is* purely historical."

"And me too," Gerard said.

Anna came out into the garden to say that dinner was ready.

The dining room, with large, open glass doors, gave onto the garden, where the light was fading from green to gray.

Their talk was surrounded by sounds from the darkening garden of nighttime insects and birds, and, as if they had sounds of their own, by their complex thoughts. David Sasson said quietly, as if now very tired, "Do I have any reason to be optimistic about the world, given the history of the world's horrors? Only that at some time, someone, somewhere had a sense of the universal, of everything all together and at once, and the idea of everything together and at once spread and spread throughout the world. There's very little that separates the universal from the mystical. I'm not interested in the out-of-the-world, the heavenly mystical, but in this terrestrial phenomenon. And I believe the most amazing terrestrial phenomenon is the occurrence of the idea of the universal, which idea may, just may, inspire—" He raised his arms. Gerard and Catherine waited. David appeared to give in to his fatigue, which itself was so great it overwhelmed any embarrassment he felt in proclaiming, "Love." He let his arms fall loosely. The silence among them was filled with the outside night cries. Placing his napkin by his plate, he asked them to excuse him. He would like to get back to his hotel and sleep.

Before he left, Gerard asked him, "What did you do with your wife's papers?"

"I burned them all."

Catherine showed David out, then rejoined Gerard at the dining table, where he sat with his elbows propped on the edge, his fists at his temples. She sat across from him.

Without lowering his arms, as if talking to the silver bowl in the center of the table, he asked, "Why couldn't you get yourself to ask him for a copy of the meanings of the figures that Charles dictated to him?"

Sitting straight up in her chair, Catherine said, "We don't want to know."

# FOURTEEN

As Catherine and Gerard approached him in the lobby of his hotel, Gerard noted that David, sitting in a corner beyond an Arab in a head cloth reading an Arabic newspaper, was reading a book he immediately recognized as *Histoire de L'Ecriture*.

David didn't stand; he indicated chairs before him, and Catherine and Gerard sat. David closed his eyes for a moment, shook his head, opened his eyes to look beyond Catherine and Gerard. He again closed his eyes and shook his head before he once again opened his eyes and fixed on Catherine and Gerard.

David was very agitated, and, agitated, he placed the book on a jerking knee.

Gerard stared at the cover, on which, below the large blue letters of the title was a yellow upright rectangle in which stood two figures of men in profile with long hair and earrings, both wearing robes, one writing apparently on a loose sheet and the other incising a tablet. He did not want to give the book any more consequence than David seemed to, but he could not help saying, "I had a copy of that book."

David's knee jerked so that the book almost slid off.

That was the only reaction David had to Gerard, who, as if to use the book as a way of overriding David's agitation, said, "I found it in a store for used books in my hometown."

"Where is that?" David too seemed to be trying to override his agitation.

"Manchester, New Hampshire."

"I don't know it."

"Only the people who live there know it."

"Where is New Hampshire—named, I imagine, after Hampshire, England?"

"It's a state in New England."

"*New* Hampshire, *New* England, *New* York, and no doubt many other European places made new in America."

"New Bedford, New Haven, New London, New Rochelle, New Jersey, New Many Places."

"Do those places have any connections to the places they were named after?"

"None at all."

"They must have a connection to the origins of their histories."

"I'm pretty sure no one living in New Hampshire ever thinks of the history of the state's name originating in Hampshire, England, and would wonder why the name was chosen. The connection is lost."

"And yet, there had to have been, originally, a reason for the choice."

"I guess I myself have never wondered, but, yes, there must have been a reason."

"Do you know if there are in America such places as New Athens, New Cairo, New Constantinople, New Damascus, New Baghdad, New Tehran?"

"I wouldn't doubt it."

"And the people in those places wouldn't have any idea why the places they live in have such names?"

"I'm pretty sure they wouldn't."

"They don't know their own immediate history?"

"They don't."

This conversation, which Catherine listened to attentively, was, Gerard knew, a way of referring to the book without referring to its contents, as though its contents were what had agitated David so much.

Gerard said, "I don't know what happened to my copy of the book. Did I throw it away? If I did, why did I?" As no one responded to this, Gerard dared himself to ask David, "Where did you get your copy of the book?"

"I found it in a secondhand-book shop in the Charing Cross Road."

There was nothing more for Gerard to say, and Catherine, as if trying to act on social adeptness she was no good at, asked, "May I have a look into the book?"

His finger still inserted in its pages, David held it out to her, and as she took it his finger slipped out.

"You've lost your place," she said.

"It doesn't matter."

Catherine opened the book, and held it out, spread open for everyone to see:

"What does *that* mean?" Gerard asked.

"I'd rather not know what it is and what it means," Catherine answered, and she closed the book. "Let it all remain a secret."

"All?"

"Yes, all."

"It *is* all too much," Gerard said. "We shouldn't have tried to take on so much." He hesitated, but David's agitated silence made him go on, again to override the agitation. "I sometimes feel that I myself got rid of my copy of the book without remembering that I did, because it was all too much for me to take on."

"Yes, too much," Catherine said.

She handed the book back to David, who simply stared at it in his hands. His entire body jerked. He held the book out to Gerard and said, as if as an imperative to himself to get rid of it, "You take it."

Gerard raised his hands and placed them on his chest. "It's yours, not mine."

"I don't want it."

"You don't want it."

"It was forced on me."

"Who forced it on you?" Catherine asked.

"Who? You must know who. It was forced on me, as this whole business of the alphabet was forced on me without my in fact wanting it. I think that not one of us wants it. Well, I won't have it."

"You'll give up?" Gerard asked.

"Oh, give up, give up. I *want* to give up, that's what I want. I want the choice of giving up." He thrust the book towards Gerard repeatedly. "Take it, take it, take the book."

But Gerard now put his hands behind his head.

David thrust the book towards Catherine. His voice rose. "You take it."

"No," she said abruptly.

He threw the book onto the little table by the side of his chair and stood and, as if in an effort of defiance, walked to the other side of the lobby, towards the entrance where the commissionaire waited to open the door for him, but he turned back and walked towards Catherine and Gerard, not to them, but away from them again, pacing, Gerard saw, because he was too agitated in his anger to sit. When he did come towards them it was to pick up *Histoire de L'Ecriture* from the table and, in a fury, he slammed it down on the table, as if to destroy something. He slammed the book again and again against the table, so a small bouquet of flowers fell off. The receptionist behind the reception desk came round, but stopped to stare, as did others in the lobby, including the Arab. David shouted, *"Agh, agh, agh,"* with every blow of the book against the shaking table.

Panicked, Gerard jumped up and rushed quickly to David and placed a hand on his shoulder, and with that gesture David threw the book down and turned to him, his face a face of agony.

"Sit with us," Gerard said.

Sitting, David said, "I once knew two sisters who lived with their brother in Damascus and who, when their beloved brother died, destroyed the house they'd shared with him, cracked mirrors, smashed vases and lamps, slashed pictures. I understand them."

Catherine, too reserved to understand such a display of violent emotion, leaned forward and reached out and touched David's hand, then sat back.

After picking up the vase and replacing the flowers in it, leaving the puddle of water, Gerard also sat. As though the other people in the lobby had been taken out of their lives for a moment, they returned to their previous lives, as did, for the moment, the receptionist.

"I know why you came to see me," David said to Gerard and Catherine.

"Why?" Catherine asked.

"You want from me the list I wrote out of the letters represented by figures that Charles Craig recited."

"We found the figures in the room, at King's, where my daughter Susan killed herself."

"I knew that your daughter killed herself." He looked at Gerard. "And I knew that your son was killed."

"You knew," Catherine and Gerard said together.

"I knew when we first met." He hit his forehead as though to break his skull. "I knew, I know."

"We want to know what the figures mean—four figures drawn in a row that correspond to letters."

"And what I scribbled down will let you know."

David reached into the inside pocket of his jacket and took out the thin, leather-encased notepad with the slim gold pen inserted in loops at its side, the scribbled-on first page of the notepad exposed. He read the writing on it to himself, then he looked around and pulled the notepad close to his chest as if to keep it from being snatched out of his hand. But then, defiantly, he held the notepad out for anyone to take it. Nevertheless, he didn't read from it.

They all needed the reassurance that the figures didn't contain a message.

Too agitated to sit, David again stood, and Gerard thought that, possessed as he was, David would again rage, but, pacing back and forth, he held the notepad up to his eyes.

Gerard said, "We know the ox head means *A*. Tell us what letter a door stands for."

As if he were hardly capable of concentrating, his eyes darting about the page, it took David a moment to read, *"D."*

"And an eye?"

*"O."*

"And the sign of the division of day and night?"

*"G."*

*"A, D, O, G,"* Gerard recited.

Catherine appeared to withdraw, as if from an insult, into herself.

"A dog!" Gerard exclaimed. "A dog? Not a god? That's all it means—a dog?"

David turned away.

"Shouldn't we laugh?" Gerard asked. "Shouldn't we be howling with laughter for making pretentious fools of ourselves?"

# FIFTEEN

Staying in Catherine's house, David said to her and Gerard at the ritual of tea, "I know about embarrassing oneself. All my life, I sometimes feel, has been an embarrassment to me. Even as a boy, I didn't believe in the evil eye, because my own mother told me she didn't believe in it either; and yet, she must perform the ritual to break the spell of the evil eye and I must submit to it, because that was what was done. As I lay in bed, I watched her arrange on the bedside table, on a white napkin spread open, a pin, a little pile of cloves, a glass of water, a candle and matches, all of the instruments, I felt however many times I witnessed it, of a sinister religious act; I watched her light the candle and, carefully taking up a clove, impale it on the point of the pin, and I heard her in Greek say, 'If I gave you the evil eye, may my eyes pop out,' which I hated to hear but which I knew must be said, however cruel, for the spell to be broken, for only those with blue eyes, which my mother had, could give the evil eye. I could not, with my blue eyes, give myself the evil eye, but I could to others. Holding the impaled clove delicately by thumb and index finger, my mother inserted it slowly into the flame, and, though I knew that her eyes would not in fact pop

*179*

out, I drew back in horror at the image of my mother's eyes hanging by slimy, twisted cords from their sockets. Never did it happen that she was the medium for casting the evil eye on me. But there was Manos, the gardener, originally from the island of Páros, who had blue eyes, because Páros had once been a Venetian island. Again, I was assured by my mother that Manos couldn't be guilty of intentionally giving me the evil eye, but would have been used by the forces of evil without his even knowing to cast their evil intentions through his blue eyes; yet I held myself in tense suspense, anxious that Manos—whom I liked for letting me open the little earth dams in the ditches he had dug in the garden to let the water run from olive tree to olive tree—would not be the one whom the evil powers had used to make me ill. But as much as I was sure that Manos hadn't himself intended me to be ill, how could I be so sure, because I had no idea what went on in Manos's head? I was relieved when the clove simply sizzled as it burned. My mother would then drop that burnt clove into the glass of water, slipping it from the point of the pin by dragging it across the rim. She would impale another clove on the pin, and say, 'If Olga gave you the evil eye, may her eyes pop out,' because Olga, a friend of my mother, was from another Aegean island that had also once been Venetian and where most of the inhabitants had Venetian blue eyes. That my mother could pronounce the name of her close friend as a possible suspect should have reassured me that the evil powers were acting through her without her knowing—certainly, a close friend of my mother could never, ever herself intend to do me harm—but, again, how certain could I be? The clove fizzled out in the flame and again my mother dropped it, still smoking, into the water. I sometimes watched my mother go through a number of cloves, as many as ten or twelve, until it was difficult to think of people, however distantly related as friends or help in and around the house or shopkeepers, who had blue eyes; and if, after more cloves than I could remember had simply fizzled out in the flame when a name was pronounced, I would want to say to my mother, *Let's stop*, because I would see, in the now automatic way she continued, with her arm slack from having done it so many times, that she wanted to stop. But she wouldn't stop, and I wouldn't ask her to. And finally, after the repeated plea to whatever power that was meant to counter the power of the evil eye was pronounced with the name of the someone with blue eyes who might have given it, a clove held in the flame did pop, the tiny fragments like shrapnel exploding in the light of the candle, the spell would be broken, and I would get better. The final act of the ritual was that I drink the water now flavored with burnt cloves. Most often, I didn't get better, not as quickly as the breaking of the spell on me should have made possible. And always, as my mother blew out the candle and cleared away the objects of the ritual by placing them on a tray, I would feel silly, and embarrassed by the silliness of the ritual, as embarrassed as my mother was. I have no idea where it derived from. We knew it did no good, and, remembering it now, I think that perhaps we wanted the powers that be to know that we did it in defiance of them, to let them know we knew it did no good. Yet, we never stopped the ritual.

"As, I suppose, we won't stop," David said, "and we won't stop if only just to make fools of ourselves."

"Fools of ourselves," Gerard repeated quietly.

But Catherine was vehement. "Fools."

"We make fools of ourselves," David said, "as a way of not being helpless. I am willing to make a fool of myself, but I'm not willing to be helpless. Not I, no, not I. I'll never give in to helplessness. One can be a fool, but that does not mean that one is helpless. I know how ridiculous I am as a businessman, as a man of culture, as even a member of the Rotary International Club. I know how affected it is of me to come to London to stay at the Connaught, to dine at the Ivy, to have my suits made in Savile Row. I'm ridiculous in my affected knowledge of wines ordered from Berry Bros. & Rudd. And I'm most affected in my use of English. But all of this keeps me in the world, and I will not, *will not,* give up the world. I *will not* be made helpless. I am not, will never be, a negative person, but as positive as it's in me to be, however embarrassing that is."

He stood and walked back and forth before the fireplace, on the mantel of which was propped a little girl's doll.

David said, "Fools that we are, we can't give in to hopelessness, we can't. Nothing matters, of course nothing matters, but we have got to believe something does. I'm most foolish in insisting on a place in the world, which I believe will be destroyed, will be devastated, inevitably, by massively destructive and devastating powers which humankind invented but over which humankind has no control, because humankind can't control the impulse to destroy and devastate. But until it happens, I'll go to my tailor, go to fancy restaurants, drink vintage wines. And all the while, until it happens, I'll go on reading Plato, insisting that Plato matters."

Gerard laughed as though to add slight derision to his question. "Plato? Why Plato?"

"Because, if I am Greek, I have to see Greek as having a history deeper than Christian history, its Christian history itself derived from pre-Christian history. I read Plato, not for philosophy, but for history, because history is more relevant to me than philosophy, than ahistorical ideas, and there is more history in Plato than the philosophy he's known for. In *The Protagoras,* Socrates mentions people who simply browse around on their own like sacred cattle, on the chance of picking up virtue automatically. What's most striking about the passage are the sacred cattle, the religious respect for which came from where? India? Plato didn't know much about India, if anything, as he didn't know Greek and Sanskrit were related languages. He knew about Egypt, and he knew the influence of Egyptian culture on Greek culture. Again in *The Protagoras,* he talks about the Egyptian town of Naukratis, a site given to the Greeks by an Egyptian pharaoh to set up a trading post with the Egyptians. In fact, Naukratis means, in Greek, 'new ship.' The Greeks had their own temples to Aphrodite, Hera, Apollo. Not that the town was exclusively Greek—nothing, I think, can be exclusively anything—not even, I'm sure, the religious ceremonies, which must have incorporated Egyptian rituals in them. And the Greeks, being as enterprising as Greeks of course are, in Naukratis manufactured Egyptian faience scarabs, and Egyptian pottery too, for the Egyptians. And during all the centuries of Pharaonic Egypt, when the entire economic system was based on bartering, the only known coinage—silver and bronze coins from different parts of the Greek world—was introduced into Egypt by way of Naukratis. Plato knew that one of the Egyptian gods called Theuth lived in Naukratis, and the ibis was sacred to him. Theuth invented numbers and calculations—and it is interesting to note that in Greek and in Hebrew the letters of the alphabet served as numbers—and astronomy, and, good for him, also draughts and dice, because there had to be something of a game about all the inventions he thought up. Most important, he invented writing. The god Theuth, an Egyptian god in a Greek site, invented writing."

"And what do we know about the god Theuth?" Gerard asked.

"Isn't that for us to find out?"

"Historically?"

"Yes, historically—because all gods exist in history, of course they do. If we're going to do research, it will have to be our own, discounting all that the scholars say to us about the impossibility of what we're looking for and go our own way, and my way—based on what I consider the most irrefutable evidence—is to believe that writing came from the god Theuth. What can be more idiotically foolish than this? What can be more foolish than to be drawn, drawn as though I were being pulled by a force, to believing that writing came from a god, and the historical evidence for that is, simply, gods date back so far into the history of mankind that there is no separating them from history? The history of humankind is the history of gods. Why not believe, for the sake of believing in belief, that a historical god revealed the first alphabet? And why not Theuth?"

"Why not?" Gerard asked, but he saw that his agreeing with David only made David think he was as affected as Gerard, or so Gerard felt about himself.

David sat again, picked up his cup from the red lacquered tray on the ottoman, and, holding the cup so as not to spill the tea, crossed and uncrossed his legs, seeming to try to take a position that would allow him to sip delicately.

Then, to assert himself against his embarrassment, he insisted, "We have got to believe in what most embarrasses us. We have *got* to. All we have is history, and history is terrifying, but, given that it is all that we have to prove to ourselves that we have any meaning, history proves the existence of God—or, if you will, gods—and that proof is enough for me to believe." He was still holding the cup, and the tea did spill from it in a small splash onto his jacket when his arm jerked, but he laughed. "Oh, I am a fool."

Catherine remained silent, as though embarrassed for him.

Worried about the tea staining his linen jacket, David dabbed at the wet spot with a napkin.

The white napkin in his hand, he looked up and said, "But do I know what I believe in? Is it up to me? Even as I speak, I feel that I'm being taken in directions I don't intend, openings occurring in my words that lead effortlessly to other unintended words, and these openings synchronically leading to other openings, as in a labyrinth through which I'm being guided in unexpected turns, each opening unexpected. I don't mean to say what I say, not at all."

"What pulls you?" Gerard asked.

David looked down for a long moment, then up at Gerard, his expression one of pleading that caused a movement in Gerard of pity for this cultivated man, who believed he was, after all, a fool.

"You don't know?" David asked.

"Yes, we know," Catherine answered for Gerard.

# SIXTEEN

In the taxi to the British Museum in Bloomsbury, David silently looked out the window at his side.

Catherine sat between the two men in the backseat. She said to David, "What is the name of the god of writing?"

David didn't say.

"What is the god's name, David?" Catherine insisted.

Looking out the window, he said quietly, "Theuth."

The high, wide gallery, with a coffered ceiling and pillars, resounded with the voices of children.

David, who was between Gerard and Catherine, appeared to be most aware of having come on stupid, truly stupid, pretenses, but it was he who stopped before an Assyrian figure to examine it closely, with Catherine and Gerard next to him, they too stressing the examination of the figure, which had a long beard with rows of curls in it and a curling moustache, and the hair too was long, flowing onto the shoulders with many curls. He wore a cap that appeared to have horns on either side. His blank eyes were wide. One hand clasped the other at his waist, and the bracelets tight about his wrists were decorated with rosettes. From the waist down, his long robe was incised densely with cuneiform.

He dated from about 810 to 800 B.C., and was from Nimrud, from the Temple of Nabu, and he was the Assyrian god of writing. He had been stationed on one side of the entrance to the temple, and his duplicate, the distance of a wide doorway between them now, had centuries before been stationed on the other side of the entrance, so the god of writing in identical manifestations had guarded the temple.

In the silence among the three of them, Catherine said, "Another god of writing." David turned away for the others to follow, but he stopped before a black Assyrian obelisk, also inscribed with cuneiform, listing the tributes paid to Shalmaneser III from: Gilzanu, now western Iran; Jehu, the king of Israel; Musri, perhaps eastern Iran; Suhi, on the Middle Euphrates; and Patina, in south Turkey.

With a sudden tone of mockery that surprised him, Gerard said, "Oh, interesting."

"Oh, very," Catherine repeated with more mockery, "oh, very interesting."

"Come," David said impatiently, as if to get through the gallery as quickly as possible, "come along, both of you."

A group of schoolchildren, all wearing blue pullovers, were led past by their female teacher and between two monumental Egyptian figures of smooth black stone, seated on thrones, hands on knees, each with a slightly bulging belly over a stiff kilt, their chests bare and with small nipples, wearing false beards and headdresses that pressed their ears forward, staring out above the crowd. David and Catherine and Gerard entered into the Egyptian gallery.

Among children moving animatedly about and calling to one another, Catherine insisted that they read the placards next to battered statues of figures sitting and standing, the walls of flat, incised figures standing stiff and sideways in the midst of hieroglyphics, the false doors to tombs, the stelae and heavy stone slabs carved with texts in hieroglyphics, trying to spot any reference to the Egyptian god of writing, and then, as if only a reference would justify their having come, they would leave and never again mention a god of writing, or any god.

Standing huge in the middle of the gallery was a black sarcophagus, open, with thick walls, and clambering about it, trying to see inside, was a class of shouting children in red pullovers. Catherine and Gerard and David waited until the students rushed off, and they examined the outside and inside of the massive sarcophagus, both surfaces carved with incised hieroglyphics and figures in low bas-relief. The placard informed them: the 345 B.C. sarcophagus, meant for a certain Nectanebo II, had never been used to entomb him, but in the much later Christian era was used for baptism by total immersion in the church of Saint Athanasius in Alexandria, the church still later having been turned into an Islamic mosque, where the sarcophagus was used for ritual baths. Holes around the bottom had been made to drain the water out. All together, they leaned far into the deep, stark depth of the sarcophagus, and as they did their heads met.

David said, "This was once thought to be the tomb of Alexander the Great, because history needed the tomb of Alexander the Great, which, in fact, has never been found. History still needs it."

"The needs of history get a lot wrong," Catherine said.

And Gerard added, "Get almost everything wrong."

They drew back.

As if now all interest had left them, they wandered away from one another, but they came together at another sarcophagus, huge, in black schist, its massive cover raised above it on blocks. They didn't even read the explanatory placard by it, but, instead, looked at three youths crouched before the sarcophagus as if it had been the youths who had attracted them, because one of the youths, in a school blazer, his striped school tie pulled down and his collar unbuttoned, was explaining to the other two a vertical line of hiero-glyphics, pointing at the deeply incised images in the black stone with the tip of a ballpoint pen. He was dark, maybe Indian, and his intelligence showed in his refined face. The other youths, white and also in school blazers, were making fun of the youth who was now pointing at a jagged line and smiling at the fun being made of him, "Goor, aren't you the clever one," while explaining that the line—〰〰〰〰—represented water.

Clearly, he was sincerely interested, and he sustained his sincere interest against the teasing of his fellow students.

Catherine interposed herself by stepping closer to the boys to ask, "Water?"

The Indian boy, if that was what he was, looked up at her, and his dark face became darker with a blush. He followed her with his wide, black eyes as she crouched down among them.

"You can read the pictograms?" she asked.

"Some," he answered.

"Where did you learn? In school?"

"I've been teaching myself. On a basic level, it's not very difficult if you have a pretty good memory."

"How many pictograms are there?"

"It depends on the period. In Ptolemaic and Roman times, there would have been more than six thousand. In the Pharaonic period, a much longer period, there were fewer than a thousand, and an even smaller number were being used regularly."

He had a faint moustache.

David joined in to ask, "Where are you from?" this, it seemed, the only information he was interested in.

The boy frowned, as though this was an odd question, as it surely had to be obvious where he was from. "From London." He spoke with a clipped upper-class English accent. "But if you're wondering, my grandparents were from India."

"I see," David said flatly, and he stepped back.

"Do you read Sanskrit?" Gerard asked.

"I don't. My grandfather did, but I don't. I've never been to India."

"Have you at least read the Bhagavad Gita in English?"

"I haven't."

"Thanks," Gerard said.

Still crouching among the boys, Catherine asked, "Is there any order to the hieroglyphics?

"You mean, as in a dictionary?"

"Something like that."

"Not that I know of, but I doubt it very much. There's no alphabet of hieroglyphics, or of cursive hieratic, or even of cursive demotic."

Catherine said, "Chinese doesn't have an alphabet either."

"I know."

One of the other boys said to Catherine, "He really doesn't know everything," and the other said to this boy, "You'd like to know a fraction as much."

The Anglo-Indian student raised the tip of his pen to indicate an

inscription in small hieroglyphics along the upper edge of the cof-
fer, and he said, resuming his lecture, "The pictogram 'water,' pronounced 'mem,' became the long sound *M*. Separate two waves of
the pictogram and what do you have? You have M."

"He's making this up," the skeptical boy said.

"Making up history?" the convinced boy asked, and answered
himself, "Ramesh wouldn't do that. Would you, Ramesh?"

"I'm making connections," Ramesh said.

Catherine and Gerard joined David to continue haphazardly
along the gallery.

The Anglo-Indian boy had shown them up for what they were:
not even amateurs, for not willing to do any real research to acquire
sound historical knowledge, as if research were incidental to the
expectation that historical knowledge would come to them of itself,
a sudden revelation in a flash of light. In fact, they knew nothing. What stopped them from doing any serious research was the
sense, the overwhelming sense, that to know anything required
knowing everything, and there was no way to know everything.
The connections were too many to be made. Of course they had
become disenchanted.

But David stopped before a glass case in which a terra-cotta
baboon squatted, and he said, "That's Theuth."

"That's a baboon," Gerard exclaimed.

"Theuth was sometimes manifested as a baboon."

"So writing came originally from a baboon."

"Is there any reason why we've come here?" Catherine asked.

"Perhaps not," David said.

At the very end of the gallery, on either side of a door with a
heavy architrave, were white limestone statues of female sphinxes,

their breasts sharp, their claws sharp too. They were from the Roman period, second century A.D., and must have once marked the entrance to the grave of a Greek inhabitant of Egypt.

Gerard tried to make a joke. "A Greek inhabitant of Roman Egypt. What religion could he have had? Could he have possibly been—why not?—Confucian?"

"Anything is, I suppose, possible," Catherine said, not laughing.

"Anything," David repeated, and he did not laugh.

He moved away from Catherine and Gerard, who remained before the exit from the gallery and watched him go to a glass case on a side wall; he stood for a long while before this case, and they, with hesitant steps, joined him.

In the case was an inscription of instructions to invoke a god: write on a lamp's wick BAKHUKHSIKHUKH, light the wick, and in the penumbra of the lamplight the god will appear.

Studying the invocation closely, his forehead almost pressed to the glass, Gerard, to say something, said, "It must be the ancient Egyptian form of 'abracadabra'."

A playfulness came over Catherine. "Do we dare to write on a wick the invocation BAKHUKHSIKHUKH and light the wick to find out what, in the penumbra, is revealed? Do we dare? Maybe it would invoke the god Theuth."

"Dare?" Gerard asked.

David abruptly turned away. "Let's leave," he said.

Catherine said quietly, "No, we don't dare."

# SEVENTEEN

**B**ut they must dare, Gerard thought, they must, all together.

Alone, he walked through Hampstead Heath.

If they didn't dare to go on there would be no reason for their being together, for they were too different from one another to stay together.

Or, he thought, he was too different from Catherine and David, who, in their multidimensional worlds, had more in common with each other than he had with them. They could take differences for granted, as they took it for granted that they had been born into and brought up in worlds both different from other worlds and at the same time open to so many other worlds in which languages, manners, cuisines, spices, revolved one about another. He had been born into and brought up in a world that was so self-enclosed, such spices as oregano, red pepper, garlic, were of another world he could only fantasize about. They thought of him as naïve. Well, he *was* naïve.

Wind flashing through the dense trees along the sides of the narrow path he walked up dislocated his thinking; the stones and ruts in the earth of the path dislocated his thinking; and so too the sudden appearance of other early-morning walkers, one with an old gnarled stick to steady him, passing Gerard from the opposite direction and for whom he stood back among the shaking bushes to make room. It seemed to him that these dislocations, made portentous by the wind, were more important than his trying to think of some way to make them stay together, to make them dare to believe in something that would make them stay together.

Here a squirrel, running across the path, distracted him. Its claws lightly clattering, it climbed the trunk of a tree on the opposite side of the path and disappeared among the windblown, leafy branches.

Would anything? he asked himself.

It was as if their very worldliness had defeated Catherine and David. They knew too much, had experienced too much, had been too exposed to differences—as he had not been—for them to be able to imagine another world beyond what they knew and had experienced, beyond all the manifold differences they had been exposed to. There was for them no other world to dare to believe in.

Was there for him some other world in which everything came together as one?

The path led to the top of a hill, from where he could see, through the narrow opening of the descending path, a field of tall green grass and cow parsley in white bloom. Slowly, he walked down the rutted path, gusts of wind pulling him forward.

He was born into a world that was premised on the longing for some other, totally ahistorical world, eternal. He had never before seen as he saw now how his religion, which he had so self-consciously disavowed, surrounded him with his religion's own intention, far beyond his own, far beyond his repudiation. So little—nothing more than his self-consciousness—kept him from giving in to the eternal world as the only way to give meaning to the temporal world, and he was prepared—if alone—to give up his consciousness of himself to believe in what was far beyond himself, far beyond the temporal world. He stopped on the footpath. He looked down at the field in the wind and, at a slower pace, continued towards it.

No, he thought, not alone. On his own he was, oh, too lonely in his giving in, as lonely, he felt, as a suicide must feel at the point of death. He needed Catherine and David—here his thinking jolted—to commit suicide all together, for the daring that was needed to give in, beyond doubt, beyond embarrassment, beyond cynicism, was close to the daring he imagined was needed to commit suicide. His doing this alone would be as meaningless as he was in himself totally disconnected. He must, he must, he must connect, and he must be connected to the two people he was most disconnected from. He must make every effort to convince them that there were connections to be made that brought them to the outside of a vast globe from which they looked out at the universal.

He halted at the edge of the field, in which the round, convex blossoms of the cow parsley shook in the constant wind.

Grief, he thought. Grief. Grief seemed to have concentrated itself to exist in itself apart from them, though still in their midst, a globe about which they talked and gestured and moved, a small group of lonely people distanced from the world, aware only of another world englobing the world, which was grief.

The blasting wind seemed to blow up from the ground; it circled round him, and, rising, impelled him up and forward. He held himself against it as it rushed out from him across the field, bending the stalks of the cow parsley so they seemed about to break, and at the center of the field, as though it were fated to do so, it turned round on itself, swirling round the grass and weeds, then stopped. A great, transparent globe appeared where the wind had stopped in the field—a great globe that kept its place above the field, an invisible but radiating globe.

He turned away from the sight with difficulty, his body suddenly too heavy and fixed to move, and with slow steps he climbed back up along the path he had descended, to the top of the hill, and from there along the narrow streets of Hampstead to Catherine's house.

He told himself that the appearance of that globe was most likely caused by the sunlight.

In the house, clutching the banister as if in anticipation of something he could not imagine, he climbed the stairs to the landing, and without knowing quite why went towards the front of the house, towards Catherine's room. The door was open to her study, the room in semidarkness, the blind pulled down. He stopped. David, his back towards him, was standing at a desk, and Gerard could tell by the movement of an elbow that he was writing. Beyond him in the deep dimness was Catherine, standing still and watching David write. She saw Gerard and made a gesture to David that seemed meant to stop him from what he was doing because Gerard had appeared. David did stop, turned, a ballpoint pen in one hand and a sheet of paper in the other, and, seeing Gerard, stood as still as Catherine once again did.

Trying to be matter-of-fact, Gerard stepped into the room and asked, "What's going on?"

Catherine and David glanced at each other.

"Is it something you don't want me to know about?"

Catherine emitted an "Oh, we—" and nothing more.

"What are you doing, and why don't you want me to know about it?" Gerard now insisted.

David said, "We thought that you wouldn't want to know."

"Not want to know? Why?"

David shrugged.

"Why did you think I wouldn't want to know?" Gerard again insisted.

Catherine said, "We thought you'd given up and wouldn't dare."

"Wouldn't dare?"

"Wouldn't dare," David repeated.

Gerard went to David, and, as though he had been holding it out for him, he took the paper and in the dimness read, in large, awkward letters jammed together:

BAKHUKHS

Handing the sheet of paper back to David, he said, "Finish it."

Saying nothing, David continued to write at the desk, now with Gerard watching him along with Catherine. David held up the paper for them to read:

BAKHUKHSIKHUKH

They watched as he folded the paper into a narrow, thick strip, and, with matches and a ceramic bowl at the ready, he lit the end of the strip, which burst into flames and smoke. He dropped the flaming paper into the bowl, and from it emerged a sudden rage of fire so that, on the walls, the drawn blind, the doors of the wardrobe, moving light and shadows appeared, and the room filled with smoke.

Coughing, they all went to the window as if together to raise the blind and open it to the outside air, and then they stood still.

Then David reached for *Histoire de L'Ecriture,* which was on the chest of drawers next to the bowl with burnt shreds of paper. He flung the book across the room, so that, its pages flying open, it hit a wall, from which it fell, fanned out. Catherine and Gerard watched David go to where the book lay and pick it up. In his hands, it fell open, as though it had a will of its own and insisted on attention to its pages. His eyes hardening with rage that the book should be so insistent and, more, with rage against himself that he should read again pages the book insisted he read, forcing him to give up his will to its will, he grasped the two open sections of the book and, twisting them one against the other, broke the paper spine.

The cheap paper of the pages was almost blotter soft, and the book was broken in two. One section tucked under his arm, David tore out page after page of the second section and threw them to the floor, then he did the same to the first section. Stepping now on the scattered pages, he reached down to pick up random pages and tear and crumple them until he was surrounded by a heap of torn and crumpled sheets.

Calmly, not to object but to finalize David's rage with calm, Gerard crouched to begin to gather the paper, but David stopped him. Catherine's cleaning lady would clear up the mess.

As if they had nowhere else to go, they remained together in the room.

# EIGHTEEN

He must, David said, return to Athens.

And Gerard thought of returning, if not to Manchester, to America, maybe New York, to get a job, because he was not sure of the amount of money he had in his account in Manchester, which he was drawing on sparingly with his credit card, more and more using his card without knowing how he would pay the debt. The account was Margaret's too, and he did not want to start taking her money, and, God knew, he didn't want her to have to pay his debts. He was dishonorable towards her, but not that dishonorable. She had not blocked his access to their account, though she could see, from the bank statements she received in his absence, where he was, far from her without any explanations of why he was so far, and maybe her not blocking his access to their account meant she thought he would come back to her. He should telephone her, just to make contact with her, just to say he was all right, in case she was worried about him. He might say to her, "Give me time, please give me time," without promising to return, but to try to leave everything open between them. He might try to persuade her to leave

Manchester too, leave everything there behind, and move with him to New York.

Catherine seemed at moments to wish that they would leave.

They were in the garden at the back of the house, Gerard and David on the white, filigreed, but heavy cast-iron garden chairs, and Catherine, in the midst of the flowers, deadheading withered blossoms. From time to time she stomped on the ground as though to crush something.

They did not have to communicate to one another what they, each one, knew: that if they abandoned one another the dead would abandon them, and they needed the dead as much as the dead needed them.

David took his small mobile telephone from a pocket in his jacket as it began to ring, but what the subject of the call was he revealed no more than a repeated *né né né,* as if this were all that was necessary to conduct business. He switched off his mobile telephone and placed it on the garden table.

In a quiet voice, apparently to himself, he said, "I do have to return to Athens."

"And I should return to Margaret," Gerard said. "I really have been unfair to her."

Approaching the men with a long, narrow, slatted basket of broken blossoms, Catherine said to Gerard, "You'll have some work to do to explain your disappearance."

"And will she understand?"

"Most likely not, especially if she knows about us all. Does she?"

"No."

"Then how can she understand?"

"She can't."

"Who could?" David asked.

"So what should I do?" Gerard asked.

"I think you should do what you need to do," Catherine said.

"Oh," Gerard said, "What I need to do—"

"Need," David repeated.

Catherine placed the basket of deadheaded flowers on the ground and sat on a garden chair between the two men.

"The gardener is upset whenever he finds me smashing a snail," she said. "I tell him, more spiritual in my practical way than he is, that I'm simply helping the snails along in their reincarnated afterlives."

On the garden table, also white, filigreed cast iron, were a pair of sunglasses with a lens missing, one garden glove, and a red, crumpled rag.

"Come to Athens with me," David said. "Both of you, come."

Catherine immediately stood and walked in among the flowers and stopped to study the peonies.

Gerard said to David, "I'll come only if Catherine comes."

"Come to Athens," David called to her.

She stomped on what must have been a snail, then she picked a peony, and carrying it upright she returned to the men. "I'll come," she said.

They left the next day, and at the exit from the Athens airport the dead were among the living waiting for the arrivals, the dead both visible and invisible, as though beside each living person there stood a double, a shadow, the shadow-double immediately invisible the flashing moment it was glimpsed. They quickly appeared and disappeared, these shadow-doubles, among the crowd David led Catherine and Gerard through. And they appeared and disappeared along the highway into Athens—in the shadow of a dead cypress tree, of a rusted car chassis, of a heap of broken slabs of concrete—their presences gathering more and more deeply, but fleetingly as they appeared and disappeared among the pedestrians on the pavement when the taxi entered the outskirts of the city.

The faintly flashing sights of the dead both reassured the three friends and made them apprehensive. The dead reassured them because they knew that something was going to happen, something essential that could change the very way life was lived, at least for the three members of their society. And they were made apprehensive because they had no idea what that happening would be. But the presence of the dead made it clear to the members why they had had to come to Athens for that happening.

The dead had taken them in thrall, but, giving in, they all now wanted the dead to enthrall them with what the dead wanted from them. The dead wanted this: to count on the living, not to resurrect them back into life (the dead did not want resurrection), but for meaning. Along the sides of the streets, raising ghostly hands, they heralded the arrival of the three death-obsessed and death-bound friends, and as the taxi neared David's place, in Palio Psychiko, an area of large villas behind high white walls and narrow guard-houses beside the entrances of the residences of ambassadors, the dead, alternately visible and invisible, massed on the otherwise deserted pavements, more and more excited.

The taxi left the friends off behind a car parked directly in front of the spiked metal gates of the block of flats where David lived, and the taxi driver hefted their bags from the boot onto the pavement and, paid by David, drove off, leaving the parked car in full view. About to pick up a bag, David went rigid, then, staring at the parked, passengerless car, slowly stood up straight to examine it more closely.

He walked along the side, then to the front of the bonnet. In its windshield were many holes from which radiated, in bursts of exploding white lines, cracked glass. He stepped back to examine the car from a distance, as though distance would allow him to take it in—take in what was too much to take in—but the dead were pressing him forward. Gerard knew that they knew what that something was before David himself was able to take it in: it was the car in which his wife had been shot to death. The dead waited for his reaction. David swerved round on a heel to look at Gerard and Catherine, as though, before he was able, they were able to tell him what the car was, were able to explain to him why it had reappeared, here, in front of the gates to his house. But all they were capable of was looking back at him. The dead began to agitate around them, agitate for some reaction, because, to the degree the dead had any energy, they were energized by the living, were energized by reactions the living had to what they themselves could not react to. The dead had no other interests than their interest in the living. Turning back to the car, David dropped the keys and raised his hands high to protect himself from the shocking sight. Gerard picked up the keys and he and Catherine moved close behind David, whose shock was their shock. David did not have to explain to them that there, in the front seat of that car, behind the windshield filled with bullet holes, his wife had been murdered, murdered by terrorists who had not yet been found, who would never be found. Gerard and Catherine advanced with David as, finally, he went to the door of the driver's seat, looked into the interior of the car through the closed window, then leaned his head against the glass. Gerard and Catherine stood close behind him and waited as the dead waited for David to draw a little back from the door and place his hand on the door handle and slowly open the door. With the door half open, heat, fetid heat so hot it made David step back so he was pressed against Gerard and Catherine, blasted from the interior, and with the heat a smell of rotted lilies. David remained leaning against Gerard and Catherine, who held him up. He was shaking. The door opened all the way of itself, revealing, on the seat, the rotted lilies, and on them rested a plain white card, which was blank.

The movement among the dead was the movement of their own communication with one another. Excited, they communicated that, really, they had known, they had known all along, what there had been to expect.

No message was the worst message.

David's house was near a roundabout in Palio Psychiko, and in the center of the roundabout was a garden. Lurching, David walked towards the garden, Catherine and Gerard following. At a kiosk on the edge of the garden he bought a newspaper, and inside, among orange trees, he sat on a bench, Catherine and Gerard on either side of him, and, fastidiously, David spread the newspaper out on the ground before him, leaned over, and vomited.

When, after a period of silence, they returned to the gate of David's apartment building, the car was gone.

# NINETEEN

The only explanation for the appearance and the disappearance of the car was that the terrorist gang had managed to get hold of it—implying some collusion with the police who had impounded it?—and, knowing when David was to return to Athens, had left it as a warning to him. But a warning against what? That he himself must stop any investigation into his wife's murder? He had no more information than he had already given the police.

David said blankly, "Shall we go in?"

"Yes," Catherine said, "we'll go inside."

Gerard said, "Please, let's get inside."

David opened the wide metal gates with spikes along the top. The three didn't look at one another as, carrying their bags, they went through the gateway into the front garden of lawn and palm trees and then into the spacious foyer, nor when they stood close together in the lift, nor in the penthouse and the more spacious sitting room with white sofas and white armchairs, where they didn't sit. There appeared to be nothing Greek.

Instead of the central occurrence removing them from daily

events, it made them concentrate fixedly on daily life. David asked Catherine and Gerard if they would like a coffee. They would.

While he was in the kitchen, Catherine and Gerard looked separately at paintings hanging on the walls.

One was of a sunset over an island.

David brought in a tray of tiny coffee cups, a clear glass jug of ice water, tall glasses, and three tiny crystal dishes each with a small green orange preserved in syrup on it, and beside each tiny crystal dish a tiny silver spoon. The preserved orange, in Greek called *gliko tou koutaliou*, was to be eaten with the spoon, then the ice water drunk, and then the thick, froth-covered coffee.

To concentrate on the daily events, that was what mattered, to concentrate on the momentary particulars.

"Where does this delicious preserve of green oranges come from?" Catherine asked David.

"From the island of Chios, famous for its fruit preserved in syrup. One can even get Chiote preserve of rose petals."

"They have a long historical tradition of making the preserves?" Gerard asked.

"Long," David said, "very long. That and mastic. Chios was famous even in medieval Europe for gum from its mastic trees."

"Interesting," Catherine said.

David said, "There is a special milk pudding made even to this day flavored with mastic, though made more and more rarely. It's called—" He stopped. "I can't recall what it's called."

"It doesn't matter," Catherine said.

"No, it doesn't matter."

"It matters," Gerard said. "It matters very much."

But David couldn't recall.

They settled silently in the room. When David spoke, he seemed to be reflecting, for he spoke quietly.

"We live in an unreal world, but it is only in the unreal world that meaning can be found for the real world, if meaning matters at all."

David spoke in generalities Gerard envied.

# TWENTY

Gerard and Catherine were with David in his office on the spacious top floor of the high glass building he had recently bought for his expanding import company in Marousi, part of the developing outer area of Athens. From the floor-to-ceiling windows could be seen, far below, a scruffy yard of bare red earth where huge terra-cotta pots, used marble sinks, and the marble decorative parts of destroyed neoclassical houses were for sale, everything looking harsh in the harsh light. Beyond the yard were cypress trees and highways.

What was David aware of, looking out the windows? Was everything to him so familiar it appeared to have no significance, or was it all, as it was for Catherine and Gerard—and especially for Gerard—foreign, and in its foreignness vivid, and in its vividness somehow significant?

Perhaps, staring out, he was not seeing anything.

When, down a passageway off his office, there sounded the *ping* of the arrival of the lift at his floor, he turned towards the sound with an expression of fear, fear of the unexpected.

"Who's that?" he asked Catherine and Gerard. "All my staff are off."

Catherine and Gerard didn't answer, for how could they know?

They gathered together to wait. A guard looked into the office and spoke in Greek, and David, frowning, answered in Greek. The guard left.

"What was it?" Catherine asked.

David raised his chin, then lowered it.

"What does that mean?" Gerard asked.

"It was nothing," David said, and added, "come along now, I'll show you around Athens, then we'll have a late luncheon."

Catherine and Gerard nodded, as if submitting not to him, but to what he had to submit to, which left him and them with only the choice to go into the center of Athens and look around and have lunch, and nothing more.

In his evident fear, David, it seemed, had to know everything that was going to happen, every step of the way.

He took them by taxi to Kolonaki Square to sit at a café. The awning over the café cast a deep shade in which people lounged, slouched back into armchairs, still, hardly speaking, while outside, in that crude sunlight, was the frantic movement of pedestrians and traffic.

At the next table were three middle-aged women, with tinted glasses and gold bracelets, eating croissants with the tips of their fingers, and in their occasional talk switching from Greek to English, and sometimes French.

Quietly, as if only to introduce a subject that David would find ordinary, Gerard asked him, "What does *vamvaki* mean?"

"*Vamvaki?*"

"What does it mean?"

"Why do you want to know?"

"I've heard one of those women use the word over and over, and think it must mean something important."

David smiled. "It means 'cotton'."

"Just that?"

"Just that."

"What is its etymology?"

"I don't know."

"Don't you think it's a strange word—*vamvaki*—for 'cotton'? Doesn't it make you wonder what its etymology is?"

"I'd never before this moment wondered. But, then, what is the etymology of the word 'cotton'?"

"I don't know," Gerard said.

Clearly, to try to bring them all out of their cautious silence and engage them in some incidental talk, which Gerard would of course try to do, he asked David to teach him some basics in Greek, such as "please" and "thank you" and "the bill." David seemed amused when Catherine, as if to demonstrate that she already knew the basics, preempted his teaching.

He said, "Listening to you, I hear Greek as I hadn't quite heard it before, so I do wonder about the derivation of *parakalo* and *efharisto* and *to logariasmo.*" He looked around the café. "In point of fact, I find myself wondering about everything here. Is this because I'm with you both?"

"It can't all seem as strange to you as it does to me," Gerard said.

"I think it does, as though, suddenly, I'm a foreigner here, and don't know what to expect. And, yes, I'm rather frightened."

"Don't you have reason to be?" Catherine asked.

"Yes, I suppose I do. But why now more than ever?"

"That's for you to say and to tell us," Gerard said.

"If I can."

David led Catherine and Gerard away from the café and across Kolonaki Square and down to Queen Sofia Avenue and to Constitution Square, and Gerard, though not Catherine, kept asking him for information. The wide, stark, neoclassical building on the north side of the square was the Parliament, and the rifle-shouldering evzones, in their tasseled caps and pleated kilts and upturned shoes with pom-poms, stood on either side of the tomb of the unknown soldier, a bas-relief of an ancient Greek soldier, dead but still bearing his shield.

On the south side of the large square was Ermou Street, a pedestrian street, which brought them past fancy shops to those less and less fancy, almost stalls, with bolts of cloth and shoes and electrical heaters displayed outside on the uneven pavement. From time to time Gerard stopped at a shop window, as if the window framed a culture he must find out about, even though the only information that could be derived came from rows of bottles of shampoo with English and French and Italian names. He stopped at a window of metal trays of dry rusks, toasted slices of bread, a kind of pretzel covered with sesame seeds he asked the name of—*koulouria*—which David went into the shop to buy for each of them to eat as they continued down to Monastiraki Square. The square was overlooked by a disused mosque, at its base small shops that sold sandals, sweaters made of goats' wool, cheese pies. In answer to Gerard's questions about the mosque, David said that it dated from four hundred years of Greek history during which Greece was occupied by Turks, an occupation that Greeks wanted to obliterate, as if it were possible to obliterate history, and he left his answer at that.

"Are there any active mosques in Athens?" Gerard asked.

"Hidden, perhaps, the way Orthodox church activity was hidden during the Ottoman Islamic occupation. But I don't know."

David, it seemed, was less than half attentive to this talk, and more attentive to something that Gerard—and Catherine too, in her glances at Gerard—could only sense in him, something that Gerard wanted to distract him from by his questions. David, frowning, kept looking about, and would from time to time stop to listen to what two people passing said.

He took them up around the sunken, ancient Agora, along the side of the metro tracks, and up past a pine-wooded knoll, into a paved street called Smith that led to a dirt path that brought them through pine trees up into a hill of bare, white rock, from where the city below was no longer visible. The still air smelled of resin. A chain-link fence ran along one side as they walked over the rock. David led the others to an open gateway to the Athens observatory, which he said he knew from walks he had often taken here, to see—but he didn't explain to see what, for, from the top of the hill, there appeared, in the distance above another pine-covered hill, the Parthenon.

Catherine asked him, "What does it mean to you?"

"Mean to me?" he replied. "Does it mean anything more to me than it does to you? What does it mean to you?"

Catherine shook her head.

"What does it mean to you, Gerard?"

Any reply Gerard might have had ready would be, he knew, banal. And then he thought, But is David not banal? A little urge came to him to be aggressive in his pretensions, but it was an urge he couldn't give in to, because Gerard must always be agreeable, even complaisant. He said, "I can't say."

Now David was aggressive. "What can that mean? You can't say because it means more than you can say?"

"You don't know?"

"What do I know?" David said, lowering his voice as he again looked up at the Parthenon. "I'm frightened of the Parthenon. You know, it happens often enough that guards on the Acropolis are wary of people—people from all over the world—going too close to the steep west wall to jump off and commit suicide. What does the Parthenon mean to *them*?" He turned away. "Come along," he said.

He led them round the base of the Acropolis to the Panathenaic Way, the ancient road that once connected the marketplace below to the temples above. They walked on the thick, black paving stones, those that remained, into the Agora, the site of the daily life of ancient Athens, the generating center of the history of the Western world. Strewn on the bare earth were marble fragments. Some were stored on shelves behind wire mesh, and these were numbered, as if with the hope of their being sorted out and connected, to reconstruct the entire site as it had once been. But against a far wall, not numbered, was a heap of broken marble fragments of classical, Hellenistic, Roman, Byzantine capitals, cornices, and too the shafts and turbans of Ottoman gravestones.

In the Stoa of Attalus, reconstructed from its ancient Greek fragments, were glass cases filled with the objects of life: pots, stone buttons, a razor, a wine cooler, a holy-water basin, standard weights of bronze and lead, an official liquid measure, jurors' ballots, a water clock for timing speeches in law courts, and a peculiar machine, now only a broken marble slab with fine dots, for choosing Athenian officials by lot.

David led them back along the Panathenaic Way out of the Agora, across a bridge over the metro tracks, and into Monastiraki again through a narrow passage into Abyssinia Square and the junk market of Athens, the stalls around the square filled with jumbled objects, not categorized: brass pots, door knockers and glass lamps and old straight razors, battered dentist's equipment, hammers and planes, stoves, folding beds, old coins and paper currency, bells, rusted flat irons, and scales with round weights.

All of these made up a civilization, and something beyond civilization. They were aware of this, aware of every single object as an icon of some greater meaning than each object had in itself, so that to study an old, empty gilded frame was to study it for its iconography. And, out in the streets again, to see a woman carrying a round pan of stuffed tomatoes, to see the balcony of a small, crumbling neoclassical house, to see on a wall the graffito of a political slogan, wasn't that, in each case, to see an icon with an iconography so vast it took in all of Greek history, and, more, all of Western history, and, even more, all of world history, and even more than that?

What did it all mean? What did it all *mean*?

From Monastiraki to Plaka, they stopped at a churchyard to hear the singing of nuns, and as they listened a nun, animated, wearing a gray apron and a black cloth tied around her gray hair, came out of the churchyard and, noting them, asked if they would like to see inside the church. David left it to Catherine and Gerard, and Gerard raised his hand. The nun unlocked the church. Inside, the icons were decorated with sprigs of basil, and pots of basil were on the floor. The nun made a gesture towards the candles, the thin, yellow-brown candles of beeswax, to be lit after an offering and inserted into a round brass tray of sand, and David and Catherine and Gerard lit candles while the nun watched. Then there was the icon of the day, exposed on a stand, to be kissed, which the nun again gestured at, and the three, touching their noses to the glass, kissed the icon of a faith that they had no faith in.

Not one of them mentioned the lighting of the candles or the kissing of the icon when, in a small Plaka square shaded by a eucalyptus tree, they sat for their late lunch.

After a silence, Gerard said, reflectively, "I was thinking—"

"What were you thinking?" Catherine asked.

Gerard said to David, "You asked me, looking up at the Parthenon, what it meant to me and I said I couldn't say. Someone I knew once told me that all we can ever know of something, if this can be called knowing, is to have an impression of that something, nothing more than an impression. He said we don't *understand*, we have *impressions*, in the same way we can only have an impression of everything all together and can never understand everything all together, because everything all together, everything in the world all together, is an impossibility. And that's the most we can expect of our reasoning minds, which can't say what anything really means."

David paid the bill and said, "Let's go back to my house now," as if he had had enough of being out in the streets of Athens, where anything could happen.

They walked down from Plaka to Monastiraki, after centuries still bazaar-like with its small shops, their wares displayed on the pavement: military boots and camouflage fatigues; gauzy, multicolored scarves; small reproductions of ancient vases and statues. Gerard first, then Catherine and David with him, stopped to look at old magazines and books heaped on the pavement on either side of stone steps down to a basement shop; old magazines and books in Greek, French, English, German, Russian, Arabic, and God knew what other languages that David and Catherine and especially Gerard did not know; old magazines and books that were yellowish, partly disintegrating, soggy with damp so they looked as if they had been washed up from the basement shop on a flood of water and deposited on the stone pavement. Gerard picked up an English grammar book on the pages of which were written translations in Greek, and David and Catherine studied the book with him over his shoulders. Gerard replaced the book, and the three were about to walk away when David stopped because he saw, among another pile of books, the corner of a book he recognized: *Histoire de L'Ecriture.*

David opened the cover, which was half detached from the binding. On the blank first page was written, in Latin cursive, in pencil, the name *Aminat Dayeyer,* and under the name was written, in the same handwriting: *Grozny, Chechnya.*

A slip of paper protruded from the closed pages, and David opened the book to that slip of paper, which was narrow.

Catherine said quietly, "Close the book, David, close the book and put it back, and then let's leave."

David held the book open in one hand, and covered the outspread pages with his other hand. When David removed his hand, this is what they, standing on the pavement, read: *Ougarit était le nom d'une ville, dont les ruines ont été touvées à Ras Shamra . . .*

Ugarit was the name of a city the ruins of which were found at Ras Shamra. Ras Shamra, or "The Cape of Fennel," is situated in northwestern Syria, a dozen kilometers north of Latakia. The ruins take up parts of Ras Shamra itself, one part situated some seven or eight hundred meters into the interior, another part on the site of the ancient marina of Ugarit, called today "The White Port," Minet el

Beida, because of the blazing whiteness of the rock formations about it.

The discoveries made at Ras Shamra represent without any doubt a capital event of recent years, not only for what they reveal of ancient Phoenician civilization, but also of the history of the alphabet.

Here, briefly, are the facts.

In 1929, at Ras Shamra in Syria were found the remains of a palace and, in one of the chambers, tablets covered with cuneiform characters that had been hitherto unknown. The only conclusion possible to the question of what they were, given the small number of these characters, was that they were letters of an alphabet. What was this alphabet? What language was hidden beneath this fancifulness? More excavations led in 1930 to further discoveries of new tablets, inscribed with the same mysterious writing.

In August of 1930, a German scholar, H. Bauer, announced that he had discovered the key to the alphabet of Ras Shamra. In September of 1930, E. Dhorme published in a brief article his interpretation of the alphabet of Ras Shamra. The Semitic nature of the language suggested by the writing became evident. It was left to Ch. Virolleaud, in 1931, to announce that he had deciphered the alphabetic writing of Ras Shamra, bringing to an end the decipherment except for two or three doubtful signs.

The Ugaritic alphabet is strange. It is written in cuneiform, traced by pressing the point of a sharpened reed into tablets of wet clay, so each sign has many "corners." This is the case with all cuneiform writing, but all other cuneiform writing is syllabic, and the Ugaritic alphabet is different, not only in the form of its characters, but in the fact that it is not even semi-syllabic, but is written in *letters*. This alphabet comprises thirty of these letters.

There has been a great deal of discussion about the origins of the Ugaritic alphabet. K. Ebeling is intent that the derivation is Sumero-Akkadian syllabic cuneiform. This is far from evident on first sight, but K. Ebeling invokes certain aspects of Japanese katakana writing, believing it possible to establish that the inventor of the Ugaritic alphabet must have cut in two the Akkadian syllabic signs that would have served the inventor as a model, and that he would have retained the first half and that he would have given the letter the value of the initial consonant of the syllable. Certainly, writing based on a purely alphabetic prototype does frequently re-create or borrow from elsewhere certain syllabic signs, as, for example, Coptic, Glagolitic writing, and also, perhaps, Persepolitan and various indigenous North American writing. But the origins of the Ugaritic alphabet are unknown.

However, it is known from a tablet—most likely used by a student for an exercise—that the letters of the sixteenth-century B.C. Ugaritic alphabet begin with the equivalent of A B C.

David bought the book, and then, as if he didn't want it, he handed it to Gerard, who in turn handed it to Catherine, and she, with no one else to pass it on to, slipped it into her shoulder bag.

Back in David's flat, Catherine placed the book on the glass coffee table among large seashells and small marble obelisks and silver bowls.

Raising a hand to his forehead, David said, "Please don't leave me. Please. Won't you spend a weekend with me in my house on the island of Páros, for no other reason, I promise, than the daily pleasure of the island, for no other reason at all?" He pleaded again, "We can't leave one another. You know we can't."

# TWENTY-ONE

As a teacher, Gerard had insisted that his students in their assigned French papers keep to the particulars—making their ideas as particular as tools, such as *une clef, un rabot, un fil à plomb*—because in the particulars ideas were given objectivity, whereas all vagueness would be read as subjective, and only the objective was interesting because it was more complex; the merely subjective was limited to one's self. Why had he taught that? Why had he burdened his students with so much awareness?

The pleasures of the three friends, if they were to have any pleasures, must be small and so self-contained they would evoke no associations; they would not be allowed to evoke any associations.

But there was the arrival at sunset on the island of Páros, the drive across the island, up a mountain and down the other side, and along a road by the sea to a village called Dryos, the arrival at dusk at David's house among other houses overlooking the sea, the windows of his house alone lit up for their arrival by the housekeeper, an Albanian woman, who came out to help them bring their bags from the car to the terrace. A violent wind was blowing.

And there was the sight of a eucalyptus tree thrashing in the wind.

They ate at a local taverna, inside, out of the wind. They went to bed early. They woke early. The wind was still blowing.

From time to time, Gerard noted fallen red bougainvillea blossoms, an empty carafe, a smooth beach pebble on a marble-topped table placed out of the wind on the terrace.

No more, no more, no more.

Unable to bear so much awareness, they, in the cool, still, white sitting room, revolved about one another, not restlessly, but within the orbits of one another; and they remained within the orbits of one another when they went out to the taverna to eat, and even, after eating, when they reclined among pillows on the banquettes that lined the sitting-room walls to doze; and when, as they rose from half-sleep, the housekeeper came into the room carrying a tray, covered with a lace cloth, with preserved apricots and all the accoutrements for serving them, and tiny cups of coffee, and they gathered around the round, embossed-copper coffee table surrounded by tasseled hassocks.

No, nothing must be evoked beyond the small pleasure of the preserved apricots, the ice-cold water, the coffee.

"What is that?" Catherine asked, pointing to a side table on which, among other unrelated items, was a long, narrow box, its cover removed to expose a line of balls.

David laughed a little. "Oh, that—that's a box of juggling balls."

Catherine rose from her hassock to examine the balls. She took one out and turned it round in her hands. "Where are they from?"

"Some young man, the son of a friend from my Cambridge days, visited us one summer holiday and forgot them. I contacted his father to find out where he was—he was supposed to be studying at King's, but he was rather feckless—to send them back to him, but—" David paused. "Well, his father told me his son had died and to keep the juggling balls; he couldn't bear to have them remind him of his son. That's all there is to them."

"What did his son die of?"

"An overdose."

Silently, Catherine replaced the ball in line with the others, then she placed the lid over the box.

In the afternoon, David drove Catherine and Gerard around to see sites on this side of the island: the ruins of a Venetian castle, a church with an icon, the Cycladic village of Marpissa, with narrow, whitewashed streets. In a square at the top of the village stood, on a plinth among pine trees, a clear marble statue of a youth, naked to the waist, his arms tied behind his back: Nicolas Stella, who, on a sweet morning in May, at the age of twenty-three, had been hanged by the Nazis who brutally occupied the island, who brutally occupied Greece.

After a moment, David turned away, Catherine and Gerard with him, to get back to the car.

The wind died down when the sun set, and the moon rising over the sea brought with it calm. After their supper in the taverna, where they were the only customers, David suggested a walk down to the deserted beach, illuminated palely in the moonlight. They walked one behind the other—Catherine following David, and behind her Gerard—down the narrow path among the closed-up houses and, beyond a row of tall reeds, onto the beach, along which the low surf slurred as if almost silenced by the calm.

At the far end of the beach was a fire in the moonlight. They stood together to look for a long while at the fire. The flames were constant, so someone must be feeding it with wood. Without any single one of them prompting, they began to walk along the beach, as always close together and in silence, towards that fire. As they approached, the fire appeared to throw its light against the curved inside of a globe, illuminating the sea, the moon, the stars. A spark exploded from its midst and burst in all directions. David and Catherine and Gerard, side by side, kept away from the fire, as though they must not step on the beach sand that surrounded it so smoothly, the sand wet and reflecting the flames. No one appeared to be tending the fire.

Yet, on the other side of the fire, seen through the flames, was a crouching figure.

The men stood back as Catherine, stepping onto the smooth sand as if so lightly she would not leave footprints, was the first to advance, and Gerard, and last David, followed her to the fire and round it to the other side, where a woman with long, tangled hair obscuring her face was crouching and, with a broken piece of reed, inscribing short, crisscrossing marks in the wet sand. The light was bright on one side and her shadow, cast at her dark side, appeared to extend to a distance too far to be seen. She ignored the people who were looking at her, if she was aware of them. As she crouched, her only movement was of the arm and shoulder that inscribed the marks, and her long, tangled mass of hair, falling forward, shook with this movement. She wore only a halter and shorts, and was barefoot. She remained intent on making the marks, each one an extended wedge, starting with a blunt insertion of the reed and tapering into a fine point. Beside her, on the sand, was a ragged khaki military haversack. Only when she threw down the length of reed, having, it seemed, finished inscribing the marks, did she put her hands to her hair, draw it back, and, confronting them, look at the three people who had appeared above her as though they were phantoms who did not belong to this world.

# TWENTY-TWO

She was from Grozny, Chechnya. She had walked from Grozny to Tbilisi in Georgia, from Tbilisi into Turkey, where she sometimes got lifts for favors, to Erzurum, Diyarbakir, Sivas, Ankara, by which time she had saved enough from her favors to take a train from Ankara to Istanbul, and from Istanbul to the Greek border, where she was found trying to cross over and was turned back; she went into Bulgaria, and across the Rhodope Mountains into Greece to Kavála, down to Thessaloníki, hitching rides again for favors, to Larissa, to Lamía, to Athens. As in the other countries she had passed through, she was in Greece illegally, with only an old Soviet passport from her teens. She could not speak English, but Greek, having been in the country for six months, mostly in Athens, where she had earned her living as a prostitute, until she heard that jobs were available for waitresses and cleaning women in hotels on the islands. She had come to Páros a week before, but had found no work. All that she wanted before she died—because she wanted to die—was to go to Syria, to Ugarit.

She spoke French fluently, which she had read at university. Her name was Aminat.

As Aminat spoke, a woman appeared in the darkness behind her—a woman who was also Aminat, carrying two large plastic jerry cans of water down a battered street, the trees on either side shattered to stumps, the buildings broken down to expose rooms and brick chimneys, the woman following trolley tracks in places torn up and twisted and in others piled with rubble. There was no one else, not one living person, but the woman walking away.

David and Catherine and Gerard followed Aminat's double through the desolation, off the main street, to a building that still had a ground floor, the top floors destroyed and fallen in.

They followed her into a room where she lived, and where she put down the jerry cans of water next to a stand with an enamel washbasin and an enamel pitcher and they sat on wooden chairs at a wooden table. They listened to her describe an armored vehicle moving slowly down the main street of the town, on board a young, brown-haired man, covered in blood, standing surrounded by soldiers; listened to her describe the vehicle stopping and the man being pushed off by the soldiers then thrown against a chain-link fence, the soldiers then running back to the vehicle; describe the sound of either a grenade or dynamite exploding, and the young man's head flying up into the debris-filled air.

She said that blowing up people, dead or alive, was the latest tactic of the army. She knew of a village where twenty-one men, women, and children were bound together and blown up, their remains then thrown into a ditch. This method of killing was highly practical, for it prevented the number of bodies from being counted, or even, the army hoped, ever being found. Often, however, they were found by dogs digging up body parts. What had always been, she answered, over and over and over. Ditches were discovered that contained the mutilated bodies of the dead: missing eyes, ears, limbs, genitals. Mass graves were found.

At any time of the day or night, Aminat said, a village will be encircled by tanks, armored vehicles, and army trucks. One of the trucks, known as the purification car, will be designated for torture. Torture is, as always, the preferred method of gathering intelligence. The army's best hope of finding out about guerrilla activity is by grabbing citizens at random, and coercing from them whatever information they may have. Defeating the guerrillas is their objective. But it is a distant objective. The more immediate objective of the federal army is theft of personal property, of cars, refrigerators, television sets, jewelry, clothes, pots and pans, and of course money. Theft occurs when the raid is in its most benign form. Frequently the raids turn ugly. A raid on a village began at five a.m. There were about one hundred vehicles, all packed with soldiers. Everyone ran out to meet them with their documents. God forbid that you should encounter an impatient federal. If so, the best-case scenario for you would be that you'd be shot dead on the spot. In the worst case, you would be taken away. About twenty federal soldiers, armed to the teeth and wearing masks, climbed over the fence and into the yard and broke into the house. As always, they were dirty, unshaven, and reeking of vodka. They cursed horribly. They shot at everyone's feet. They demanded identity papers and shredded them. Identification papers for one person cost five hundred rubles. That was all the money anyone had. They left, no one knew why, perhaps because everyone there was too old for them. They went to the neighbors' house. Shots were heard from there and the screams of fifteen-year-old Aminat. "Let her be," screamed one of her brothers. "Kill us instead." More shots. Through the open doorway of the house, a half-dressed OMON commander was seen lying on top of Aminat. She was covered in blood from bullet wounds. Another soldier shouted, "Hurry up, Kolya, while she's still warm."

"Sometimes those who survive wish they were dead," Aminat said, "as in Zernovodsk this summer, when townspeople were chased onto a field and made to watch women being raped. The men who tried to defend them, their husbands and lovers, were handcuffed to an armored truck and raped too. After this, many of the men joined the guerrillas in the mountains. One older man, Mirdi Dayeyer, who was nearly blind, had nails driven through his hands and feet because it was suspected he was in contact with the guerrillas. He was a Muslim. When relatives later retrieved his remains, he was missing a hand. The relatives of another villager, Aldan Manayer, picked up a torso but no head. The families were forced to sign declarations that Dayeyer and Manayer had blown themselves up.

"Usually groups of people simply disappear. Shortly after, their families begin feverish searches in all the army headquarters and watch posts. If they can track down a missing family member, they may be able to buy him or her back. The going rate for a live person is in the thousands of dollars. For a dead body, the price is not much lower. If they cannot find the person, family members mail letters to the president of the Federation. And they wait. Those who do return are often crippled, with bruised kidneys and lungs, damaged hearing or eyesight, or broken bones. It is almost certain they will never have children, man or woman.

"What makes the soldiers into such monsters? They are mostly boys, wearing uniforms that exude the stench of their filthy bodies. One will tell you that he tried and tried to get a medical exemption to avoid conscription, because he knew about the brutality of life in the barracks. Because that didn't work, his mother tried to get him certified mad so he would be sent to a madhouse, where conditions would be safer, less brutal, where he wouldn't be murdered by his fellow soldiers. But he will say he hadn't been able to be certified as mad, and his basic training was made worse than the others as a punishment. He will tell you that if he hates the federal army, he hates the Chechen rebels more for forcing him into a war against them, and to be free he would happily kill them all, rebel or not, man, woman, child. This soldier's blond face has only a light down. Another soldier, who has grown a straggly beard, will say that his mother, to get rid of him, told the military that he was not exempt from conscription. Though in fact he was taking a year's leave from college, his mother thought he was lazy, doing nothing but reading, and costing her money she couldn't afford. She gave the keys to the apartment to the police, and one morning at dawn, his mother out, he was woken by officers standing over his bed, handcuffed, taken to a police station, and from there by lorry to a conscription center. He will laugh, recounting how another student within the yard of the conscription center jumped over the wall because he was a champion trampolinist, and ran. Being press-ganged into the army happens all the time, he will say; if you're young, it's dangerous to ride the Moscow metro, because in the stations you could be accosted, forced to go to a barracks, and no one, not even your relatives, will be told where you are. He was, literally, beaten into being a soldier. Beaten, and more—he had been made to stand leaning against an army vehicle, naked, his ass up in the air, and he'd been raped by his commanding officer, and what had been done to him, which made him want to kill, he will do to others, whom he *will* kill. Given that his pay is no more than two dollars a month, of course he steals, of course. He sometimes enters houses and kills everyone, which makes it easy to steal. And a third soldier, with a shaved head as well as a shaved face, will recount stories of happenings among the soldiers themselves: the stupid accusations, the obscene bullying, the violent fights, the stabbings and shootings. He will smirk, telling you of the amount of vodka drunk, the drugs smoked, swallowed, injected. And he will smirk more, remembering an incident when a soldier ate a mass of magic mushrooms and, in an hallucinogenic fit, shot and killed eight fellow soldiers and wounded more. And he will say that he was more and more convinced that the final and lasting way of freeing himself from the world he had been forced into is to kill himself."

# TWENTY-THREE

As soon as Aminat entered David's house, in which the lights had been left lit, she saw *Histoire de L'Ecriture,* which might have transported itself from Athens to Páros, there on the coffee table. She fell towards it, and, on her knees, grasped it in both her hands and pressed it to her breasts. The book held tightly against her, she rocked back and forth, now moaning and in a hoarse voice babbling in what had to be her native language, Chechen. She was crazed, and, crazed, frightening to the others.

Fed, bathed, and wearing a loose, clean shift that Catherine gave her, she talked obsessively of Ugarit, the book held close to her. As she spoke, she appeared to go into and out of different states of consciousness, as though she were, for flashing moments, in many different places; and, listening to her, David and Catherine and Gerard seemed, to themselves, to go into and out of different, flashing states of consciousness, her presence apparently multidimensional, those dimensions shifting constantly. They at one moment found themselves with her in Grozny, another in Tbilisi, another in Istanbul, another in Athens. Wherever she and they were—in Grozny, in Tbilisi, in Istanbul, in Athens—her subject, which she insisted upon, was the Ugaritic alphabet. She had become a fanatic; and, in the midst of all the flashing dimensions, her fanaticism made her rave about the Ugaritic alphabet.

With the breakup of the Soviet Union, religious books that had previously been suppressed by the atheistic Soviet Communist Party began to appear publicly, as if they had all along hidden themselves away and now emerged, to the surprise of everyone. The appearance in her grandmother's apartment of the Koran surprised her, a young woman who, though a Muslim, had never seen a copy of the holy book. If the Koran had been hidden away in her grandmother's apartment, she wouldn't have known; her grandmother no less than her father would not have told her, for her father was a Party member and abided by the Party's suppressions to his advantage as a professor of petrochemical research at the University of Grozny. The Koran that appeared on a lace-covered table in her grandmother's small apartment was in Russian. That it was in Russian her grandmother regretted, because true inspiration came from the Koran only if the book was read in the language in which it was dictated by God to Muhammad, which language was Kufic. So Aminat, named after the mother of Muhammad, read the Koran in Russian, and she was not, she admitted to her grandmother, inspired. The book, after so many years of forced disassociation from any practice, seemed too foreign, even too exotic, to have any relevance to her, any message for her to live her life by. Her grandmother sighed. But Aminat married and had a daughter, named after her, and when her daughter was able to read, her very old great-grandmother, as though disappointed in her granddaughter, gave the holy book to her great-granddaughter, who was inspired by it, and even quoted from it. Of course this pleased Aminat's grandmother, but if it pleased Aminat, it was because her daughter was free to read whatever she wanted. She would bring up her daughter to do whatever she wanted, whatever, on the absolute principle that to do what one wanted was to be free. She then saw this daughter killed and, dead, raped. Her grandmother saw the murder and the rape also, and her grandmother retreated, in silence, to read, hour after hour, day after day, the holy book. At times this annoyed Aminat, and she would snatch the book away from her grandmother's hands as if to throw it across the room; but every time, instead of flinging it away, she opened it and read here and there. What struck her—and this she didn't tell her grandmother, because her grandmother would certainly have thought the inspiration totally irrelevant to a way of life in belief—was the Kufic Arabic letters, transliterated into Cyrillic letters, that started out some of the chapters of the Koran, preceding the repeated invocation to every chapter, "In the Name of Allah, the Compassionate, the Merciful." Such letters (here transliterated into Latin letters) were: *alif lām mīm; alif lām mīm ṣād; alif lām rā; ḳāf hā yā ain ṣād; tā hā; tā sīn mīm.*

Aminat asked her grandmother what they meant. Her grandmother answered that she didn't know, and not because she couldn't read the Kufic Arabic, but because no one knew what they meant, no one but Allah. The meaning of the letters, as they appeared in different arrangements at the beginnings of certain chapters, was incomprehensible to humankind, and was Allah's meaning alone. Aminat would not, could not, accept this. Nothing was incomprehensible to humankind. Though a Muslim, she had been trained in the rational atheism of Soviet communism. She would find out what the letters meant. She didn't get far, only so far as researching the alphabets from which Kufic Arabic was derived, assuming that some pre-Kufic alphabet would make sense of the Kufic letters—some past alphabet from which the Hebrew and Greek and Latin and Cyrillic alphabets were derived. Though it was closed, she managed to get into the university library, where her research, helped by work already done by Russian writers on philology, led her to Ugaritic, and from Ugaritic back to her own language, Chechen.

She was fanatically sure of this: Chechen was derived from Ugarit. Her voice broke with hysteria when, at a higher pitch of intensity, she went on, her black eyes bulging from a face that appeared to be made up of the hard, thin, separate muscles of forehead, cheeks, mouth, jaw, chin, held tightly together by skin that glowed, as if she were in a fever, or as if she were in something more than a fever. She would not give up.

The dead surrounded her and compelled her, compelled her by their own attention to the horrors of the world to survive the horrors, and, more than to survive, to realize the longing roused by such horror. The vast longing of the dead, aware of the world's horrors far beyond the awareness of the living, could only be realized for them by the living. The living *are* compelled by the dead, even to the point of madness.

Spasms began to shake Aminat, first her head, then her shoulders, then her body, and after a shudder passed through her she suddenly went still for a moment before her jaw appeared to be wrenched open by a yawn, followed again by a shudder that passed through her.

Yet she didn't want to sleep. She wanted to go on talking.

What was the vast longing of the dead that only the living could try to fulfill for them, but always fail to fulfill? What was it? What?

She let her head fall against the chair back.

She would find out at the ancient site of Ugarit. She was sure of that. Yes, she did ask herself, what did she expect to happen to her at Ugarit? Surely, all the tablets had been removed from the site, were in museums in the cities—perhaps cities in different parts of the world—and nothing was there but the remains of corroded stone walls and desert. But she must go there, she had sworn an oath, an oath to the dead, that she would find a way of getting there. Before she died, which she hoped would be soon, she must find a way of getting to Ugarit. Ugarit was her Mecca.

Ugarit was her Mecca not just because there the first evidence of the arrangement of the letters of the alphabet was found, but, more so, because Ugarit had been destroyed, had been devastated, had been left desolate by its enemy, had been left in ruins thousands of years before by invading Philistines and had never recovered, as Grozny would never recover. She would go to Ugarit, the city of such high civilization it had developed the alphabet, developed the arrangement of the letters of the alphabet into one that existed to this day, asserting what was arguably the oldest cultural continuity of civilization; but a city in which civilization had been reduced to nonregenerative ruins. There, the dead gathered; there, the dead grouped in ring upon ring upon ring, to the horizon, there where civilization had had a beginning.

Still shivering from exhaustion, she closed her mouth, but did not wipe away the saliva. Slumped back into the chair, she shivered in her sleep.

# TWENTY-FOUR

In the deep chair, Aminat's body was turned sideways and doubled up, her knees bent, her face now crushed into the padded arm. A beam of moonlight isolated her in the darkness of the room, then, as the beams shifted, she merged into the darkness.

As the night passed, Gerard, Catherine, David, sometimes walking about one another in the room, waited for her to wake and announce to them what she must do, and they would do as she did; they would follow her.

The moon set, and the room became entirely dark, but a clear darkness that was itself a strange illumination. In it, David and Catherine and Gerard, moving about slowly, appeared to one another transparent, as if they could walk through one another. And in their midst Aminat slept, a figure they might, in this strangely luminous darkness they themselves were a part of, have conjured up.

Perhaps because they hadn't slept, the thin gray light of predawn didn't change the impression—the very mood, because even thinking became a mood—of effervescent strangeness. The thin gray deepening to a brighter gray, this gray slowly suffused with pink light, then the rays of the sun startling the gentle pink into aggressive red, and, suddenly, the appearance of the radiant sun over the bay, all confirmed the state of strangeness, particularly when a beam of sunlight struck Aminat as she slept and exposed her, not to the ordinariness of a day, but the extraordinariness of this day.

She would do, of course she would do, what none of them—Gerard, Catherine, David—had been able to do.

She opened her eyes to the glare, but closed them immediately to go on sleeping.

Her attendants reclined on chairs and sofas and closed their eyes and half fell asleep, as if day were night, and they would now sleep with Aminat through the day.

They woke to her standing in the room, looking about with a severe frown, and, clothes twisted about them, they rose to approach her.

Yes, she was crazed, and she would dare herself to do anything.

Her time among them was taken up with studying the Ugaritic cuneiform, which she wrote out on sheets of paper, over and over, the *A B C* of which she taught to David and Catherine and Gerard:

They needed her, their own phantom of suffering.

# TWENTY-FIVE

The dead, and no one else, were waiting for them inside the gate at the site of ancient Ugarit. They marched in wavering columns among the crude stone ruins, surrounding the small group of Aminat, David, Catherine, Gerard, as they walked, themselves wavering in the distorting heat, up the great mound of city upon city upon buried city to the entrance of the royal palace. The visitors had come early, they had hoped, before the great sun, but the sun, white or black, seemed always to be radiating directly overhead. They were alone with the marching dead, who raised dust that became a part of the heat.

Aminat led the way around the ruins of the palace as if she had been there. Perhaps she had been, when the city was famous throughout the East; when it was a major port for trade with Canaanites, Phoenicians, Egyptians, Hittites, even the Cypriots and Mycenaeans, the trade as refined as the mass importation of glass vials of scent; when it was crowned by the royal palace with courtyards and gardens and fountains in the courtyards, and room after room, their walls hung with cloths woven with gold thread, the furniture inlaid with ivory, the floors strewn with rose petals; when it had temples dedicated to the god Baal, the son of the supreme god El, where foreigners came from afar to worship; and, above all, when it had factories where the clay tablets were produced, had schools where the cuneiform letters were taught, had libraries of vast collections of the tablets.

The dead were always with them, joined by millions and millions more in disordered masses, in the shimmering heat.

In this place of former gods—where, commemorated year after year in the ritual thickness of incense and beaten drums, the god of the living, Baal, descended into the depths to the god of the dead, Mot, and rose—the gods were now gone, both the god of the living and the god of the dead, leaving only the dispossessed and desolate dead.

Aminat wrapped her head in the head scarf she had brought, and tied a handkerchief about her mouth and nose, and David and Catherine and Gerard copied her. Their clothes dripped with sweat, and they often stopped to drink from bottles of water they carried in shoulder bags.

To rest from the more and more pressing dead in the heat, Aminat and David and Catherine and Gerard entered a tomb, the entrance a high, steep, stone triangle, the stone steps down into the vault very worn. They sat on the floor, leaning against walls.

In her confusion and fatigue, Aminat leaned her head against the inside wall of the tomb, and the others did the same. They watched her closely.

Aminat took from her bag *Histoire de L'Ecriture* and held it to her forehead, then, unaccountably to the others, she threw it on the floor.

As if to rouse Gerard and Catherine and David and Aminat, a wind entered into the tomb, and in the wind, with many reverberating echoes, voices seemed to call, to call and to cry. The dead were calling, the dead were crying out. Aminat, straining against the weight of her body, was the first to get up and climb the deeply worn steps out of the tomb, then David followed, then Catherine and Gerard. Outside, the wind bound all the dead together in a great, undulant cloud of dust, the windblown dust of the dead.

The wind wailed across the desolation, beyond the ruins, where now was scrub and a few loose stones from walls that had ceased to stand, it seemed, against the wind.

In the distance, beyond a chain-link fence, was the sea, its surf rising and falling, but there was no access to the sea, as the shore was a military zone, where soldiers trained for war.

The wind shriveled their sweat-wet skin as it dried it, so, parched, they had often to stop to drink water. They wrapped their head scarves about their heads, over their foreheads and eyebrows, as protection, now, from the blasts of wind. From time to time, they turned their backs against the wind, and, facing it again, pressed themselves against it to enter it.

Perhaps uncovered by the wind were scattered small, angular stones, or what appeared to be stones, jutting out from a patch of earth among scrub, but too regular in their angularity to be stones.

Not for themselves, no, but for the dead, Gerard and Catherine and David and Aminat must—again, *must*—realize the longing of the dead. This was the greatest imperative of life, about which there was no choice: that the dead must be fulfilled.

And here everything becomes, literally, unreal.

Gerard was the first to reach for a buried tablet—a tablet because the part that stuck up above the earth was square—and to try to pull it out. It wouldn't be pulled out. As the others watched, he dug around it with his fingers, but the earth was as hard as baked clay. Outside the circle, he searched for and found a stone with a sharp edge, like a prehistoric flint tool, and with it he scraped the hard earth away from around the tablet, the others intently attentive to him and, beyond them, the anticipating, impatient dead. The farther down he got, scraping away the earth, the more what he had believed to have been a tablet revealed itself misshapen, and he abandoned an irregularly shaped stone.

Aminat impulsively grabbed the flint from him and she, with the movements of a woman who had learned hard labor, applied herself to digging out a tablet, a corner of which stood out, just enough for her and the others and the dead to see that it was indented with, surely, almost effaced inscription. Not deeply embedded in the earth, it came out easily, but it was not clay, and had no inscription.

They were slaves to the dead. The more stones, not tablets, were unearthed, the more the dead, their agitation making the air shiver, pressed their demand that Aminat, David, Catherine, Gerard, go on digging.

The sun, as always directly overhead, became black, no longer able to bear the brilliance of its whiteness.

In this unreality, no guard came to stop the manic excavations. Only once a figure appeared—a blond boy exposed to the sun and wearing only shorts—and looked at them for a short while from a distance, a hand shading his eyes. He disappeared as quickly as he had appeared.

Gerard knew that what he was digging up with the jagged edge of the flint could not be a tablet—it was too big and irregular—yet he was driven to unearth it, to unearth everything about him, not to find some long-buried tablet, but to bring everything up, simply to expose to the dead that there was no tablet to be found, that there was no explanation, no revelation, however much they demanded one.

He hated the dead for what they demanded, without pity for his grief—for the grief of all those here, reduced to this ridiculousness—because the dead had no interest in grief, which was merely human. Here he was, commanded by them, but he must let them know, finally and forever, that their tormenting him for their own meaning only made him want to expose to them their own meaninglessness. He was here not to satisfy them, as if with blood, but to prove that no sacrifice, however bloody, meant anything but blood. Leaving this site, he would leave the dead behind, they who denied him his human grief. He would allow in himself what grief did to make him human—in himself and for himself, and too in and for Catherine and David and Aminat, because they needed, all together, to be free of the dead. That was why they were here—not to satisfy the dead, no, but, defying the dead, to be free of them.

Aminat shoved him aside with a shoulder to take his place, though she had to have seen that what he had half unburied was not a tablet. Her muscles shaking, she dug a trench around the small rock, then, straddling it with splayed legs and grasping it with dirty hands, she used the last of her strength to lift it out of a hole and hold it up for a moment as if for the dead to see it, and, contorted at her waist, she tried to throw the rock away from her. It fell right by her, and she fell with it, sideways away from it, and immediately turned over facedown. Her arms outstretched, she lay motionless. David, Catherine, and Gerard sat on the ground around Aminat, who remained motionless until, slowly, she clenched her hands, then she let her fingers loosen, as if she were letting go of something.

The living suffered, and the dead withdrew from the living, in pity now, the spears of the soldiers lowered, the points dragging, as they turned away. They left the living to despair. A few remained— perhaps those dead who, if they had any vestige of individuality, would have been recognized by the living as the people they'd once known and lost forever—but they too vanished.

Aminat rolled over slowly onto her side. Her face was dripping with tears and saliva and mucus. Weakly, rising only to a low crouch, she stumbled about the circle to collect the unearthed stones and, one by one, piled them together, and as she did she sobbed, sobbed more and more violently. David and Catherine and Gerard watched her gather and pile the stones, rocking back and forth, keening, as if this were a ritual, inspired by despair, which had no intention but to pile together a heap of coarse stones.

# TWENTY-SIX

All of them stayed with David in his large apartment in Palio Psychiko. The housekeeper prepared meals, laundered clothes, put order in the rooms, but she, who had been with David for twenty years, spoke to him as minimally as he and Gerard and Catherine spoke to one another, and she didn't speak at all to Aminat, aware as much as the others that Aminat had become deaf and dumb as well as blind, because for Aminat there was nothing to hear or say, and nothing to see.

During the three days of their all being together at David's, she came to meals partway through or left partway through, or sometimes she was at the table before the others and stayed on after the others. She moved slowly; she was gentle. She spent most of her time in her room.

Early on the fourth morning, Gerard was woken by a high-pitched shout that he thought came from David, and, as startled as he was, he remained tensely still. The following silence was more portentous than the shout, and he jumped out of bed in boxer shorts and T-shirt and rushed out of his bedroom and into the living room. The sliding glass door to the terrace was open, and there at the railing were David, in a bathrobe, and Catherine, her nightgown clinging to her. Their backs to him, they were looking over the railing. Gerard approached them silently, and, standing between them, looked down into the forecourt at the body of Aminat, face down, her arms outstretched, motionless.

As they were, together they went down to the forecourt and, whether or not they were doing what was right, David and Gerard turned over Aminat's slack body slowly. Her eyes were wide. David lifting her under her arms and Gerard by her legs, they raised her. On her forehead was a great bruise, and from her broken nose blood dripped down the side of her face. Her eyes were open, but she was dead. Catherine walked ahead to open doors to the foyer and the lift and to the apartment; Gerard and David carried Aminat up and into her bedroom, and laid her on her unmade bed.

Shockingly to Catherine and Gerard, David, standing at the foot of the bed, picked up from a chest of drawers a crystal vase and hurled it so it smashed against a wall, kicked over a chair, and pulled at a curtain so it tore from its rod.

Gerard stood on one side of the bed and Catherine on the other, and Gerard saw Catherine lean over Aminat to stare, starkly, at her face.

He turned away, walked to a wall and pressed his forehead against it.

This thought occurred to Gerard: The impression *nothing* was as phenomenal as the impression *everything*.

Without saying anything or looking back, Gerard went out. In his bedroom, unshaven, he dressed, and left the apartment. Out in the streets of Psychiko, he noted that the guards in the booths outside the residences of ambassadors from different countries were changing. They watched him as he passed them to go out to Kifissia

Avenue, where he took a bus crowded with passengers going to work down into the center of Athens.

The sky was heavy with what seemed hot clouds.

From Constitution Square, he walked down Mitropoleos Street. Though he was among many pedestrians along the narrow pavement, he felt that not he but someone else he hardly knew was being careful not to bump into people. He was light-headed.

Passing a tiny Byzantine church, crowded into a space under the portico of a modern office building, he noticed that the doors were open, and he went in. The inside walls were almost completely soot black, with here and there highly polished silver hands hovering in the blackness.

Outside, studying the façade of the little church, was the boy who had appeared at the site of Ugarit. In the Athenian heat, he was wearing his shorts and also a T-shirt and sandals. As if he had expected to meet Gerard, he smiled at him, and Gerard smiled back.

As they walked together, Gerard asked, "Did you go to Ugarit because you're interested in the origins of the alphabet?"

"I did, yes."

"Do you wonder why the alphabet is arranged the way it is?"

"I do."

"And do you have any idea why?"

"I don't, and no one will ever know. It will be a secret kept by history."

"What, then, is the reason for wondering about it if we'll never know?"

"Perhaps, just to wonder, just to ask why."

"Is that enough to live by?"

"For me, yes."

"How old are you?"

"I am nineteen years old."

They walked on in silence; sometimes separated by pedestrians, into the crowded Monastiraki Square. They walked past the high mosque up to Hadrian's Library, before which Gerard asked the boy if he would like to go inside among the ruins. The boy nodded yes.

They were alone among the ruins of the library. There would have been a long reflecting pool and a colonnade around the pool for walking and discussing, and as they walked around what would have been the pool along paths over which there would have been a colonnade, rain began to fall from the heavy clouds, cool rain. The boy motioned Gerard to follow him to stand under the only surviving arch, from where, in silence, they watched the rain fall on shattered slabs of marble. A large black tortoise emerged from along the slabs and lumbered across one very slowly, to disappear under an overhanging slab. The rain continued to fall. A dull church bell rang at a distance.

The boy frowned a little, as if a thought came to him. "I remember," the boy said, "remember from a long time ago, so long ago I was still a baby, ringing a bell. I remember the sound of the bell ringing, ringing and ringing, as if someone else, not myself, were swinging the clapper with a rope, ringing the bell to make the whole world hear."

"Your name is Harry," Gerard said.

"Harry, yes."

The rain stopped, and they left the ruins of the library and, out in the street, both turned in the direction of Plaka. There, among gift shops, old neoclassical houses behind scaffolding were being restored.

One of the houses they passed was derelict, some of its antefixes—

terra-cotta sphinxes along the edge of the roof—missing, its small balcony, behind a rusted fancy iron railing, half collapsed, its old shutters, with gaps among the slats, closed. But the narrow double front doors were open. Gerard stopped to look inside, to a marble stairway and, by it, a long passage from the front hall into rooms at the back.

Gerard climbed the worn steps to the entrance to look more deeply into the house, hesitated, then stepped in, and he sensed the boy behind him. As if they were invisible and made no noise, not even along the bare but dusty wooden planks of the floor, they went along the passage, the walls covered with graffiti, into a room that was filled with sunlight, so filled the light flickered on the stark plaster walls. The only piece of furniture in the room was a marble-topped coffee-house table on which, as though just placed there, was a gleaming glass of water.

Now the boy led Gerard out of the room and back along the passage to the front hall and a stairway with neoclassical banisters. Ascending, the boy did not use the banister, which shook when Gerard grabbed it to take one step up. He met the boy waiting for him on the landing.

Off the landing were doors to rooms at the front and at the back of the house. The door to the room at the back was locked, and would not give way to the boy's thrusting his shoulder against it. As Gerard waited, the boy turned away from the locked door to go along the narrow landing to the door at the front of the house.

This opened onto a fully furnished room, though covered thickly in dust and cobwebs strung out everywhere. The walls were papered in faded stripes, and hanging in heavy, dark frames were blown-up, brownish photographs, vague about the edges, of men with whiskers and women in tightly buttoned bodices. Over the brass bed, its quilt gray with dust, was a long, brownish photograph of a city dominated by a dome and minarets, and written cursively in ink on its lower border was "*Constantinople*." Covering a table with complicated legs was a lace cloth, and on it a tarnished samovar and tea glasses in metal holders; two chairs, their rattan seats sagging, were at either side of the table. In a far corner hung an icon and an icon lamp. A dirty Turkish rug, rucked, lay on the warped wooden floor. Threadbare, swagged curtains, the folds gray with dust, hung over the windows, the curtains outlined with tiny pom-poms. The shutters behind them were closed, but where slats were missing bands of sunlight shone through the curtains. In a corner of the room was a heap of old books and papers. Again, Gerard followed the boy to crouch over and examine illustrated cardboard-covered books with titles in Cyrillic letters, old account books in French, postcards from Baden-Baden and Vienna and Prague in German, a volume of Italian poetry, an exercise notebook in rudimentary English, and a school notebook the boy picked up and opened to reveal in a child's uppercase letters, over and over.

ΑΒΓΔΕΖΗΘΙΚΛΜΝΞΟΠΡΣΤΥΦΧΨΩ.

The boy raised the notebook to read the letters, pronouncing them carefully out loud:

"ΑΛΦΑ, ΒΗΤΑ, ΓΑΜΑ, ΔΕΛΤΑ, ΕΨΙΛΟΝ, ΖΗΤΑ, ΗΤΑ, ΘΗΤΑ, ΓΙΩΤΑ, ΚΑΠΑ, ΛΑΜΒΔΑ, ΜΙ, ΝΙ, ΞΙ, ΟΜΙΚΡΟΝ, ΠΙ, ΡΩ, ΣΙΓΜΑ, ΤΑΥ, ΥΨΙΛΟΝ, ΦΙ, ΧΙ, ΨΙ, ΩΜΕΓΑ."

Gerard felt a flash of joy. His grief did finally what grief does: grief expands into phenomenal love.

# Acknowledgments

All the specific information about the alphabet in *ABC* comes from *Histiore de l'Écriture,* by James G. Février, which book is itself something of a character in the novel. My reading has included: *Forgotten Scripts* by Cyrus H. Gordon (in which I underlined a comment about the importance of Ugaritic, tablets of which were found containing the ABC of thirty letters already arranged in the fixed traditional order inherited by the Hebrews, the Greeks, and the Romans); *The Alphabetic Labyrinth* by Johanna Drucker; *The Story of Writing* by Andrew Robinson; *Language Visible* by David Sacks; and, of course, *The Alphabet* by David Diringer.

The account of the Chechen horrors is almost word-for-word from an article I read in *The Observer* of London, by Krystyna Kurczab-Redlich. I wanted this account to be based on fact to break through whatever horrors fiction can invent into the more horrifying inventions of history.

Friends have contributed information: Irene Andreae, Robert Perrault, Iossif Sasson, Serena Tang, Fani-Maria Tsigakou.

I am deeply pleased to have Deborah Garrison, my former editor at *The New Yorker,* back as my editor now. And I thank all those at Pantheon who have helped to bring this book about: Katharine Freeman, Iris Weinstein, and Caroline Zancan. And many thanks, too, to my agent, Peter Matson.

Grateful acknowledgment is made to the following for permission
to reprint previously published material: Editions Payot & Rivages:
Brief excerpt, title page, two graphs, and passages translated by
David Plante from *Histoire de L'Ecriture* by James G. Février, copyright ©
1948, 1959, 1984 by Editions Payot, copyright © 1995 by Editions Payot &
Rivages. Reprinted by permission of Editions Payot & Rivages. Viking
Penguin and Barbara Levy Literary Agency: Excerpt from "I Stood with
the Dead" from *Collected Poems of Siegfried Sassoon,* copyright © 1918,
1920 by E.P. Dutton. Copyright © 1936, 1946, 1947, 1948 by Siegfried Sas-
soon. Reprinted by permission of Viking Penguin, a division of Penguin
Group (USA) Inc. and Barbara Levy Literary Agency, on behalf of the
Estate of George Sassoon. John Wiley & Sons, Inc: Graphs and definitions
from *Webster's New World Dictionary, Second Edition,* edited by Michael
Agnes. Reprinted by permission of John Wiley & Sons, Inc.